THE
FILIPINO STATE
— AND —
OTHER ESSAYS

Is Rodrigo Duterte the Savior
Of the Filipino Nation?

GUILLERMO GÓMEZ RIVERA

Published in the United States by CentiRamo Publishing
First edition, New York, New York
www.centiramopublishing.com
info@centiramopublishing.com

Book formatting and design: Pierce Centina
Art consultant: Janet Frances White

ISBN: 13-978-1-7327815-1-1
ISBN: 10-1-7327815-1-6

Library of Congress Catalogue Control Number: 2018960697
LC record available at https://lccn.loc.gov/2018960697

Printed in the United States of America

10 9 8 | 15 14 13 12 11

Dedication

This book is dedicated to President Rodrigo Duterte y Roa with the humble hope of helping him get a fair view of the true history of our country so that he can establish an independent and just language policy in our educational system as well as an accurate culture policy for the new generations of drug-free Filipinos who need to know their national identity as a factor of today's progress. It is likewise dedicated to my late parents Francisco Gomez y Vital Wyndham and Lourdes Rivera y Celo and to my son Guimó, my late daughter Mayén, my grandchildren and all my former students.

ALSO BY GUILLERMO GÓMEZ RIVERA

NOVELS
Quis ut Deus
Por Dios y por España
Vicente Ilustre, el tagalo español de Taal, Batangas (typescript)

POEMS
Con címbalos de caña (Colección Oriente, Barcelona, Spain)
La nueva Babilonia (Colección Oriente, Barcelona, Spain)

TEXTBOOKS
Español para filipinos (módulos 1 a 8)
Español para todo el mundo, 2

ESSAYS
The Conflict Over Territorial Sovereignty on the Malvinas, Georgias and Sandwich Islands of the South
La literatura filipina y su relación al nacionalismo filipino
Filipino: origen y connotación y otros ensayos

RECORDINGS
Villacincos filipinos y cantos de patria y fe
El collar de sampaguita
Zamboanga hermosa
España en el alma

PLAYS
El caserón
Por los fueros filipinos
El Armagedón filipino

Author's Note

This book was originally written in Spanish but upon the prodding of a couple of friends whose opinion I treasure, I translated it into English. One of these friends was the late Philippine National Artist Nick Joaquin, himself a Spanish speaker. Writing this book in Spanish, he argued, would be like preaching to the choir. He persuaded me that it is really the English-speaking Filipinos who need to know more about the origins of Filipinism rather than the Filipino population which still speaks Spanish today.

Titans of Philippine letters in Spanish, led by national hero José Rizal and nationalist Sen. Claro M. Recto, wrote in Spanish in defining Philippine national identity and in advocating for reforms and freedom from foreign interference. Spanish-speaking Filipinos, therefore, naturally hold the advantage of discovering the philosophical thoughts of these heroes and patriots on what they envisioned Filipino nationhood should look like.

Besides Nick Joaquin, Elizabeth Medina, a writer, researcher and translator, also encouraged me in this endeavor. She is fully convinced that Filipinos trained to speak, write and think only in English will benefit from this project. Without any working notion of Spanish, she argued, these Filipinos are likely the unwitting victims of a broken educational system that has brainwashed them into thinking that the English language and the American culture, as portrayed in Hollywood movies, are superior to any other language or culture.

This kind of thinking has, without any doubt, contributed greatly to the widespread ignorance among Filipinos even of their own culture and the rich legacy that *Madre España* had handed down to the Philippines for over three centuries.

Introduced into the country by the Thomasites, the first American Protestant missionaries who arrived in the country on board USS *Thomas* after Spain had ceded the Philippines to the United States in 1898, the present educational system is responsible for spreading ignorance rather than enlightenment on the essence of Filipinism.

In encouraging me to write this book in English, Liz Medina, who is based in Chile, wrote me the following: *"En realidad el mayor legado de los Estados Unidos en Filipinas ha sido la ignorancia. Sí, en inglés. El español es totalmente necesario para poner fin a nuestro lavado de cerebro* (The greatest legacy of the United States in the Philippines has been ignorance. Indeed, in English. Spanish is necessary to put an end to this brainwashing)."

The essays included in this book were written over a period of time. Some of them had been published in both online and print publications. Others were written for lectures I delivered on Filipino-Hispano culture before various groups. I have updated the articles in light of the emergence of a new political force in the Philippines, President Rodrigo Duterte y Roa. His muscular leadership and independent foreign policy, if harnessed correctly, may help Filipinos discover their true national identity.

If the true national identity of the Filipino nation is rather elusive to some academics and writers, it is not for lack of trying on their part; rather, it is because of their failure to discover the treasure of nationalist sentiments hidden within the Spanish language, which is just waiting to be discovered.

Restoring Spanish as an official language of the Philippines is important to lift the veil of ignorance among Filipinos about their true roots as a nation. Spanish holds the key in mining the gems left behind by José Rizal, Claro M. Recto and other Filipino heroes and patriots. But doing so is difficult without the knowledge of the Spanish language which they used as a tool to define our national identity.

—GUILLERMO GÓMEZ RIVERA
Makati City
November 21, 2018

Contents

Contents

THE
FILIPINO STATE
— AND —
OTHER ESSAYS

Is Rodrigo Duterte the Savior
Of the Filipino Nation?

GUILLERMO GÓMEZ RIVERA

PART I

EL ESTADO FILIPINO:

THE BIRTH OF THE FILIPINO STATE

Desembarco de Magallanes (oil on canvas, 1893) by Telesforo Sucgang (1855-1916), a native of Aklan, depicting the arrival of Ferdinand Magellan in 1521.

1. WHAT IS A STATE?

A small dictionary defines a state as "a territory with laws." The word "laws" in this definition naturally implies that there are people living in that territory. This also means that the territory is the patrimony of the people living in it for which they have laws.

And the very fact that a territory has its own laws indicates that it has a basic attribute of sovereignty to make such laws for itself.

The word "laws" in this definition also suggests that there is a government in place, backed by both police and military forces to defend it and to impose those laws upon the inhabitants of the territory under its control. The form of government of that state may be monarchical because the ruler is a chieftain or a king or by whatever title such a ruler may be called.

The origin of the Filipino State is not discussed and taught in Philippine schools

Let us now find out the origin and evolution of the State that everyone today calls the Filipino State, *Ang Estado ng Filipinas.*

2. WHEN WAS THE BIRTH OF THE FILIPINO STATE?

WHEN PHILIPPINE HISTORY is taught nowadays, the origin of the Filipino State is not discussed. It is deliberately omitted.

By whom? — you would ask. And we would answer pointblank: by our White Anglo-Saxon Protestant (WASP) masters who by their undue interference in the linguistic and economic policies of the Filipino State threaten, or violate, its attribute of sovereignty.

Why? — you would again ask. In order to turn Filipinos into strangers in their own country for the purpose of better exploiting them economically in the midst of their confusion about themselves. And this charge can be proved true by the un-Filipino results of the educational system principally conducted in English which most often makes relative, or insecure, the attribute of sovereignty of the Filipino State.

The birth of the Filipino State can be traced to the founding of the city of Manila

But let us go back to the main question. When was the birth of the Filipino State? The answer is very easy: At the same instant that Manila was founded and established as its capital city. And the date given to that event is June 24, 1571.

It is, therefore, a fact that the Filipino State was simultaneously founded with the establishment of Manila. For, why should there be a capital city, seat of a central government and of law, without a corresponding State to govern?

And due to this fact, we come across a grave error being committed in the manner Philippine history is being taught in our schools.

We often tell our students and children that Manila was founded on June 24, 1571 as the capital city of the Philippines but we always fail to teach that with its founding, the Filipino State was also established.

We also fail to underscore that from that day onward, the Filipino State began to exist as a jurisdictional reality up to the present time as we find ourselves talking about it in this new millennium.

Miguel López de Legazpi

3. WHAT WAS THE STATUS OF THE FILIPINO STATE IN 1571?

ITS STATUS WAS that of a province of Spain administered through the vice-kingdom of New Spain which is Mexico today. At the beginning, the Filipino State was treated as a missionary and a military outpost by its creators. The military, composed of both Spanish and Mexican elements, was there to guard and to protect the missionaries and the scant Spanish and Mexican civil population that came to settle in the islands.

But this situation does not affect the other fact that the constituents of the newly formed Filipino State were primarily the Spanish and the Mexican *conquistadores* followed by the indigenous (mostly Tagalog, Pampango and Visayan) and Chinese populations that accepted the King of Spain as their sovereign.

Artist's rendition of Manila's original coat of arms.

Naturally, by accepting the Spanish King as their own, all those people became Spanish citizens in fact. And as Spanish citizens they shared in whatever attribute of sovereignty that Spain had at that time.

Spain is the Mother Country of the Philippines for forming the present Filipino State

This is the reason Spain was referred to as their State's Mother Country. And this also may explain why Filipinos stood arm in arm with Spain, for almost 400 years, against all the several invasions of their islands launched by the Dutch, the British and others.

We may add that under the United States of America, the Filipinos fought with their American comrades against Japan because they lived with the thought of sharing with Americans their country's attribute of sovereignty even if Gen. Douglas MacArthur, unlike Simón de Anda, the Basque Spanish governor-general of the Philippines who raised an army outside Manila to retake the capital after the British invasion in 1762, chose to flee from the Philippines, leaving Filipinos to fend for themselves only with his promise of "I shall return." The tragedy of the Filipino World War II veterans who waited for many long years for American compensation in the form of a grant of U.S. citizenship with all its benefits is merely noted as a footnote to the relative attribute of sovereignty due the existing Filipino State.

Going back to the establishment of the Filipino State in 1571, we note that when the reigning King of Spain became Felipe II, the name Felipeno acquired a more pragmatic connotation. Besides being defined as one who paid tribute or taxes to Felipe, it now also meant one who rendered service in his name. The Felipenos or *indios*, along with the *chinos cristianos*, paid the necessary *licencia* (a form of tax) to the King for doing business in *Las Islas Felipenas*. Also known as Felipenos were, or course, the Spanish *conquistadores* and the *frailes* who served Felipe II in the newly formed country.

> ### DID YOU KNOW?
>
> As a linguistic note, did you know that the two letters "E" in Felipeno were eventually replaced with the letter "I" because the indigenous *alíbatá* had neither an "E" nor an "O" in its composition? Being influenced by Arabic, it only had three vowels or phonemes—namely, A, I, U.

The form of government that came with the founding of the Filipino State was monarchical and it was bound to the Catholic Church by the *Patronato Real*, an agreement of unity between Madrid and Rome. This agreement assured Rome that newly discovered lands would be converted to Roman Catholicism, effectively making evangelization the main goal of Spanish colonization.

King Philip II of Spain

By 1599, or 28 years after the founding of the Filipino State, a referendum was organized, gathering the *maharlicá* chieftains, *régulos*, *principales*, *rajahs* and *datus*—in short, the heads of the different ethnic states in existence throughout the entire archipelago at the time. Assembled as representatives of the native ethnic states, they were asked one simple question (called a *requirimiento*): Do you accept the King of Spain as your sovereign?[1]

This important question was translated into the native languages of those participating

---

[1] John Leddy Phelan, *The Hispanization of the Philippines*, ed. Renato Constantino (Manila: Filipiniana Reprint Series, 1985), 25.

in the referendum so that it could be fully understood. After the chieftains had consulted one another on how to respond, they raised an important question of their own to the Spaniards, acting on behalf of Philip II who ordered the referendum to be held: If they accepted the Spanish monarch as their sovereign, what was in it for them? The Spanish and the Mexican *conquistadores* responded along these lines:

(1) They would have better control over their respective domains for they would benefit from the superior organizational set-up and backing of the Catholic Church. Acceptance of the Catholic faith through baptism would save their souls. But perhaps what appealed more to the native leaders was the idea of strengthening and expanding their power through the creation of different, more orderly political units. Under this scheme, their *barangays* would be grouped into *sitios*, sitios into a *barrio*, barrios into a *municipio*, *municipios* into a *provincia* with a *cabecera* and several *provincias* into an *estado regional* (*capitania general o provincia de ultramar*) under a *Concejo de Indias* of the Crown of Spain. By the late 1800s, *Las Islas Felipenas* would fall under the *Ministerio de Ultramar* with the status of an overseas province (*Provincia de Ultramar*), along with Cuba and Puerto Rico.

(2) The indigenous people would have a world power as their protector. The tenor of the *requirimiento* that they heard read to them made it clear that their friends and their enemies would be the friends and the enemies of Spain as well.

(3) They would enjoy a better economy that would elevate their way of life

LASTING GIFTS FROM SPAIN AND MEXICO TO EARLY FILIPINOS		
PLANTS	**TOOLS**	**FARM ANIMALS**
maiz, coffee, chocolate or *cacao*, patties, *camotelc* (*camote*), tobacco, cassava, papaya, *maní* (peanut), *lanca* (jackfruit), *calabaza* (squash), tomatoes, onions, *incamatelc* or jicama (*sincamas*), *camachictelc* (*camachile*)	*arado* (*araro* or plow), *azadón* (*asarol* or hoe), *sistema de cajón* of planting rice, a working irrigation system	horse (*kabayo*), cow (*baka*), carabao (imported from Vietnam), sheep, *ganza* (geese), *pavo* (turkey) and a new breed of *pato* (duck)

The perilous voyage of *adelantado* Miguel López de Legazpi across the Pacific from Mexico was plotted by famed Augustinian navigator Fray Andrés de Urdaneta. The successful expedition led to the establishment of permanent Spanish settlements in the Philippines.

from a mere subsistence level to one that would be self-sufficient by producing goods and services. This would occur later upon the arrival mainly from Mexico of new industrial tools, agricultural plants, root crops and vegetables (see table on preceding page).

(4) From Manila, the capital city, a national system of government would improve the local pre-Hispanic system of governance for every ethnic state since with Christianization and the founding of the *pueblos* or *municipios*, the integration into one single Filipino State of all the previously different local, or ethnic, nations would be achieved.

(5) Other relevant issues were most likely discussed in order to convince any wavering native leaders. These would have included the introduction of European infrastructure; the organization of parochial schools and even of a university (University of Santo Tomás); the strengthening of foreign commerce (Manila-Acapúlco galleon trade); the introduction of an inter-island transportation system and of a land ownership system through the *encomiendas* that would be partitioned into *haciendas*.

(6) The gradual spread of Spanish, along with the principal languages (Tagalog, Visaya and Ilocano) as the primary official language of the courts and of public documents would be the hallmark of progress. These principal native languages would also be developed with a common phonetic and Hispanic alphabet in order to convert them into better tools of Christianization and the propagation of basic European civilization and education for the indigenous people.

4. THE INTEGRATION OF THE PRE-HISPANIC ETHNIC STATES INTO THE FILIPINO STATE

THE MAJORITY OF THE chieftains who took part in the 1599 referendum liked the potential benefits they would derive from Spain and overwhelmingly voted "yes" to accept the Spanish King as their sovereign. Even the Muslim chieftains of Manila, Joló and the rest of Mindanao assented to this proposition, thereby integrating their own local ethnic states into the recently founded Filipino State. The favorable vote of these early Muslim groups was affirmed years later by Sultan Alimuddin of

Joló when he visited Manila, although the local Moros half-heartedly participated in the establishment of the Filipino State from the start.

The 150 or so Chinese residents in Mayi-in-i-la also said "*sí*" to the proposal for they correctly saw it as a golden business opportunity. And their vision would not fail them as they subsequently assumed an important role as *aparceros* (partners) to the Spanish and the Mexican *conquistadores* during the Manila-Acapúlco galleon trade that lasted for 250 years. The Filipino State started out with three diverse groups consisting of the Spanish and Mexican *conquistadores* and *frailes*, the Tagalog, Visayan and Capampañgan *katutubô* or indigenous (*indios* according to the Spanish records) and the Chinese who migrated from both China and the destroyed Orang Dampuan settlement in northern Mindanao.

As the zealous Spanish *frailes* set out to establish Catholic *pueblos*, they also introduced the cultivation of *maiz, camote, kamatis, sibuyas, ajos* and *calabaza*. They also added

The zeal of the Spanish frailes helped consolidate the Filipino State founded in 1571

to the local lexicon such gastronomic terms as *guisado, asado, pinirito* (*frito*), *salseado, enjamonado, embutido* and *puchero tinola*. By enlisting the help of the *chinos cristianos* in building a new nation, they indirectly enriched Philippine culture with Chinese influences, most especially in culinary art.

Backed by their indigenous flock and their *chino cristiano* assistants, the *frailes* tapped the natives' *bayanihan* spirit—through the *polo* and the *falla* system—to construct hundreds of Catholic churches throughout the archipelago, as well as roads, bridges and *casas tribunales* and *casas reales* that used to be the pride of place of every Filipino *pueblo*.

If the Filipino State became quickly consolidated, it was due in large measure to the patience and the determination of the Spanish *frailes* as leaders of their *indio* and *chino cristiano* flock.

In 1812, a significant event occurred: the Filipinos became full-fledged Spanish citizens along with the granting of equal representation to all Spanish colonies in the highest councils of government in Madrid by the Spanish Constitution ratified by the *Cortes* in Cadiz, Spain. This bold

TAX TRIVIA

During Spanish times, there was not a lot of oppressive taxes to worry about such as the yearly income tax to pay at source and to declare every March and April. No EVAT, no gasoline tax, no electrical and water distribution tax, no amusement tax, no 70 percent inheritance tax, no confiscatory land and business taxes, no court, litigation, entertainment, gambling, prostitution, cigarette and liquor and beverage taxes, etc. These taxes are now being levied mainly to service the atrocious foreign debt borrowed from neo-colonizers and to pay for the salaries of a bloated bureaucracy mired in corruption.

act was occasioned by changing attitudes in Spain with the growth of liberal ideas there in the early 19th century.[2]

Then in 1849, Filipinos were given Spanish surnames for identification and tax purposes during the term of Narciso Clavería y Zaldúa as governor-general, further embedding into our DNA our Hispanic identity as a people. Those who wanted to keep their *indio* or *chino cristiano* surnames were free to do so as long as these were spelled and pronounced in Spanish. *Indio* last names like Macaspac, Maglaque, Agcaoili and *chino cristiano* surnames like Tantiongco, Cojuangco, Tanjutco, Locsin, Lacson and others were entered into the registry of Spanish surnames.

Spanish authorities imposed only five different taxes: *cédula personal*, *licencia*, *amillaramiento*, *aduana* and *herencia*.

In the late 19th century, Filipinos rose up against Spain in their desire for political reforms but unfolding events halfway across the globe overtook them. When they were tantalizingly close to victory, the outcome of their revolution dramatically changed when the United States declared war against Spain in order to grab Cuba, Puerto Rico and *Filipinas*, the last three remaining *provincias de ultramar* or Spanish overseas provinces.

The U.S. invaders tried to minimize the widespread destruction they caused during the Filipino-American War by calling the conflict

---

[2] Robertson, James Alexander, "The Evolution of Representation in the Philippine Islands," *The Journal of Race Development* 6, no. 2 (1915), 155-66. doi:10.2307/29738120.

a mere insurrection. But no amount of sanitizing it could countenance the brutality of that uneven fight. Not only did it abort the flowering of the first freely established republic in Asia that had its roots in 1571 but it also forced Filipinos to be educated only in the English language. The imposition of an unphonetic language completely alien to the Filipino tongue would have a dramatic impact upon the Filipino soul for generations to come. It is to blame for the current dysfunctional educational system that we have inherited from the Americans, producing generations of Filipinos who can hardly speak or write properly in English, nor in their native

Macario Sacay

languages, placing them in some kind of a language limbo that erodes our national identity.

5. MATURITY OF THE FILIPINO STATE IN 1898

AFTER 333 YEARS OF SPANISH RULE, the Filipino State by 1898 had evolved from a mere far-flung missionary outpost to become a proud colony with a vibrant culture and economy due to its abundant natural resources. It became an overseas Spanish province under the *Ministerio de Ultramar* until it declared independence with the establishment of the 1898 *República Filipina* which proved short-lived, however. The invading American forces of the early 1900s oversaw its destruction during their iron-fisted pacification campaign which killed up to a sixth of the total Philippine population at the time.[3] With their arm superiority came impunity to do as they pleased with the Philippines, including plundering its national treasury and emptying it of its gold and silver reserves

---

[3] James B. Goodno, *The Philippines, Land of Broken Promises* (Atlantic Highlands, NJ: Zed Books, 1991), 33.

which, as alleged by eyewitness Soledad Vital de Luna in a 1952 letter, were worth as much as a hundred billion U.S. dollars.

From being a full-fledged state in 1898, the *República* was reduced into a servile U.S. colony ridden from the start with graft and corruption as described in the historic editorial of *El Renacimiento*, "Aves de Rapiña (Birds of Prey)," in 1907.

The *República Filipina* of 1898, the legitimate owner of the Filipino State with a well-defined national territory, gallantly defended itself against the invasion in a protracted war that began in the Santa Mesa-San Juan Bridge, where U.S. Private William Grayson fired the first shot directed at Filipino soldiers. The armed hostilities of the Filipino-American War more or less ended with the capture and secret execution of the second President of the *República Filipina*, Macario Sacay, in 1907.

> *U.S. policy during its colonial rule withheld the granting of citizenship to Filipinos*

6. BUT IN 1900 THE FILIPINO PEOPLE WERE DEPRIVED OF THEIR OWN STATE BY FORCE OF ARMS

WHEN THE AMERICANS had at last succeeded in imposing their military and colonial rule, James A. LeRoy, who was connected to the Philippine Commission and an authority on Philippine history, honestly concluded that the Filipinos became stateless as a result of U.S. expansionism.[4] The Americans claimed the Philippine Islands as a territory of the United States but they never extended U.S. citizenship to the Filipinos as Spain did from the very beginning of its rule.

While the Spaniards and the proto-Mexicans laid the foundation for what was later to become a state for all Filipinos, the Americans in contrast came to strip them of their basic national patrimony and human rights, especially their independence.

American humanist James A. LeRoy pointed to this historic injustice as the reason Filipinos were being kept in the dark, as they are still even to

---

[4] Epifanio de los Santos, *Filipinas para los filipinos,* (np: 1908).

this day, we must add, about the Spanish citizenship their forebears had enjoyed under Spanish rule which stood in sharp contrast to the manner the United States treated the Filipinos in the way of citizenship.

When the Americans tried their hands in empire building with the invasion of the Philippines, they attempted different tacks to eliminate resistance. Among the Americans' rigorous efforts to win the hearts and minds of Filipinos was trying to convince them that they were better off under the Stars and Stripes. And broadcasting the fact that they were being deprived of U.S. citizenship would have, of course, eviscerated that propaganda line. To achieve their goal of fashioning themselves as *the savior* of the unfortunate Filipino people, they had to put blinders on those things that made the Spaniards look good. Blaming the Spaniards for everything that was ailing Philippine society suited their purposes of making themselves smell like roses to the Filipino people who were resisting their presence in the Philippines.

Yet our history books are purposely excluding these historical facts. And we have reached the present pathetic situation—that of being ignorant of our own real history—because our obsequious education authorities of today continue to distort the true picture of our history as a proud people by uncritically adopting the American narrative.

U.S. President William Mckinley's benevolent assimilation policy in the conduct of military rule in the Philippines was far from benign. Besides the atrocities it perpetrated against the Philippine population, it withheld from Filipinos the very basic human right to citizenship. They refused to grant U.S. citizenship to Filipinos to replace 1) the Spanish citizenship they lost when Spain ceded the country to the U.S. and 2) their own Filipino citizenship under the 1898 *República,* which vanished when the same U.S. invaders brutally destroyed and plundered their nascent republic.

The denial of U.S citizenship to Filipinos was driven by fears of lawmakers in the U.S. Congress that non-white immigrants would be flooding into the United States and would threaten the Americanization policy they were seeking to advance in order to create a cohesive and homogeneous society.[5]

---

[5] Cabán, Pedro, "Subjects and Immigrants During the Progressive Era," *Latin American, Caribbean, and U.S. Latino Studies Faculty Scholarship*, vol. 16 (2001). http://scholarsarchive.library.albany.edu/lacs_fac_scholar/16

Although denied U.S. citizenship, Filipinos and Puerto Ricans who fell under American imperialistic control in the early 1900s nevertheless became a big part of the American social experimentation to create Americanized societies in its overseas possessions. Author Pedro Cabán drove home this point in an instructive article he wrote for an American journal as gleaned from the following excerpt:[6]

The process of Americanizing the new immigrants and colonial subjects was interrelated. The experience of assimilating millions of Southern and Eastern European immigrants influenced the U.S. government's efforts to Americanize the inhabitants of Puerto Rico and other colonial possessions. In turn, the experiences acquired during the first two decades of colonial rule also influenced the Americanization campaigns on the continent during the years preceding U.S. entry into World War I and until about 1920.

Americanization of the Philippines was predicated on WASP racial superiority

The goals and content of the Americanization campaign in the United States and in Puerto Rico were similar in that both emphasized English language instruction and sought to build loyalty for the nation and its institutions. While Americanization entailed absorption into the dominant culture and acceptance of a new political identity in both Puerto Rico and the United States, in the latter Americanization focused on individual assimilation.

In Puerto Rico it entailed the transformation of an entire people and the imposition of new institutions. The Americanization of Puerto Rico, the Philippines and Cuba was the U.S. empire's first attempt to implant its legal [system] and government overseas. Americanization of the inhabitants of the former Spanish colonies was predicated on the militaristic ideology of Anglo-Saxon racial superiority. It also relied on a morally based judgment that the people of the tropics were culturally inferior and consequently should be denied those political rights reserved for the white male citizens of the United States.

In the Philippines and Puerto Rico Americanization included implanting a new system of governance and law and an educational campaign to win acceptance of the legitimacy of the new sovereign power. The ambitious Americanization program included compulsory universal public education that included mandatory English language instruction, patriotic exercises, civic classes and

---

[6] Ibid.

gender-based manual training programs… Through the education system Puerto Rico's youth would learn to accept the legitimacy of the radically different economic and political order that the United States would install and administer.

Besides this transgression, the imperialistic Americans also exposed an ugly underbelly when they introduced Filipinos to extreme racism in their own land, which provoked a famous newspaper writer at the time, Tirso Irrureta Goyena, to expose it and to demand answers as to why Filipinos were being deprived of U.S. citizenship and treated as second-class citizens in their own country.

The American occupation government in the Philippines ought to make it known that the Filipinos now live under the American flag but are not American citizens nor can they call themselves Filipinos since no Filipino State is presently allowed to exist; that this people therefore are like the Jew, robbed of national personality; but that under the Spanish rule the Filipinos were Spanish citizens and could occupy, as many occupy still, important posts in the Motherland.

It ought to make it known that now the Filipino cannot command American troops, white troops, because the brown color of his skin forbids it, but that this color never was an obstacle under Spanish rule to keep a native Filipino from commanding white Spanish troops, as several of them actually continue to do up to now in Spain.

It ought to make it known that the Filipino, on account of the color of his skin, can neither be a member of a white association of Christian young men, now being organized as such into a common center but in a separate building for Filipino associates, when there already exists one for Americans and foreign whites. This is a reflection of what occurs in the Southern States where the Negroes have to form, if they can, their own circles, their own clubs and societies apart from the whites.

It ought to make it known that the present U.S. government here is not like that of unfortunate Spain, the old Spanish one being 'by and for Filipinos' with the aggravating circumstance that the presently best figs in the budget, the best positions and the best salaries are, in their majority, primarily being enjoyed by Americans, whilst the inferior posts of clerks, messengers and porters are exclusively reserved for Filipinos, even if better educated and instructed than the Americans.

The grant of independence in 1946 was farcical as the U.S. continued to hold sway

It ought to make it known that, formerly, Spanish missionaries used to evangelize the savage tribes of the interior, forming them into village and town communities, converting them to Christianity and infusing into their souls the spirit of civilized beings; but now, one Worcester[7] puts it himself to 'civilizing' those same tribes with glass toys and with cinematic projections, to get them to fashionably part their hair in the middle, whilst in their interior they remain savages like before.

The Filipino State continues to be a U.S. colonial territory even after its independence

It ought to make it known that now many more millions of pesos are extracted from the Filipino people than in Spanish times, and a pile of money is spent in Public Instruction only to have those thousands of supposedly instructed young men, that yearly come out of those schools, find themselves unemployed because they have not been given, in reality, any other future in their own country save that of dependents and petty clerks in American concerns that economically exploit the Filipino natural resources; that the lucky student who is sent to America with money wrested from the Filipino people, has to pay for what they tell him is a U.S. privilege when, in reality, the money that was spent for him he really owes to his own people, whom he later betrays when he makes over his personality to become a half-baked American that has to give undue thanks to the American administration.[8]

It ought to be known that in many public employment positions, competent and intelligent Filipinos are put below incapable Americans, and have to obey American superiors whom these Filipinos must instruct because they really know nothing of their charge.

It ought to be made known that the miserly pay which the Filipino school master gets in the public schools is a pittance when compared to the splendid salaries drawn by principals, supervisors, superintendents and high American functionaries in the department of education funded by the tax money arbitrarily collected from Filipinos.

It ought to make known that here, it is the American Government itself that functions to the detriment of the interests of individuals, because it is the American government here that goes into the business of freighting vessels,

---

[7] Dean Conant Worcester (1866-1924) served as interior secretary during the American colonial period. An ardent supporter of American imperialism, he conducted controversial studies of the Igorots that many Filipinos considered racist.

[8] This refers to the so-called *pensionados*, Filipino scholars sent to the United States to study under a government grant.

of supplying ice, of manufacturing furniture and of printing textbooks; and that in public biddings and awards, the bid of 'the local firms' are accepted, but Filipino money still leaves the country because those bidding firms are, in fact, American companies since the companies which first enjoy franchises and privileges are the American ones, or those enjoying American patronage, whilst the enterprises of Filipinos and other foreigners are without any protection. Finally it should make known that all, absolutely all Filipinos who now occupy high positions in the Assembly[9] in the courts, in commerce, in the arts, and in the administration are products of the Spanish educational system which the Americans and their lackeys here treacherously attack in newspapers and school textbooks at every turn.

It is but a fact that all the Spanish-speaking Filipinos who are today's honored statesmen, noted writers, distinguished priests and recognized artists—which is an impressive intellectual phalanx of greatness—are precisely the ones who do so much honor to the Filipino nation thereby vindicating for it a high place among the most civilized nations and not the miserably confused lot that have now graduated from this colonial system

Our economic dependence on foreign banks makes us vulnerable to dictation

of miseducation; that, in order to provide intelligent pupils for these present-day American schools of reinforced concrete now being built upon American orders, but at the expense of Filipino money, Spain had to first succeed in giving existence here to a cultured, Christian and civilized Filipino society; and, that if Spain had not accomplished this gigantic and sublime work, America would not need to build schools of concrete now, but would have been forced to erect barracks of wood and strongly fenced iron pens to herd in them an uncivilized Filipino people, like they often do to this day with the Redskins that are still penned up in the so-called U.S. State Reservations, because in contrast to what the present Spanish educated Filipinos are in this first decade of the 1900s, Anglo-Saxon Protestant civilization has reached absolutely nothing higher with the original natives of the American continent.[10]

---

[9] The Philippine National Assembly which, from 1902 to 1916, consisted of an upper house composed of the appointed Philippine Commission and of a lower house which was elected by popular vote.

[10] Tirso de Irrureta Goyena, *Por el idioma y la cultura hispanos* (Manila: UST Press, 1917), 122; also reproduced in the *Canadian Catholic Letter* (n.p.: 1918).

7. LEADERS IGNORANT OF THEIR COUNTRY'S HISTORY HAVE WEAKENED THE FILIPINO STATE

WITH THE FARCICAL grant of independence to the Filipino people on July 4, 1946, the White Anglo-Saxon Protestant interlopers at the same time exquisitely laid out an economic debt trap which would place the Philippines into a perpetual state of indebtedness to their banks.

> *The best way to keep a people ignorant and poor is to confound their language*

Despite our "independence," the country's economic subordination to these banks allows the neo-colonizers to continue dictating policies, including in the field of education, that are harmful to our national interests. With our so-called leaders at their beck and call, they have poked their fingers even into our own alphabet, ramming into Tagalog-based Filipino the entire English alphabet retaining Ñ as its only concession.

The Philippines became independent in name only in 1946 because the Filipino State continues, in fact, to be a colonial territory of the United States of America without the majority of Filipinos realizing it in the midst of their miseducation and stifling poverty.

The neo-colonizers and their local flunkeys have laid out a language policy that would confuse the Filipino people about themselves and their own national identity.

The neo-colonizers know that the best way to keep a people ignorant and poor is to first confound their language.

8. EDUCATING AND TRAINING FILIPINOS IN ENGLISH ONLY IS A NATIONAL TRAGEDY

SOME OF OUR SO-CALLED THOUGHT LEADERS fail to see how important preserving the Spanish language is to our national identity. On top of that, they are even the first to repudiate the fact that it was used by our patriots and heroes as a powerful tool in their fight for reforms and eventual freedom. For example, the late Andrew González, a La Salle religious brother and former secretary of education, denied the fact that Filipinos of the 1898 revolution had chosen Spanish and Tagalog as their "national linguistic symbols."

In a book he authored, he claimed that "this search for national identity, however, did not focus on language as an issue. Nor did it associate the search for national identity with a specific Philippine language."[11] The first part of this statement can be deemed false since it is easily disproved by José Rizal himself when he discussed at length the issue of language as central to Filipino national identity in *El Filibusterismo*. In the seventh chapter of this novel, Rizal used the characters of both Simoun (who argued in favor of the native languages, including Tagalog) and Basilio (who batted for Spanish as a common language that will unite Filipinos to their government and to one another) to debate about the role of Spanish with regard to the 40 or so native languages. And the books of Rizal, it must be stressed, are directly relevant to any discussion of the Filipino Hispanic identity of the 1898 *República de Filipinas*. How, then, could González have asserted that the search for national identity did not focus on language during the 1898 *República*? Did he perhaps overlook this very apropos chapter of *El Filibusterismo*?

In the same book, González cited the Constitution of Biak-na-Bató as stating that "Tagalog shall be the official language of the Republic."[12] Yet, in the same breath, he asserted that there was no "search for national identity with a specific Philippine language" during the time of the First Filipino Republic. The data he himself provided about the Biak-na-Bató Constitution proclaiming Tagalog as an official language diametrically contradicts his opinion that there was no search for national identity with a specific Philippine language.

His opinion is wrong because it defies the real existence of a native language like Tagalog. For, what, then, is Tagalog? Is it not a "specific

> *Rizal discussed the importance of language to Filipino national identity*

---

[11] Andrew Gonzalez, FSC, *Language and Nationalism* (Quezon City: Ateneo de Manila Press, 1980), 1.

[12] Ibid.

Philippine language"? In fine, González, by saying that the First Philippine Republic had a "nationalism without a national linguistic symbol," appears to justify the neo-colonial imposition of English upon the mindless Filipino people at taxpayers' expense. In this matter about language, it looks like this La Sallian linguist and author joined the efforts of some American Protestant groups like the SIL (formerly known as Summer Institute of Linguistics, Inc.) in pushing an agenda, which works against the development of a real Filipino national language.

González, well-known for opposing the inclusion of Spanish in the college curriculum even as a mere foreign language subject, is remembered by local Hispanista circles as one of those who appeared before the then Salvador Británico Committee at the Batasang Pambansa (1985-86) to ask for the repeal of the Miguel Cuenco 12-unit Spanish language law. And the reasons he gave then were just as contradictory as the ones he supplied in his book, *Language and Nationalism*. Through a De La Salle University professor, Cornelio Villacorta, who was appointed by Corazón Aquino to her 1986 Constitutional Commission, González is also known to have influenced the abolition of Spanish courses in college through the much-criticized Cory Constitution.

> *So-called linguists do not give any serious thought to the importance of Spanish*

What looks like a González bias against Spanish is akin to his stand against Tagalog, or Filipino, with regard to the compulsory use of English as a medium of instruction in all levels of Philippine schools. It is argued that if he were for Filipino, he would be the first to demand for the restoration of the 32-letter alphabet used by Francisco Balagtás in the original *Florante at Laura* in lieu of the English, or Taglish, alphabet invented by the late Ponciano B.P. Pineda, who led the national language commission. Its adoption is being promoted in Filipino, the national language, as well as in Tagalog, in Visaya and in the other principal native languages.

González was known as a member of the local board of SIL,[13] a USAID funded entity that some have alleged is responsible for the

---

[13] David Stoll, *Fishers of Men or Founders of Empire?: The Wycliffe Bible Translators (Summer Institute of Linguistics-SIL) in Latin America* (London: ZED Press, 1982), n.p.

use in Tagalog, or Filipino, of the unphonetic English alphabet which contains vowels or basic phonemes contrary to the basic sound of the five absolute vowels of Tagalog.

Despite his credentials as a linguist, it appears that he had failed to fully appreciate and grasp the need to teach Spanish in our schools as a foreign language and the practical value of using Tagalog-Filipino as the medium of instruction for all subjects taught in our schools.

If the wrong practice of spelling Tagalog words in English is now acceptable, it is because we have linguists in our midst who do not give any serious thought to the importance of preserving Spanish and other Philippine languages in our national life. It is this sort of linguists and educators who abet the rise of a pidgin language (that is, Taglish) with their permissive attitude toward forcing into Tagalog-Filipino the entire unphonetic English alphabet and syllabication, which is the cause of the overt destruction of the very foundations of the Filipino national language. By giving it their blessing, these linguists and educators are deliberately promoting the pidginization of the English language in the Philippines.

At the bottom of this destruction of the Filipino language, initially based on Tagalog, is the sectarian and racist hatred of Spanish because what we call the Balagtás alphabet or the *abecedariong Tagalog* is, to a large extent, derived from the Spanish alphabet—albeit added with letters that symbolize particular Tagalog and native consonants like NG (*nang*) and ÑG (*ñga*).

The misrepresentation and distortion of the Filipino-Hispano native alphabet is eradicating our linguistic heritage. Its corrosive effects are eroding our culture and national identity and will eventually lead to the ruination of the Filipino State itself.

9. THE FILIPINO STATE BECOMES MUTE IN ITS OWN COINED LANGUAGE

AS WE SAID, THE NEO-COLONIZERS who desire to control the Filipino State have used language as a tool to confuse the Filipino people in order to keep them ignorant and poor so that they will forever remain putty in the hands of their former masters. The bastardization of our national language and the exclusion of the teaching of Spanish in our schools

The imposition of English as a language of instruction was carried out by force

have the effect of muffling the real voice of Filipino self-reliance and freedom.

Why is the Spanish language being targeted by those who want to keep the Filipinos ignorant of their own history? It is because Spanish, which was maintained as an official language by the Malolos Constitution, represents the continuation of the basic nationality and nationalism of the Filipino from 1571 to 1898 and even onward to the 1935 Constitution.

The importance of Spanish to our identity as a people was not lost on President Ferdinand E. Marcos, who was branded in certain U.S. liberal circles as a dictator the moment he defied foreign dictation, especially on the continued stay of U.S. military bases in the country. In a move that foresaw the importance of Spanish not only in the world of diplomacy but also in a global world where Spanish-speaking countries are being courted as markets for goods and services, President Marcos preserved

Unable to find work at home, Filipinos turn overseas to look for jobs.

Spanish as an official language of this country through a decree he issued reportedly to spite the neo-colonizers who wanted to pull the strings using the country's indebtedness to U.S. banks as a leverage.

During the American colonial period, there were Filipino leaders and thinkers who were already questioning the deliberate moves made in official circles to take away the Spanish language from our national life with the imposition of English as the only medium of instruction in our schools. One such enlightened mind was Modesto Reyes y Lim, a newspaperman and Manila labor leader. In his

President Ferdinand E. Marcos

Rizalist newspaper *ISAGANI*, he clarified two important things that our present-day history textbooks willfully disregard:

> Well, in our humble judgment, the Philippines used to have a national language when it formed part of the Spanish nation. And that national language was Castilian or Spanish, which is also the national language of Spain because the Philippines was an integral part of Spain and we used to be Spanish citizens like those born in the Peninsula. But came the United States and without first making us part of its territory nor wishing us to become American citizens like themselves, they have, however, imposed upon us English, their national language.[14]

Reyes Lim further expressed astonishment at how long it took for the American authorities to realize that their grand social and cultural experiment to impose their own language upon the Filipino people was ill-conceived:

---

[14] Reyes, Modesto L., *ISAGANI, Revista mensual de asuntos generales* 1, no. 5 (June 1925), 24 and (September 1925), 22.

It had to take a quarter of a century and a Commission[15] of wise men, chosen from millions of U.S. citizens, to know that the Filipino people cannot be forced to speak the language of another people no matter their wealth and power. Here are the eloquent words of that Commission:

'Upon finishing school, more than 99% of the Filipinos will not speak English in their homes. Probably ten to 15 percent of the next generation might use this language in their occupation. In fact, according to this estimate, English in the Philippines will not be the language of the Filipino people.'

Filipinos are stateless in their own country due to globalization and cultural ignorance

At most, it will only be the language of the people in the government service who may use it among themselves, which is why there shall always be the need to use the vernaculars (and Spanish) to address directly the people...

If only some reflection had been duly done when the actual [American] rule was implanted here and if only there was a measure of equanimity and respect toward what was previously in existence in this country, namely the accomplished work of occidental civilization [Spain] for over three centuries upon the strong base of Catholic Christianity, all that exists here would not have been considered bad and despicable, as seen from the lens of egoism and ignorance, since so many great institutions could have been appreciated, such us our legal system along with our other institutions which are just as sacred and which are the envy of other nations that are greater than the Filipino nation itself.

Among those other sacred institutions is the Spanish language of Alfonso el Sabio and Cervantes, el Manco de Lepanto.

Outside of the right (if any) of the [U.S.] Master to impose his language upon the people subjected by him, due to the design of Providence according to him, and the Treaty of Paris and the twenty million dollars according to history, what other right and just motive does he have to erase the Spanish language in this country and replace it with English?

---

[15] The Monroe Commission on Philippine Education was formed in 1925 to assess the progress of the Philippine educational system under American rule. It interviewed thousands of students and teachers across the country and criticized the dismal performance of pupils in English-language related subjects. "Pupil performance was generally low in subjects that relied on English, although the achievement in Math and Science was at par with the average performance of American schoolchildren...," it concluded.

Is it not of plain common sense to know that it would have been far easier to further propagate Spanish, which was already the official language and the mother tongue of so many pure Filipino families, in and out of their homes, and from whom were born so many writers, poets and distinguished men of letters?

There is absolutely no doubt, says a Filipino jurist of today, that if the same time and money, and the same teaching systems and methods, now employed in the teaching of English were instead dedicated to the teaching of Spanish, the latter would have been propagated in a much larger proportion in comparison to the much less present proportion in which English has been propagated! Now, with that failure with English, it is but natural to think in the adoption of one of the native dialects as, first, the official language and, later, as the national language of this country.

In short, the American colonizers very capriciously forced the English language upon the Filipino people without any respect for the wishes for Spanish. To make matters worse, the imposition of English was carried out by force without the U.S. WASP colonizers spending a single dime from their own treasury—since the funds needed for the obligatory teaching of English were taken from Filipino taxpayers. A Puerto Rican writer once posed this question: What effect, upon the matter of language, did the terrifying military operations, as launched by the U.S. invaders, really have upon the Filipinos since 1899?

10. THE FILIPINO STATE, HOCKED BECAUSE BETRAYED

THE IMPLACABLE REQUIREMENT of forcing the teaching of English as the "first and only" official language—over Tagalog-Filipino and Spanish—has done incalculable damage to the psyche of the Filipino people. As a consequence, the Filipino State has ended up being a lost property to the Filipinos. Forcing them to learn English, to the exclusion of Spanish and other native Filipino tongues in school, was—and remains—a bad idea because it prevented them from learning concepts in their own native languages which are inextricably linked to their notion of nationhood.

The language policy instituted by the American colonizers has resulted in the mortgaging of the Filipino State to mostly U.S. banks and other lending institutions, making us vulnerable to foreign dictation. The solution to this betrayal could, perhaps, be the outright rejection of the use of the English language—unless, of course, the United States all of a sudden decides to make the Philippines its fifty-first state and assumes all its debts. Shouldering these debts would be the moral thing to do. After all, it was the American neo-colonizers, acting through slavish Filipino politicians, who created the environment for the Filipino State to be saddled with such ginormous financial obligations.

Is being a domestic helper the reserved place for Filipinos in the English-speaking world?

But given the near impossibility of achieving U.S. statehood for the Philippines—or the status of a free associated state like Puerto Rico—the rejection of English must nevertheless be immediately started by the Filipino people themselves. It will pave the way for their own national language becoming the medium of instruction in schools and will gain them real freedom and independence, at least in language and culture. When these goals are achieved, the Filipino State will strengthen and enhance its national sovereignty.

The sorry state of the Philippine economy and the supine, nay, doormat position of the Filipino State—threatened, as it is, with the specter of becoming a narco-state—call for a drastic solution such as the one recommended here. If our incurably pro-American politicians insist on the madness of continuing with the same failed language policy, they do so at their own risk.

Most Filipinos have no economic interest in pursuing the same failed policy. It is only a few Filipino quislings who benefit from corruption through political power and the illegal drug trade. Their ill-gotten wealth somehow enables them to avoid the moral suffering, the actual poverty and the miserable penury imposed upon the majority. The rest of the Filipino people are simply being condemned to abject poverty and stultifying ignorance. They suffer from daily miseries brought about by the high prices of electricity, food scarcity, inadequate medical attention, lack of potable water and a deadly environmental destruction through systematic pollution. At the end of the day, the majority of Filipinos must ask themselves what economic and social benefits can they really get from talking in a mostly fractured English known as Taglish? Employment as overseas domestic maids, drivers, entertainers or prostitutes?

This degradation which the ordinary Filipino job-seeker is forced into has made "Filipino" and "Filipina" synonymous to domestic help or servant in the English language. Is this the reserved place for Filipinos in the English-speaking world? Can the Filipino people ever recover the national honor they once held when they were still a predominantly Spanish-speaking people? Is it necessary for Filipinos to become Chinese vassals first before recovering some honor for themselves?

In short, will the Filipinos ever be able to recover their State from the U.S. WASP mortgagees who use their lending institutions to carry out their impositions and conditions? Or, will Filipinos just go on being stateless even in their own country because economically marginalized through a whimsical globalization in unphonetic English?

11. AND NOW, WE HAVE A NEAR NARCO-STATE

OUR TRANSITION from being a Spanish-speaking Filipino State to being a pidgin-speaking nation is a national tragedy. The spectacular descent of the country from its lofty perch as a nation of highly intelligent people who expressed themselves eloquently and fluently in the Spanish language into the abyss of a bastardized form of English and Tagalog (Taglish) is too painful to watch. How did we soar so high in Spanish literature with the sterling works of Rizal, Mabini and Recto—to name but a few of our writers and speakers in Spanish—only to plunge so low into a pidgin iteration that in the vernacular is described with a nervous laugh by the made up word *ispokening*?

> *Duterte is trying to prevent the Philippines from becoming a narco-state*

It is a tragedy in the real sense of the word because the same Filipino State is now also becoming a full-blown narco-state with all its negative social implications. President Rodrigo Duterte y Roa is determined to prevent the country from sliding into the dark pit of the narco-states and has declared an all-out war against the drug menace.

Let us turn back a few pages of history to see what might have gone wrong.

First of all, the shift of language from Spanish to English disrupted the flow of the national ideology from one generation to another. This situation also severed a vital link that normally enables generations otherwise separated by age and by shifting cultural mores to understand each other through a common language despite their intergenerational differences. The English expression "we speak the same language" is so true in this context.

The pigheaded language policy of this nation has condemned many of our countrymen into a black hole of ignorance and economic poverty. We, of course, mean the present Filipino masses who are being discarded like garbage into a cultural void after their thinking and perceptions had been systematically alienated from their natural roots by a pro-American educational system that favors foreign rather than national interests. The predicament of the Filipino young was very well explained by Rosa Sevilla de Alvero, an old-school *maestra* in the mold of the 1898 *República de Filipinas*:

> In effect, the English language used as the medium of instruction in the Philippines stupefies, dumdbens or frustrates, to a great extent, the intellectual, moral, political, economic and even the social development of the Filipino students. And compulsory English is an impertinent delaying factor that obstructs the formation of their character and personality.

> Because the Filipino child has the misfortune of being forced to do the burdensome work of insecurely and unsteadily acquiring his ideas, as if he were actually blind, through the labyrinths of a language [English] which is totally unknown to him.

Let us clearly note that the introduction of the English language was not merely added as another tool for the daily life and culture of the Filipinos. It was forced upon them as part of a military strategy and used as a weapon against them because absent a unifying language, they were easier to manipulate. And the practice initiated by the American colonial government remains unchallenged to this day because our policymakers have not lifted a finger to change this odious system. The poor Filipino children today are thus bereft of any solid knowledge of their

> *The Filipino child acquires ideas via the labyrinths of a language unknown to him*

own true history and their great Hispanic culture. They noncha-lantly identify themselves either as a *Pinóy* or a *Pináy*, without fully knowing the term's pejora-tive connotations.[16] By and large,

> *The drug menace has touched all classes of Philippine society*

they are devoured by the *shabú* subculture. In some cases, their drug involvement may even have the blessing of their own parents who use them as drug couriers. Drug syndicates take advantage of the law which prohibits the incarceration of children in legal trouble who are 15 years old and below. The jobless poor among their elders not only sell *shabú* produced by local and Chinese syndicates but even use it as a rice sub-stitute to fight hunger since rice has become so expensive and beyond the reach of the poor.

Many members of the middle-class are also into drugs like cocaine and ecstasy for their exclusive parties and events. Politicians of all stripes are also engaged in the drug trade but the brainless mainstream media do not report on their illegal activities as they are either beholden to their wealth and influence or are on the take. President Rodrigo Duterte y Roa himself has made a very long list of these high-value targets.

12. THE FILIPINO STATE, WEAKENED BY THE YELLOW REGIMES, NOW IN DANGER OF DISINTEGRATION

IN 1840 A SANTA CLARA nun prophesied that the abolition of Spanish "by a Protestant power" in the Philippines will result in the dismemberment of the Filipino nation, and her prediction appears to be coming true.

·

For one, a Moro separatist movement in Mindanao presents a grave national security threat. It is led by a faction of a Muslim terrorist group which, according to columnist Rigoberto Tiglao, is being trained and funded

---

[16] *Pinóy* is coined from "Philippine" and *unggóy*, which is Tagalog for monkey or simian,

by neighboring Malaysia.[17] This reality of a creeping Muslim invasion squares with an earlier observation by the late National Artist Nick Joaquin, who warned about "the Moros wanting to dissolve what the Philippines is today."[18]

We also have to contend with the dicey situation presented by the parlous political movement to shift from a unitary to a federal system of government, ignoring the long history of our march as a people toward national unity which started with our pre-Hispanic ethnic tribes. Some of the most ardent supporters of federalism are members of political dynasties and oligarchs who want to cling to power at the expense of the Filipino masses who leave their dignity at home to work abroad as domestic servants. Screaming newspaper headlines document the maltreatment many of them suffer in the hands of uncivilized employers. Their barbaric treatment in the Middle East exploded into world consciousness with the murder of Joanna Demafeliz, a domestic helper in Kuwait whose dead body was kept in a freezer by her Lebanese and Syrian employers after she was killed.[19]

> **Federalism poses some serious security and economic risks to the country**

Adding to the threat of dismemberment posed by Muslim terrorist groups in the South is the widespread *shabú* drug trade. President Duterte's efforts to prevent us from becoming a full-blown narco-state are being hampered by our own government which is embedded with corrupt police officials and bureaucrats. One dreads to think what would happen if the single Filipino State is all of a sudden officially and quickly dismembered into the proposed 18 federated regions. We will end up with 18 narco-states instead of one!

The regime of Corazon Cojuangco Aquino who came to power in

---

[17] Tiglao, Rigoberto. Malaysians Fund Abu Sayyaf. *rigobertotiglao.com.* http://www.rigobertotiglao.com/2016/06/21/malaysians-fund-abu-sayyaf/ (accessed October 10, 2018).

[18] Nick Joaquin, *Culture and History* (Manila: Anvil Publishing, 2004).

[19] "Joanna Demafelis: Employers of Filipina Maid Found Dead in Freezer Arrested." *bbc.com.* https://www.bbc.com/news/world-middle-east-43177349 (accessed October 10, 2018).

1986 on the back of the so-called People Power Revolution had done nothing to strengthen the Filipino State. All it did was restore the oligarchs back to power and usher in a new set of public officials, relatives and cronies more corrupt than the ones under Ferdinand Marcos whom Corazon Aquino and her ilk had sanctimoniously denounced in their manic efforts to seize power. Her regime which ended in 1992 and the much despised administration of her son Benigno Simeon Aquino Jr. who came to power 18 years later introduced creative, corrupt practices on a massive scale like the constitutionally infirmed Disbursement Acceleration Program (DAP). It was a

A poster in Tagalog depicting *noy-noying* that has come to define the inept presidency of Benigno Simeon Aquino Jr.

program designed to make it easy for plunderers to commit their evil deeds against the public till. Purportedly crafted to hasten the funding of government exigencies without congressional approval, it was alleged to have been used as a tool to bribe senators to convict Supreme Court Chief Justice Renato A.C. Corona during his impeachment trial in 2012.[20] Corona displeased the Aquino-Cojuangco clan because he had ruled in favor of peasant farmers in their fight to implement true land reform in Hacienda Luisita, a vast landholding in Central Luzon owned by the Cojuangco-Aquino dynasty.[21] The Yellows' hypocrisy and insatiable greed make the corruption described in Rizal's *Noli* and *Fili* look like child's play in comparison.

> *Wanton corruption was the hallmark of the Aquino-Cojuangco regimes*

[20] "Miriam Wants Probe on Alleged Bribery of Senators." *philippinestar.com*. https://www.philstar.com/headlines/2014/07/02/1341452/miriam-wants-probe-alleged-bribery-senators#wRdFcVyTAT89UjtB.99 (accessed October 9, 2018).

[21] "Arroyo Spokesman Claims PNoy Personally Asked Corona to Block the Distribution of Hacienda Luisita to Farmers." *politics.com.ph*. http://politics.com.ph/arroyo-spokesman-claims-pnoy-personally-asked-corona-to-block-the-distribution-of-hacienda-luisita-to-farmers/ (accessed October 1, 2018).

It has also spawned cultural mediocrity and comical ignorance due to its evil Hispanophobia. It is no wonder that many thinking Filipinos today view the illegal ascent to power of the Cory Cojuangco Aquino oligarchic dynasty as destructive. From 1987, when the Cory Constitution was fraudulently imposed by a rigged and flawed plebiscite, up to the end of the lackluster, corrupt and cruel regime of Cory's own son, the inept and inexperienced Benigno Simeon "Noynoy" Aquino Jr., the Philippines retrogressed and became poorer economically in spite of its great natural resources.

> **The lumads are the real Mindanao natives, not the Muslims who terrorized them**

So failed was her son's regime that its negativity is summed up in the pejorative coined word *noynoying* which, according to *Wikipedia*, is "a play on the term planking and Aquino's nickname, 'Noynoy.' *Noynoying* involves posing in a lazy manner, such as sitting idly while resting [one's] heads on one hand and doing nothing."[22] That is why, when the 2016 presidential elections were held, the vast plurality of Filipino voters, choking in disgust, anger and indignation at the atrocities and the banalities of the American-sponsored Aquino-Cojuangco misrule, overwhelmingly handed victory to a virtual unknown, Rodrigo Duterte y Roa. His win was so resounding that no amount of massive electoral cheating by the Yellow Regime through the Commission on Elections could prevent.

The weakness of the corrupt and poor Filipino State became so obvious that the self-styled freedom fighters who comprise the Moro Islamic Liberation Front (MILF) were able to intimidate it into signing an atrocious "comprehensive peace agreement" geared at giving them a territory of their own that they can exploit economically, politically and even militarily.

Never explained in all this, however, is the madness of allowing a terrorist and rebel group like the MILF to have its own military camp within Philippine territory. This weakening of Philippine sovereignty has been allowed since the time of President Fidel V. Ramos, except during

---

[22] "Noynoying." *wikipedia.org*. https://en.wikipedia.org/wiki/Noynoying (accessed June 1, 2018).

the brief presidency of Joseph Estrada who ordered an all-out assault by the Armed Forces to destroy and capture this military camp (Abubakar). The Armed Forces successfully overran the camp to impose the country's sovereignty but Estrada had to pay a stiff political price.

He was shortly thereafter illegally ousted from the presidency by a mob with U.S. approval. What followed was incomprehensible: Camp Abubakar, for which our fighting men and women in the Armed Forces shed their blood, was inexplicably handed back to the MILF rebels and terrorists. Why? Who arranged for the unlawful return of this rebel military camp to the same rebels and terrorists? Malaysia? The CIA? Fidel V. Ramos? The UK? What happened to this country's sovereignty?

The next thing we heard was that the MILF was giving refuge to a Malaysian terrorist inside Camp Abubakar. Marwan, a bomb maker, wanted by the United States, was targeted by

Why is the government allowing a Moro rebel camp to operate in its territory?

the Aquino government. An ill-advised Noynoy Aquino sent a police team of Special Action Force (SAF) to arrest the terrorist. But the MILF forces, purportedly defending the "territorial independence of their military camp," mercilessly ambushed and massacred a total of 44 SAF elements in the vicinity of Mamasapano. They were brutally slaughtered just like that as if they were not inside Filipino territory. Perpetrators of the Mamasapano massacre remain unpunished. To rub salt into the wound, the MILF has been rewarded with the passage in Congress of the unconstitutional Bangsamoro Organic Law to purportedly correct non-existent historical injustices against the Muslims in Mindanao.

In fact, if one looks closely at history, the Muslims in Mindanao are not the true natives there but the *lumads*, who are the real victims of injustice perpetrated by lawless Muslim elements who had raided their villages and terrorized them for centuries.

The over three decades of misrule by the Aquino-Cojuangco political dynasty on behalf of the U.S. WASP neo-colonizers is characterized, among other inexcusable, unconscionable and unforgivable things, by the loss of portions of the territorial patrimony of the Filipino nation. What is even more appalling and galling is that the claim that

Ninoy Aquino created a hoax that ruined the Philippines' claim on Sabah

the Muslims in Mindanao are the victims of a historical injustice is based on a big hoax—the Jabidah Massacre which was hatched by former Sen. Benigno Aquino Sr. to discredit President Marcos. Aquino Sr. is idolized as a hero by those who malign Marcos but seen as a heel by those who know his history as the one who facilitated the founding of the violent communist New People's Army in his family-owned Hacienda Luisita. The Jabidah Massacre yarn that he spun,[23] which led to the defeat of the Sabah claim by the Philippines, is now being cited as a historical injustice against the Muslims.

Aside from the Sabah debacle, the boundary provisions of the 1987 Cory Constitution has resulted in the diminution of the Filipino's economic zone in the West Philippine Sea. The loss of Bajo de Masinloc fishing ground (Panatag Shoal) is the outcome of the miscalculations of Noynoy Aquino and his subsequent poor dealings with a belligerent China through Sen. Antonio Trillanes IV under covert U.S. WASP dictation. The loss of Sabah and the Filipino economic zone in the Spratlys is today a done deal. Will Filipinos also lose Mindanao to Malaysia due to the hasty approval of the unconstitutional Bangsamoro Organic Law?

13. DURABILITY OF THE FILIPINO STATE

MANY THINKING FILIPINOS begin to doubt the durability of the Filipino State when they see the wanton corruption, plunder, selfishness, greed and treachery of their miseducated political leaders who are in government positions not to serve the Filipino State and people, but to rob them blind. Many Filipinos often say that, by and large, there is no future in this country. For over three decades the return of the oligarchs and the ascension to power of weak and corrupt leaders after the so-called People Power Revolution in 1986 has almost totally ruined the Filipino State and also betrayed, in the long run, the hegemonic

---

[23] Tatad, Francisco S. "Clueless on Sabah, Messed Up on Jabidah, Toothless on China." *manilastandard.net.* http://manilastandardtoday.com/opinion/89468/clueless-on-sabah-messed-up-on-jabidah-toothless-on-china.html (accessed May 10, 2018).

position and dreams of empire of the United States in Southeast Asia vis-à-vis the now powerful China.

Without the destabilizing efforts of the selfish and greedy oligarchs who did nothing but to destroy the reputation of the country abroad so no investors would come, the Philippines under the strongman leadership of then President Ferdinand E. Marcos could have become a bigger Singapore in its economy and an Italy or a Spain in its culture and tourism with the visionary programs of Imelda Romuáldez Marcos. But this unfortunate country has never taken off under the Hispanophobic and thoughtless Aquino-Cojuangco regimes and their sectarian Yellow followers who wantonly abuse their ill-gotten power.

The present Filipino State is headed for disaster. The 1840 prophecy of doom by the *mestiza terciada* Santa Clara nun is coming true. After alluding to the negative outcome of the forced language shift from Spanish to English and the total denaturalization of the Filipino in his national culture (*de español católico a inglés protestante y ateo-satanista*), the nun even prophesied a more catastrophic event. She foretold the transfer to Mindanao of the capital of these islands after describing Taal Lake as the mouth itself of a huge underwater volcano whose eruption will sink more than half of present-day Metro Manila and the then former provinces of Manila, Tondo and Morong. In her horrific vision, she saw the volcanic eruption causing the waters of Laguna de Ba-í to rise, rampaging through and bringing destruction over a good part of Luzon before reaching Lingayén.

And the remedy given by that same prophecy is to pray in Spanish to the three advocacies of the Virgin Mary.[24] But the problem today is that the de-Hispanized Catholic clergy has become largely too Americanized and corrupt, leaving no room for a balanced life which could create the necessary environment to have an intellectual and cultural curiosity to learn Spanish.

---

[24] These advocacies are *la Virgen de Guadalupe*, protectress of the *indios filipinos católicos*; *la Virgen del Santísimo Rosario*, protectress of the *chinos cristianos criollos católicos*; and *la Virgen del Pilar*, protectress of the *españoles criollos filipinos* or *filipinos españoles*.

In order for them to be able to pray in Spanish as advised by the prophecy, Filipino priests should first learn Spanish. To facilitate their learning of Spanish as a new language, they should be assigned to do missionary work for several years in Spanish-speaking countries throughout the world where they can benefit from language immersion. Once they have become fluent in Spanish, they can return to our old parishes to teach and to promote the Spanish language and the culture of Recto, Balmori and Bernabé along with the Catholic traditions of the Hispanic world of which *Filipinas* is one of its original members. Upon returning home, those already Spanish-speaking priests will ultimately regain our originally Hispanic Filipino soul and national identity without the vapidities of American pop culture.

President Rodrigo Duterte y Roa

Disrupting the dream of the Yellows to stay in power to continue with their massive corrupt practices was the unexpected entry into the national political scene of the controversial Rodrigo Duterte y Roa. President Duterte won on his promise of change: to stop the illegal drug trade and to curb government corruption. He won the presidency despite efforts by the Yellow electoral cheating machine to stymie the will of the people.[25]

Right after his presidential inauguration, President Duterte implemented a bloody drug war to free millions of Filipinos hooked on *shabú* from the grip of their pushers and suppliers. Many illegal drug laboratories were raided and shut down forcing big-time drug lords to flee the country or be neutralized.

---

[25] "Duterte Supporters Allege Cheating in Presidential Polls." *rappler.com.* https://www.rappler.com/nation/172141-duterte-youth-cheating-presidential-elections-comelec (accessed October 12, 2018).

But what really rocked the nation is the case of Leila de Lima, former justice secretary under Benigno Aquino Jr. Her alleged connivance with some jailed drug lords, mostly local Chinese, converted the national penitentiary in Muntinlupa into a *shabú* drug laboratory and a national distribution center of prohibited drugs.

What is beyond the pale and worthy of a special entry in *Ripley's Believe It Or Not* was the conversion by prison inmates of portions of the New Bilibid Prison building in Muntinlupa into a country club-like

Leila de Lima

dwelling for the convicted drug lords to live in luxury. The drug lords enjoyed five-star hotel accommodations, including suites complete with jacuzzi, while directing the drug trade from inside the prison walls. In the maximum security compound, the convicted drug lords built an air-conditioned ballroom and jazz theater where celebrities were paid handsomely to entertain them. Reprehensible is a video footage showing De Lima in skimpy attire dancing before the same drug lords who allegedly contributed millions of

> *Drug convicts lived a lavish lifestyle at Muntinlupa under Leila de Lima's watch*

pesos to bankroll her senatorial campaign for which she won the seat with the apparent intercession of her Yellow patrons. After drug charges were filed against her by the Duterte administration with the drug lords testifying against her, she is now detained awaiting trial. She is referred to by conservative quarters as the measure of the "disgraceful modern advancement and triumph of the English-speaking Filipina."

De Lima is also being perceived as the degradation of the Filipina who has no longer any notion of the Hispanic Filipina María Clara. She and several other Yellow personalities are also being held as the alleged "living examples" of the American corrupted and miseducated Filipina. They have come to represent the loathsome corruption that started with the unelected and unelectable Corazon Aquino whose bogus presidency was forced upon the unwary Filipinos in 1986, causing irreparable damage to the Filipino State.

Spanish friars introduced plants, animals and farm practices from the New World into the country

Yet many international human rights advocates still listen to the likes of Leila de Lima. She also has the ear of the highly politicized elements of the Philippine English-speaking Catholic hierarchy which is critical of the Duterte administration.

14. THE FILIPINO STATE OWES A GREAT DEAL OF ITS EXISTENCE TO THE SPANISH RELIGIOUS MISSIONARIES

NOBODY CAN DENY the fact that the creation and material development of the Filipino State is due to the pioneering work of the Spanish religious orders and missionaries. Aside from giving us Roman Catholicism as a major Spanish legacy, they contributed in all areas of daily life which the late historian Pio Andrade listed in detail in an article, excerpt of which is reproduced below.[26] These accomplishments are not adequately described—if they are mentioned at all—in history textbooks.

1. THE FRIARS PROPAGATED MANY USEFUL PLANTS FROM MEXICO DURING THE MANILA-ACAPÚLCO GALLEON TRADE. In history textbooks and press articles, the Galleon trade has been simplified as the commercial exchange of Mexican silver with Chinese silk and spices. But many Filipinos do not know of the Mexican plants that came with the galleons, such as corn (*maiz*),

camote (camotl), peanuts, tomato, sunflower, *ipil-ipil*, cacao, indigo, *kalachuchi*, marigold, *kamatchili* (*quamochitl*), *kakawati*, maguey, tobacco, acacia, *caballero*, papaya, *chico*, coffee, pineapple, guava. These plants have increased the Philippines' food supply, providing us new medicines, giving rise to rural industries, and

---

[26] Andrade, Pio. Jr. "'Padre Damaso' and the Friars: Myth Versus Reality." *inquirer. net.* https://lifestyle.inquirer.net/220264/padre-damaso-and-the-friars-myth-versus-reality/ (accessed October 10, 2018).

beautifying backyards and plazas. Some of the better-known friars responsible for the introduction of such flora were Fr. José Dávila (cacao and chocolate making); Fr. Diego García (tobacco and cigar making); Fr. Tomás Moncada (wheat); Fr. Octavio (indigo and processing of indigo dyestuff); and Fr. Antonio Sedeño (mulberry; he was a Jesuit, not a friar, but just the same a Catholic missionary like the friars).

Philippine history textbooks are silent about Mexican plants being introduced locally and the big role the friars played in propagating them all over the country. Some of the plants led to the establishment of extensive rural industries such as cigar, indigo dye, tanning leather, chocolate and coffee. But the friars also propagated useful plants from neighboring Asian countries. They popularized the use of moras or vetiver for erosion control of irrigation canals and small streams; citrus plant species from China for eating and cooking; rosemary and thyme for home remedies; and sugarcane from China for the manufacture of sweets. The Dominicans brought Tonkin seeds (from Vietnam, of course) and showed the plant's medicinal potentials

2. **THE FRIARS BUILT ROADS AND BRIDGES FOR TRANSPORTATION.** Dominican Fr. Juan Villaverde built over 100 kilometers of roads in Pangasinan, Nueva Vizcaya and Kiangan. He also pointed out the Dalton Pass as the gateway to

Cagayan Valley. Recollect Fr. Pedro Cuenca built the Bacolod-Minuluan Road in Negros; Franciscan Fr. Victorino del Moral built the famous Puente del Capricho in Majayjay, Laguna; and Fr. Andres Patiño built the Tinajeros Bridge in Malabón. The friars quarried stone and introduced new building technologies.

Dominican Fray Domingo de Salazar, the first bishop of Manila, quarried at the mouth of the Pasig to come up with solid materials to replace the combustible nipa-and-wood house of the native Filipinos. Jesuit Fr. Sedeño introduced the technology of brick-making and burning limestone to make lime as mortar for brick and stones to build stone structures. These translated into the building of durable, long-lasting stone bridges, churches, schools, fortifications and *bahay-na-bato*.

3. **THE FRIARS INTRODUCED MODERN IRRIGATION.** The Philippines was a rice exporter in the 1860s until 1880s because of the irrigation systems built by the friars in many provinces. In Cavite

province, the Recollects built 18 irrigation systems that watered 21,000 hectares of rice lands. In Calamba, Laguna, under the Dominicans, eight irrigation systems watered 4,250 hectares of rice lands. In Bataan, an irrigation dam of the Dominicans supplied water to 521 hectares of rice lands. Bulacan had two friar-built irrigation systems watering 1,850 hectares. In Umingan, Pangasinan, a Dominican priest taught the farmers how to build portable bamboo water-wheels to draw water from brooks or streams below the level of farmlands. We became a rice importer because it was more profitable to raise sugarcane, abaca and tobacco than rice by the 1880s.

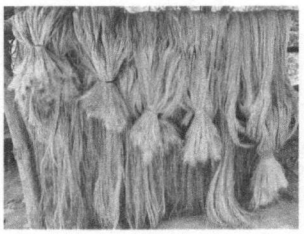

4. **THE FRIARS MADE THE ABACA INDUSTRY.** Abaca was a Philippine monopoly and a major export crop starting in the 1830s. Credit is due Franciscan Fray Pedro Espallargas in Albay for inventing the abaca stripper, which made abaca fiber extraction faster and easier while increasing the yield and quality of the abaca fiber, the best marine fiber in the world. The abaca stripper was so successful that, from 1830 to 1920, abaca became known internationally as 'Manila hemp,' and it accounted for 20-40 percent of the foreign exchange earnings of the Philippines. Fr. Espallargas is unmentioned in history textbooks.

5. **THE FRIARS ESTABLISHED THE HOSPITAL, BANKING AND WATER SYSTEMS IN THE PHILIPPINES.** Fr. Felix Huertas, a Franciscan, is unknown except for a street in Manila's Santa Cruz district, which does not identify him as a priest. He was the head of San Lázaro Hospital for lepers and he founded Monte de Piedad, a combination of savings bank and pawnshop, which was the first agricultural bank of the Philippines.

But his greatest achievement was completing the forgotten Carriedo to supply Manila with safe, potable running water beginning in 1882. I do not remember reading about Fr. Huertas in the many articles on Manila's past published in the Philippine press.

6. **THE FRIARS ESTABLISHED THE MODERN PRINTING PRESS.** Dominican Fr. Francisco Blancas de San José introduced modern printing in the Philippines. This replaced the wooden block press, also introduced by him and the Dominicans, which published the first books in the country such as *Doctrina Cristiana*. The press was a big help in education. It helped disseminate the Gospel in the native languages, which meant the friars did not destroy local languages and cultures, as most history books

virulently declare, but, rather, they studied and conserved them. The press that Fr. Blancas established is still running today—the University of Santo Tomás Press, which is the second oldest in the world after Cambridge.

7. **The friars cultivated the Filipino's talent in music and the performing arts.** Filipinos are the minstrels of Asia. One writer noted that nightclubs in Asia would always boast of their Filipino musicians. Indeed, the Philippines may be the most musical of Asians and the friars cultivated the musicality of Filipinos. Franciscan Fr. Jerónimo Aguilar was the first to teach Filipinos and deepen their musical talents. The friars taught the natives music for Mass and other religious rituals. I have seen in the National Archives a few *cuentas*, the record of income and expenses of each province during the Spanish era; they showed that choir members were paid for their services.

8. **The friars defended the Filipinos from abusive Moro attackers and slave traders and built fortifications that have withstood the test of time.** While busy building communities, the friars were also defenders of the natives from corrupt local leaders and pirates who periodically raided coastal villages to plunder and acquire slaves.

9. **The friars built a hospital and welfare system in the Philippines that was ahead of North America's.** The friars built the first hospitals in the Philippines; they built them in the first century of Spanish rule, antedating the system in the United States by 100 years. They introduced medicinal plants from Mexico and Spain and recorded for posterity the herbal cures used by the natives, so that Philippine herbal medicinal knowledge and skills were conserved.

10. **The friars built the sugar industry.** The giant sugar industry was also due to the work of the friars, particularly the Recollect missions in Negros. Sugarcane then was first crushed between two wood or stone cylinders called *trapiche* to yield its sweet juice. Fr. Fernando Cuenca introduced the first hydraulic sugarcane crusher in 1850, which began the sugar boom and made Negros a very wealthy province.

11. **THE FRIARS BUILT THE LOOMING INDUSTRY.** The Dominicans, who founded University of Santo Tomás, the oldest university and the only pontifical univer-

sity in Asia, introduced the first modern loom system, supplanting the native loom and making weaving faster and easier. Thus, the weaving industry became a big home industry in many places in the country.

12. **THE FRIARS, NOT THE NORTH AMERICANS, INTRODUCED PUBLIC INSTRUCTION.** Most Filipinos have been led to believe that Spain did not educate the Filipinos to make them submissive to Spanish officials and that the United States introduced public education in the Philippines. This is a big lie.

Formal public education in the Philippines officially began in 1863 with the Educational Reform Act. But even before that the friars had been active in teaching elementary reading and writing.

Gunnar Myrdal, in his monumental classic *Asian Drama*, wrote that the Philippines was ahead of other colonized Asian countries in education in the second half of the 19th century. The Philippines had higher literacy than other Asian countries, even higher than Spain, according to data submitted by Taft to the U.S. Congress. This was, in fact, the prime reason for the Katipunan revolution—our relatively advanced state of education and the economic progress under Spain that had been largely fostered by the friars. Revolutions are not started by uneducated masses. It is important to point out that the Philippines was economically prosperous during the last four decades of Spanish rule, thanks to the agriculture-based industries—abaca, sugar, tobacco, indigo, and coffee—the propagation and cultivation of which were pushed by the friars.

13. **PREJUDICE.** Many of the information about the big role the friars played in Philippine cultural and economic advancement are not being taught in our schools; thus, generations of Filipinos do not know of the good friars. Thus, Filipinos are culturally Catholics but are superficial about Catholicism, especially its moral teachings and the work of the missionaries.

15. IS PRESIDENT DUTERTE THE SAVIOR OF THE FILIPINO STATE?

IN SEVERAL OF HIS speeches about the anti-drug campaign he has launched with the Philippine National Police and other law enforcement agencies, President Duterte has declared that he is out to protect the new generations from destructive drugs, particularly from the Chinese-operated *shabú* laboratories. Because *shabú* is cheap, it is easily available even to children and teenagers. After a year or two of abusing the drug, the user's brain shrinks by a third of its size. Many poor Filipinos use it daily because it does not only give them pleasure but even mitigates their hunger.

It is safe to say that most crimes in the Philippines are drug related. Drug dealing has turned into almost everybody's lucrative sideline. It does not help that some policemen themselves are involved in get-rich-quick schemes, recycling and selling drugs they have confiscated in raids. Even politicians become tycoons when engaged in the drug trade. It is widely believed that Chinese syndicates are responsible for manufacturing the drugs on a massive scale and some Muslims are its most avid distributors, pushers and sellers. It is the unaware young that is enticed to use it with promises of adventure.

The ISIS-inspired and Maute-led invasion of Marawi City in Mindanao in 2017 was bankrolled by Muslim drug lords and politicians, according to some reports.[27] A Muslim Maranao mayor was recently accused of selling *shabú* to his constituents. Of course, there are also Tagalog and Visayan politicians selling drugs. Many of them are listed in a dossier that intelligence agencies have provided to President Duterte. And he has repeatedly threatened to kill them if they did not quit the drug trade. But the drug lords here and abroad are fighting back against the anti-drug campaign of President Duterte by funding, directly and indirectly, all the media attacks against his person and his family.

The drug war has become bloody because the drug lords and their henchmen are armed and dangerous. They have no qualms in killing people who get in their way, including law enforcement officers ordered to apprehend them. Drug lords have their own private armies. Armed men in their employ ride motorbikes in tandem to kill drug dealers who fail to remit profits from their illegal activities. Critics conveniently blame President Duterte and the police for the death of innocent victims,

---

[27] Morallo, Audrey. "Defense Chief: Bulk Of Marawi Siege Funding Came from Drugs." *philstar.com*. https://www.philstar.com/headlines/2017/09/25/1742536/defense-chief-bulk-marawi-siege-funding-came-drugs

even of those slain in the turf wars among the drug syndicates. The Yellow political opposition tags President Duterte as a "human rights violator," using the still powerful and prostituted Yellow media as their echo chamber to magnify their unfair and untrue allegation. To stop this irresponsible Yellow criticism against his anti-drug operations, President Duterte has armed his agents with cameras and allowed the news media to accompany police raids to witness for themselves how police lives are in danger against drug syndicates. This strategy has somehow muted most of the exaggerations and lies being peddled against the anti-drug campaign, which has curbed crimes throughout the country.

The relentless war being waged against the evil of illegal drugs is causing a lot of unintended consequences, for sure, but it must be continued to free the country from the drug trade's choking tentacles. The sheer volume of drug surrenderees has taxed the meager resources of the government given the lack of rehab centers. It has also put more pressure to the already overflowing prison system. To decongest Philippine jails and drug rehabilitation centers, the government must allow the private

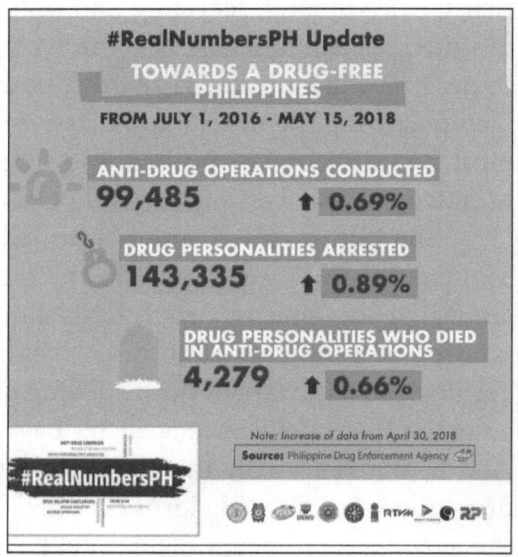

A government infographic to counter propaganda against President Duterte's anti-drug campaign.

sector to participate in building and managing new rehabilitation facilities as well as new jails and prisons.

The gargantuan drug problem has forced the hand of President Duterte to deal with it harshly. Many despairing Filipinos who worry about their own personal safety and that of their own family from the evil of the drug menace have thrust him into his reluctant role as the savior of the Filipino State. The drug problem facing the nation must be stopped at all costs. Filipinos must realize the grave danger this problem poses. Filipino national survival, even of the Filipino State itself, depends upon the success of President Duterte's drug war. The fact that he has started an honest-to-goodness crusade to stamp out the problem already makes him a savior of this country we originally know as *Filipinas*.

16. GETTING TO KNOW THE ROOTS OF RODRIGO DUTERTE Y ROA

THROUGHOUT THIS BOOK, the President's name is mostly written according to what our old Penal Code provides. When anyone is arrested in the Philippines, he or she is finger printed and his or her mug shot is taken. You must be familiar with the police practice of having the suspect display his or her name on a sheet of paper or chalkboard for the camera. The suspect's name is written the way the Spaniards do theirs. Thus Juan Ramos de la Cruz will have his name displayed as Juan de la Cruz y Ramos, the same way our elders wrote their names in the not-so-distant past. Following this naming convention, we shall call the President "Rodrigo Duterte y Roa" and not "Rodrigo Roa Duterte" or "Rodrigo R. Duterte." For the latter manner of identifying an individual is for one who is an American or a national of some other Western country besides Spain. And we know for a fact that President Duterte cannot be an American for obvious reasons.

The American way of writing names and surnames has been taught to every Filipino child. Our Americanized school system is to blame for this practice because it has unintentionally and carelessly ignored our independent Penal Code. In a perfect world, the education department would immediately take the proper measures to discontinue this folly. But for them to do the right thing will, of course, remain a pipe dream as long as they continue to fancy themselves as Americans and the Philippines as the fifty-first U.S. state.

Rodrigo Duterte y Roa first saw the light of day on March 28, 1945 in Maasin, Southern Leyte. His mother was born to a *chino cristiano* father surnamed Roa and to a Maranao mother. His father, on the other hand, was a descendant of a *mestizo español* from the *Parian de Cebú* who married a member of a *chino cristiano católico* family, a daughter of the Veloso clan from the same *parian* or *sector de mestizos*. This marriage produced President Duterte's paternal grandfather who married a pure *india* Cebuana surnamed Buot from a neighboring *municipio*. He later relocated to Maasin, Leyte, where President Duterte's father was born. From Maasin, the family moved to Davao where the elder Duterte, a lawyer, was elected Davao governor for three terms.

Growing up in Davao, the young Rodrigo Duterte y Roa briefly attended the Americanized Jesuit-run Ateneo de Davao where he came in contact with an American Jesuit priest, now long dead. This American Jesuit, according to President Duterte, was a pedophile who molested him and other Ateneo high school students at the confessional. (This ugly incident would not have happened to the young Digong Duterte if the former Spanish Jesuits of the likes of Padre Federico Faura were not hastily replaced by American Jesuits. Father Faura founded the Manila Observatory in 1869, which was so successful in predicting typhoons that not only did the country rely on his expertise but other countries in the Far East as well. American Jesuits like Finey, Zummacker, Meany and others discriminated against Spanish-speaking Filipino Jesuits like Hilario Lim and Joaquin Lim Jaramilio.)

No amount of cheating could stop the people from electing Rodrigo Duterte president

The sexual molestation he suffered in the hands of the American Jesuit has, for sure, left a lasting trauma in President Duterte, as he himself has revealed in not one but several nationally televised speeches. The sexual abuse was one more evil thing that WASP neo-colonialism has brought upon heedless Filipino students.

Similar to Claro M. Recto's "Hispanista vs. WASP case" but without the aggravating pedophile incident, President Duterte must have possibly seen in that American Jesuit, along with the shallowness of other American Jesuits and their unctuous Filipino confrères, an offending attitude of totalitarian disrespect for everything Filipino with Sino and Hispanic influences.

Right after his inauguration, U.S. WASP neo-colonizers wanted to immediately control his actions, including his war against drugs and corruption. Their arrogance obviously offended his cultivated independence. He fired back by declaring an independent foreign policy from U.S. WASP dictation, which is an old advocacy of nationalist Claro M. Recto who told the CIA to "have a decent respect for our sovereignty." This explains the new bilateral relationship with both China and Russia.

President Duterte, to defend himself and to counter the unjust demonization of his persona as the duly elected President of this country, responded very well with a masterstroke by bringing out old photos of the U.S. atrocities during the Filipino-American War. In that ruthless conflict, according to one estimate, up to three million Filipino combatants and civilians were killed either in battle, by diseases or by butcheries, foremost of which was the Balangiga massacre in Samar. The staggering number is shocking, considering that the Manila Spanish government, in a census conducted in the 1890s, had placed the Philippine population at the time at almost ten million.[28]

It is always relevant to remember that Miguel López de Legazpi, upon establishing our Filipino State as a political entity under the Spanish Crown, counted the number of native inhabitants in these islands who totaled, in the 1570s, not more than half a million individuals. He also counted no more than 150 Chinese shipwrecks. Not even the number of small Chinese traders living in junks docked around the shores of Baybay near what was later called *el distrito de San Nicolas* near Tondo escaped his notice.

In the course of over three centuries of Spanish tutelage, the original half a million inhabitants became almost ten million Filipinos in the late 1890s, consisting of the *chinos cristianos criollos*

As a young man, Mr. Duterte was molested by a Jesuit priest at Ateneo de Davao

and the Hispanic *criollos*, who were all bestowed Spanish citizenship by the Spanish Constitution of 1812 as subjects of the Spanish sovereign.

The Filipino State around that time had become, after Mexico's declaration of independence, an overseas province of Spain, like Cuba and Puerto Rico, which were all taken away from Spain as war booties after the 1898 Spanish-American War. The Philippines, which had already declared its independence from Spain, was also taken away from the Filipinos themselves by the Americans who tricked Gen. Emilio Aguinaldo.

Starting in 1898 and in the wake of their victory over Spain, the

---

[28] "The Philippines Genocide Three Million Filipinos Killed." *britsinthephilippines. top.* https://britsinthephilippines.top/philippines-genocide-3-million-filipinos-killed/ (accessed October 20, 2018).

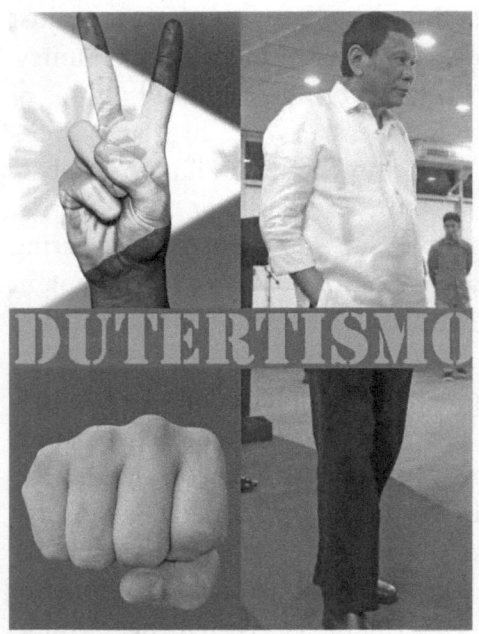

Dutertismo sums up President Duterte's no-nonsense approach to resolve issues.

U.S. colonizers took over the three overseas Spanish provinces. The first to fall was Cuba, which would be under U.S. influence for the next 60 years before getting tired of abuses under the corrupt and U.S.-sponsored dictator Fulgencio Batista y Zaldívar. Cuban revolutionary leader Fidel Castro, with the help of the Soviet Union, came to power during the 1959 Cuban revolution that ousted Batista. Since then, U.S. imperialists have imposed an economic embargo on Cuba.

Puerto Rico, for its part, remains an economically exploited U.S. colony. The utilization of its resources is hidden under the guise of declaring Puerto Rico an "associated state." Not a few Puerto Ricans are happy with the present set-up so much so that they have launched an Internet movement to return Puerto as a province of Spain.

Filipinas, now called "Philippines" or "Pilipinas," continues to be a U.S. neo-colony in spite of the grant of "political independence" in 1946. Among the unwanted results of this neo-colonialism are the economic enslavement of the country by U.S.-controlled international lending entities and the compulsory use of English as *the* medium of instruction in our schools.

In the face of pressing issues hounding the country, moves have started for a risky shift to federalism, which is also feared to be an expensive exercise as pointed out by President Duterte's own economic managers. Federalism is seen by its proponents as the answer to under-development as well as the Muslim demand for autonomy, if not independence. Pending approval of the proposed federal government, the President wants the Bangsamoro Organic Law to address in the interim the Muslim demand for greater autonomy. It cedes governmental control over areas comprising the so-called Bangsamoro ancestral lands, except control over the police and the military.

Another pressing national security concern is the stubborn and violent communist movement which has resorted to extortion activities in the countryside. Early in his presidency, President Duterte extended the olive branch to the communists, even appointing four leftist leaders to his Cabinet. But he halted the peace talks with the Communist Party of the Philippines when he sensed their insincerity in achieving real peace. No one knows how this on-again, off-again relationship of the Duterte administration with the communists will end.

President Duterte has his hands full fixing institutionalized bureaucratic corruption and addressing the threats of narcotics and terrorism posed by the Muslim terrorists in Mindanao and by the violent New People's Army. He sees the urgent need for systematically working toward peace. But recognizing the treacherous nature of the enemies of the State, he has also prepared the Armed Forces for war by further reforming and strengthening the military. In the midst of the Marawi occupation by the ISIS-inspired terrorist Maute group in 2017, he declared martial law in Mindanao.

Nationalist Sen. Claro M. Recto.

As he attends to these urgent matters President Duterte has to fend off the noisy and power-hungry Yellows, who are determined to grab power from him. The Yellows, led by the discredited Liberal Party, still control most of the local media that incessantly spouts opposition propaganda against the government.

To defend himself better, President Duterte and his administration need to have a stronger media arm to present much better television programs on Filipino nationalist culture and education, particularly in the areas of history and our Hispanic native languages. It should be done with a more dignified use of Tagalog-Filipino instead of Taglish and other bastardized versions of the language derived from the total imposition of fractured English. These programs should showcase our *parian* Chinese Christian Hispanic culture that is true to the Hispanic ideals of Rizal, Del Pilar, Aguinaldo, Recto, Quirino, Cuenco, Guerrero, Balmori, Tuason, Bernabé and other true nationalist Filipinos.

Our people's rich Filipino-Hispano poetry, along with its Filipino, Cebuano and Ilocano translations, should be dramatized in a program on government television tapping our young students as performers. Another program on our indigenous and our Hispanic dances should also be produced to preserve them so that the new generations will be informed about the Filipino national identity and its evolution. In line with the President's independent foreign policy, our government PTV 4 should also have programs emphasizing our historical brotherhood with 30 or so Hispanic nations of Central and South America, Africa, Europe and the Spanish-speaking areas in Asia such as Timor-Leste, Goa and the Moluccas. The more countries are aligned with the Philippines, the better for the Duterte administration and the new generations of Filipinos.

> *The opposition has unfairly tagged President Duterte as a human rights violator*

Dutertismo must be expanded and crystallized so that it becomes a coherent and well-defined ideology to guide Filipinos on the way forward. Then the Filipino State, *Ang Estado Filipino*, will surely be saved by President Rodrigo Duterte y Roa. And that will be his enduring legacy to his people.

17. THE FUTURE OF THE FILIPINO STATE

THE 1840 PROPHECY OF THE SANTA CLARA nun speaks of the dismemberment of the Filipino State due to the "invasion of a Protestant power" that will change our language from Spanish to English which will, in turn, lead to the country's disunity and dismemberment heralding an unnecessary return to our pre-Hispanic dispersion and into our forgotten and former mutually independent ethnic states.

The Filipino State called *Filipinas* was successfully started on June 24, 1571 by the Spanish *conquistadores* and the *frailes* with Manila as its *cabecera* or capital city but now it is imperiled by disunity out of ignorance and Hispanophobia. Of no help to preserving the Filipino State is the pernicious Americanization of the country. It forms a lethal mix when combined with other movements like the exaggerated *purista* indigenous movement and the *Balik-Islam* campaign being pushed by the separatist Bangsamoro rebel group. Some Filipinos, enticed by the Bangsamoro religious recruitment, are embracing Islam out of sheer political and sectarian opportunism. Every day, there seems to arise another minority movement that hurts and damages the unity embodied by the perfected Filipino State of 1571.

These dangers from within are compounded by the dangers from without. First, there is the threat posed by the Islamic fronts in the so-called Muslim Mindanao. Then, there is the security challenge presented by China, which has become an economic

Government television should produce programs to promote Filipino-Hispanic culture

superpower that rivals the United States. It has slowly but surely taken over a good part of the West Philippine Sea by turning some reefs and islets belonging to the Filipino State into artificial islands upon which are now built modern military bases. President Duterte has blamed U.S. inaction in the Spratlys which he said has presented the Philippines with a *fait accompli* in the West Philippine Sea because the U.S. never lifted a finger while China was just starting to build the artificial islands in the disputed waters.

Those of us who have read Claro M. Recto's prophetic *Monroismo asiático*[29] in its original Spanish can see the neo-colonizers' agenda in Asia and Oceania to build a wall of countries to contain and control the future China that would someday rise, in spite of the British Empire, to become a world power. Thus rose that wall of countries beginning with a humbled Japan, a former militaristic society which was tamed by the United States to do its bidding after becoming the first and only country in the world to be nuked, courtesy of U.S. President Harry Truman who ordered the atomic bombing of Hiroshima and Nagasaki near the end of World War II. South Korea, Taiwan and the Philippines have also been co-opted to form

---

[29] Claro M. Recto, *Monroísmo asiático (artículos de polémica) y otros ensayos* (Manila: Imprenta de Juan Fajardo, 1921).

this wall of countries against China, not to mention the cooperation of the British-influenced Malaysia, Indonesia, Singapore, Australia and the Anglicized Sri Lanka, India and Bangladesh.

The Filipino State, due to its close proximity to China, will be one of the most affected countries in case a war breaks out between the United States and China. Will the Filipino State survive?

Perhaps, a solution could be found in the long-desired American statehood—long-desired at least in the minds of some extremely pro-American Filipinos, that is—or even a return to the 1930s Commonwealth status, similar to the associated state standing of Puerto Rico. This will give the United States a solid legal foundation to be in Asia to stop the encroaching influence of China. But this idea, given the anti-immigrant sentiments within the ruling American Republican Party, a strain of which borders on racist beliefs, is a pie in the sky.

Given the near impossibility of achieving U.S. statehood for the Philippines, we are back to the solution offered by the 1840 prophecy. The Catholic clergy should begin relearning and praying in Spanish for the Virgin Mary's intercession to save the Filipino State from doom.

Una leyenda filipina

Las Tres Virgenes y la profecia

PART II

THE ENDURING LEGACY
OF THE THOMASITES

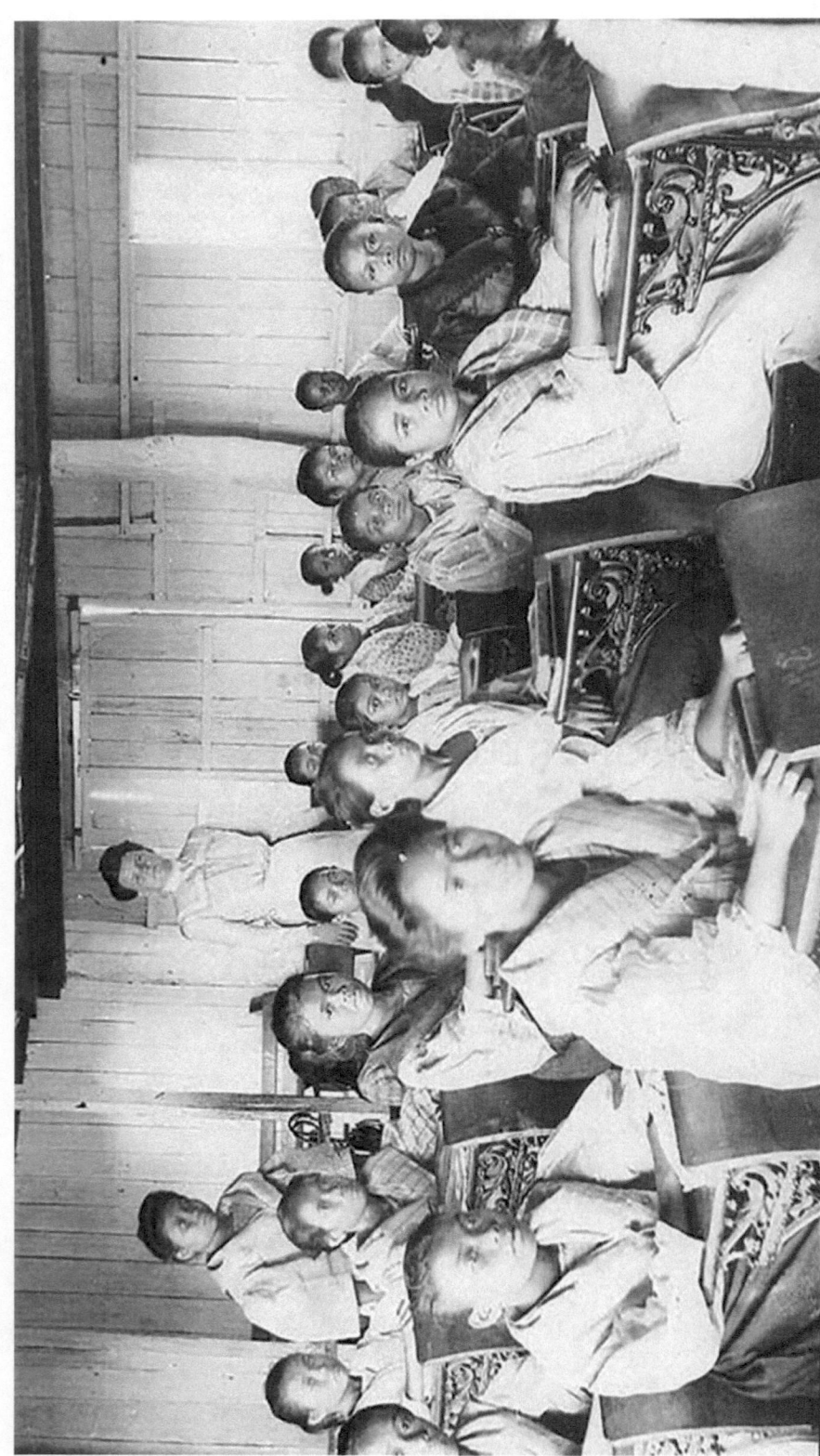

A Thomasite teacher and her students (circa 1901).

1. WHAT WENT WRONG
WITH OUR EDUCATIONAL SYSTEM

The first American teachers who were dispatched by the U.S. government to the Philippines arrived two years after the American takeover of the country. They eventually came to be known as Thomasites because they landed aboard a cattle cargo vessel called the USS *Thomas*.

The original Thomasites, a group of about 500 American teachers, were sent to the Philippines by the U.S. government in 1901 to teach English as part of the U.S. policy of attraction after the 1898 *República de Filipinas* was destroyed by invading American military forces. As most Filipinos already know, the Americans snatched victory from the hands of the Filipino revolutionaries under the country's first president, Gen. Emilio Aguinaldo, who was leading the revolution against Spain. The American invasion of the Philippines was a result of the Spanish-American War triggered by the sinking of the USS *Maine* at Havana Harbor during the Cuban revolt against Spain.

It was obvious the main goal of the so-called benevolent assimilation policy was to be advanced by mandatory universal education solely through the use of English as the medium of instruction. This Americanization of the Philippines was intended to hasten the acceptance by the Filipinos of the new economic and political order that the United States wanted to put in place.[1]

According to the new sheriffs in town, if no working knowledge of English was acquired by the native Filipinos, education was unilaterally considered not to have taken place among them. Without English, under

---

[1] Cabán, "Subjects and Immigrants During the Progressive Era."

this thinking, a Filipino is deemed illiterate even if he can correctly write and speak in Tagalog or any of his major native languages.

Before the Thomasites landed, the teaching of English to native children had fallen on the shoulders of American soldiers. They were known as McKinley soldiers after U.S. President William Mckinley who pushed for the surrender of the Philippine archipelago by Spain in 1898 as a prize of war. Some of them gleefully chronicled their tour of duty in which they bragged about educating "them Injuns with the crank and the kragg." This boast dovetailed with the Mckinleyan motto "to Christianize, to educate and to uplift" the Filipino.

The Thomasites' mission to teach English did not meet with complete success

But since the Filipinos of the early 1900s were already enjoying potable water, cheap electricity and fine silk, were interacting with friends by notes, postcards, phone calls and telegrams and grandly celebrating Christmas and Lent, who was there for the Thomasites to Christianize, educate and uplift in the English language?

An American linguist, Mary I. Bresnahan, who researched on the subject of English in the Philippines,[2] described how the Filipinos were initially traumatized when forced to learn English but over time, they learned to use the learning exercise to please their new colonial masters:

> In any case, it continues to be speculative if the Filipino's purported desire to learn English was genuine or not. Documents tell us about Filipinos trembling with fear inside their huts built on stilts as they expected the intrusion of the cruel Americans reputed to be blood thirsty giants bent on killing even the most trusting among them.[3] Unsure about the real motives of the invaders, the Filipinos did what they thought would please the Americans the most. And that was to learn their language—English.[4]

---

[2] Bresnahan, Mary I., "English in the Philippines," *Journal of Communication* 29, 2 (1 June 1979). 64–71. https://doi.org/10.1111/j.1460-2466.1979.tb02948.x

[3] To change this general perception, the Thomasites came and found acceptance by the Filipino population.

[4] Alfonso L. García Martínez, "The Imposition of English During the 1898-1901 Period," *The Americanization of the Philippines* (San Juan: Law College of Puerto Rico, 1982), 237-270.

Pleasing the new colonial masters by learning their language, it appeared, became the new norm so that even a Spanish school like *Colegio de San Juan de Letrán* released a textbook to teach the English language as early as 1902. It was a big boost to the beleaguered Thomasites because the 482-page book contained English language lessons which were effectively presented in both Tagalog and Spanish.

USS *Thomas* on dry dock for repair (circa 1916).

But the Thomasites had a hard time in their efforts to educate the Filipinos in English. While so much was expected of them by the American authorities, they faced headwinds with the passive resistance of some Filipino educators who did not shirk from showing their independent streak before a foreign power, not to mention the natural difficulty of submersing the native children in the American language. By 1916, despite their hard work, it was criticized in a report prepared by Henry Ford to U.S. President Woodrow Wilson:

> There is, however, another aspect in this case which should be considered. This aspect became evident to me as I traveled through the islands, using ordinary transportation and mixing with all classes of people under all conditions. Although, as based on the school statistics, it is said that more Filipinos speak English than any other language, no one can be in agreement with this declaration if they base their assessment on what they hear on the testimony of their hearing...Spanish is everywhere the language of business and social intercourse... In order for anyone to obtain prompt service from anyone, Spanish turns out to be more useful than English...And outside of Manila it is almost indispensable. The Americans who travel around all the islands customarily use it.[5]

What appeared to be a big deception was an earlier report of Director of Instruction David P. Barrows, which claimed that the forced study of English had benefited Spanish as more and more Filipinos were learning it:

---

[5] "The Use of English," *The Ford Report of 1916*, chap. 3, 365-366.

U.S. soldiers with Filipino women and a child.

It is to be noted that with the increased study and use of English, there has been an increased study of Spanish. I think it is a fact that many more people in these islands have a knowledge of Spanish now than they did when the American Occupation occurred.[6] Spanish continues to be the most prominent and important language spoken in political, journalistic and commercial circles. English has, therefore, active rivals as the language of trade and instruction. It is equally probable that the adult population has lost interest in learning English. I believe it is a fact that many more people now know the Spanish language than when the Americans sailed for these islands and their occupation took place...The customary prerequisite for dispatchers is for them to know English and Spanish. Through the great upsurge in numbers and circulation of newspapers and publications, there is much more reading matter in Spanish than before...[7]

Despite the challenges, the Thomasites persevered. They were determined to carry out their great task of teaching Filipinos to speak English. Their enthusiasm, however, was not universally shared by Filipino educators, especially those steeped in the Katipunan ideals enshrined in the *Primera República*'s *universidad literaria*. Among these contrarian educators were Dr. Leon María Guerrero and Don Enrique Mendiola, co-founders of the *Liceo de Manila*, Librada Avelino, founder of the *Centro Escolar de Señoritas*, Mariano Jócson, founder of the *Colegio de Manila*, *Las Maestras* Avanceña and Don Manuel Locsin, founders of the *Instituto de Molo*, Iloilo, Doña Florentina Tan Villanueva, founder of the *Escuela de Cebú*, and *Gran Maestra* Rosa Sevilla de Alvero, founder of the *Instituto de Mujeres*.

These native educators were for the use of both Spanish and Tagalog, with Visayan and Ilocano, as media of national education. They viewed English as "a language of economic conquest."[8] The Thomasites, hampered

---

[6] *The 1908 School Report*, 96.

[7] Ibid., 9.

[8] Francisco Varona and Pedro de la Llana, *The Life of Librada Avelino*, bilingual edition in Spanish and English (Manila: Vera & Sons Publishing Co., 1935), 241.

in their task by such passive native resistance, were made acutely aware of Filipino sentiments that raised doubts about English ever becoming the language of the Filipino masses. The fact that English is not written as it is spoken made it difficult for Filipinos to learn as they naturally preferred their own native languages which are written the way they are spoken. The Tagalog phrase *mahirap ispiliñgin* (difficult to spell), which was coined out of their frustration in learning the new language, attests to this reality. Mr. Henry Ford himself referred to this fact in his report:

> The use of Spanish as an official language has been extended to January 1, 1920. Its general use seems to be spreading. Natives acquiring it learn it as a living speech. Everywhere they hear it spoken by leading people of the community and their ears are trained to its pronunciation. On the other hand, they [the natives] are *practically without phonic standards in acquiring English and the result is that they learn it as a book language rather than as a living speech.*[9.]

The italicized portion in the foregoing report rings true today as it did over a century ago. What is even more saddening today is the sight of many children dropping out of primary and secondary schools due to extreme economic hardship brought about by a ballooning foreign debt and the increasing prices of fuel, electricity and potable water. The decreasing number of school-age children getting sufficient education must be the reason English is fast becoming a minority language in these islands today. This slinking reality is supported by the fact that English-speaking politicians are forced to campaign in Tagalog, or Filipino, for votes. The government and the

AS AN EDUCATOR HE SHOULD KNOW THAT SPANISH SPEAKING FILIPINOS LEARN ENGLISH FASTER. ENGLISH AND SPANISH SHARE A 65% COGNACY RATE...

Doña Librada

DEBIERA SABER QUE EL FILIPINO DE HABLA HISPANA APRENDE EL INGLÉS CON MÁS RAPIDEZ.. PERO ES EL PREJUICIO QUE TIENE...

NEWTON GILBERT EDUCATION SECRETARY AND Governor General

---

[9] Italics mine.

private schools do not have enough money to pay teachers a truly living wage to sustain a quality English language education. In other words, the Filipino language ecology has started to self-destruct, and to blame for this is the de-emphasis of Spanish, the link between English and Tagalog, Visaya and Ilocano.

The Thomasites' goal of making Filipinos fluent in English fell short. Their efforts were impeded by the fact that the Philippines was not a *tabula rasa* with regard to language. There was already an existing Philippine language ecology with Spanish as its nucleus. Therefore, the aim to replace Spanish with English as the first step to also replace Tagalog (the actual basis of Filipino or Pilipino), along with Ilocano, Cebuano and Hiligaynon, could not take off with success. And this was the case because the imposition of English was actually going against an existing language ecology. Forcing Filipinos to learn it was a tactic that would backfire many years later as proven by the continued decline of English proficiency among Filipinos today.

The forced imposition of English has backfired, resulting in its pidginization

But the early legislative commissions that ruled the islands were determined to impose English at all costs. Some sweeping measures were inevitably implemented to help the Thomasites go about their linguistic task. The *Ford Report* gives us a glimpse of these measures that came in the form of harsh laws:

> Act No. 190 of the Commission[10] provided that English must become the official language of all courts and their records after January 1, 1906... Act No. 1427 extended the time to January 1, 1911... Act No. 1946 again extended the time to January 1, 1913.[11]

In short, it was the American regime back then that started the idea of teaching a language, whether English, Spanish or Tagalog, by force of law so that no one could escape its prevalence. But while they then wanted us

---

[10] It was then acting as the country's legislature.

[11] "The Use of English," *The Ford Report of 1916*, 368.

to believe this precedent as accepted wisdom, the neo-colonizers and their local partners in crime—in a crass exercise of double standard—are now singing a different tune, lecturing to us that "the compulsory teaching of Spanish by legislation would not succeed because of its obligatory nature."

After first declaring English as the official language of the courts starting in 1906, the American colonial authorities were faced with another self-imposed deadline to make it a reality on the first day of January 1913. But as the third deadline neared without them coming anywhere close to their goal, they issued Executive Order No. 44 on August 8, 1912. The decree allowed the continued use of Spanish as the language of the courts due to the impossibility of replacing it with English, a fact that Henry Ford acknowledged in his report:

> The practical impossibility of substituting Spanish for English in court proceedings and in municipal government was such that even if English was imposed as the official language on January 1, 1913, Spanish would still continue in use.[12]

Another law was enacted by the Filipino-dominated National Assembly on February 11, 1913 further extending the use of Spanish up to 1920. On this law, Henry Ford reported:

> There is no present prospect that Spanish can be superseded any more readily in 1920 than heretofore. And from all appearances, its place as an official language is securely established.[13]

In 1925, the Monroe Commission came to the islands to assess the educational system started in English by the Thomasites. With regard to the advance of English, this commission concluded that:

> Upon leaving school, more than 99% of Filipinos will not speak English in their homes. Possibly, only 10% to 15% of the next generation will be able to use this language in their occupations. In fact, it will only be the government employees, and the professionals, who might make use of English.

---

[12] Ibid., 369.
[11] Ibid., 368-369.

The publication of this report drew a reaction from Modesto Reyes y Lim, a Filipino writer in Spanish and a companion of José Rizal in Spain:

> ...with the same funding and efforts spent, with the same system and other modern means of instruction now employed in the obligatory instruction of English, if Spanish were instead taught to Filipinos, the proportion of modernly educated Filipinos would have been greater than the number produced with English as the medium of education. Now, because of this failure with English, we have no other just and natural alternative but to adopt Tagalog as the national and the official language.

Reyes, publisher and editor of the Rizalist publication *ISAGANI*, assailed the imposition of the English language upon the Filipino people and highlighted the withholding of the grant of American citizenship to Filipinos:

> In our humble opinion, the Philippines already had a national and official language in Spanish when it formed part of Spain. And we adopted Spanish as our own language because we were in fact Spanish citizens. But came the Americans and without first turning us into American citizens, they just went on forcing us to adopt their language through an educational system paid for by our own tax money.[14]

The relentless shelling and bombing of Manila near the end of World War II by the American liberation forces killed many Filipinos. Among them was a big number of Spanish speakers and writers. And the entry of the liberating American forces suddenly made English a necessary tool of communication for grateful Filipinos who came to adore G.I. Joe with his chocolates and his pam pams.

CHED has put the teaching of a foreign language course in the freezer

But right after the U.S. granted independence to the Philippines on July 4, 1946, the Soto-Magalona-Cuenco law was unanimously approved by a still largely Spanish-speaking legislature, thereby making Spanish a regular subject in college. As many

---

[14] Reyes, Modesto L., *ISAGANI* 1, no. 5 (June 1925). 24.

Spanish-speaking Filipinos across generations were still alive then, Spanish continued, in the words of Henry Ford, "as a living language."

This assessment did not sit well with the White Anglo-Saxon Protestant segment of the U.S. presence in the country. They viewed Spanish as a threat to English in the Philippines and resurrected a black propaganda against Spanish, dismissing it as "a dead and irrelevant language." Parents and students were brainwashed into believing that the 12-unit course in college was an economic burden. (Twenty-four units were previously required: 12 were devoted to grammar and the remaining 12 to the study of Filipino writings in Spanish.)

With the 1987 Cory Constitution in place, the supposed Spanish threat to the advance of English was at last eliminated from the official and the educational spheres. Article XIV, Section 7, Paragraph 7 of that Constitution provides that "Spanish and Arabic shall be taught on an optional and voluntary basis." But the Commission on Higher Education (CHED) refuses to organize a 12-unit foreign language course for the

college curricula so that neither Spanish nor Arabic nor any other foreign language can become a regular subject in the tertiary level. This deliberate violation of the Constitution by the CHED can be easily fixed through an executive order from the President, compelling both the CHED and the education department to allow the teaching of foreign language courses in college. But will anyone in the Executive Department take up this cause?

Over a hundred years since the Thomasites landed to tutor us in a new foreign language, all that has been accomplished is the replacement of Spanish as the country's official language. Aside from this we have the almost secret policy to force into phonetic Tagalog the unphonetic English alphabet, as pointed out by Henry Ford. This is now being done by ramming the entire English alphabet into Tagalog and almost all the other major native languages through the issuance of a circular by the education department without any clear objections from the Commission on the Filipino Language.

This forced cross-breeding of alphabets has given birth to a pidgin called Taglish, which is bad news for the efforts to promote English since it can lead to the further decline in the common use of English and even of standard Tagalog or Filipino itself.

Filipinos today are still being "educated" in compulsory English first implemented in 1916 by the tyrannical Jones law. Why is the teaching of other international languages like Spanish being deliberately withheld by education policymakers, especially by the controversial CHED? Why not make either Mandarin, Spanish or Arabic within the reach of Filipino students by offering them as regular or elective courses in schools?

The answer is that our education policymakers are dominated by U.S.-educated elites who dance to the tune of the neo-colonizers seeking economic dominance through the continued brainwashing of our children with the gravely flawed and inadequate teaching of the English language as their main tool.

Is language tyranny a part of the legacy of the Thomasites?

PART III

LANGUAGE DURING
SPANISH COLONIAL TIMES

Doctrina Christiana, en
lengua española ytagala, cor
regida por los Religiosos de las
ordenes Impressa con licencia, en
S. gabriel, de la orden de S. Domingo
En Manila. 1593.

1. HOW SPAIN MANAGED THE COUNTRY'S BABEL OF VOICES

Was there a language problem during the Spanish era? The answer is in the negative: **none, zero, zilch, nada**. This is so because the early Spaniards who came to the Philippine Islands were not opportunists when set against the unbridled capitalists whose vested economic self-interests and sectarian political agenda do not serve the common good of the Filipino people.

There is no doubt that the American people are generally good and have contributed much to humanity. But some of the policies of their government have done harm not only to the American people themselves but to the world outside of the United States as well. The irony of it all is that these policies are being carried out in the name of the American people who may not even be aware of what their government is doing.

> *Foreign influence on education policies are harmful to national interests*

Just like ordinary Filipinos, ordinary American families are mostly just concerned about survival. They worry about putting food on the table, providing healthcare for their family, saving for the college education of their children and other mundane concerns that come with daily existence.

Sadly in the Philippines, despite the presence of some highly motivated individuals like the Peace Corps volunteers who project the best of America's ideals in the pursuit of individual happiness and freedom, the Ugly American stereotype is what prevails. The machinations of the WASP neo-colonizers and their lackeys here leave a bitter taste in the mouth.

Perceptive Filipinos have long alleged that the CIA has subsidized Protestant missionaries and their Filipino underlings in education to exert undue influence over the curricula of the educational system. The funding of these missionaries by the CIA to influence the policies of foreign governments is also alleged by author David Stoll in his book, *Fishers of Men or Founders of Empire?*:

x x x evangelical missionaries are the most dedicated U.S. presence in the Third World. This fact has not been lost on their Government, which subsidizes mission relief and gives technical aid through the U.S. Agency for International Development (USAID). Nor has this reality been lost on the Central Intelligence Agency (CIA). Following exposure on church protest in 1976 the CIA said it would stop recruiting missionary collaborators. A proposed CIA charter would prohibit paid use of U.S. missionaries but permit voluntary contacts or voluntary exchange of information.

> *Neo-colonialism casts a long shadow over all facets of Philippine society*

In another book, Stoll reveals how a Protestant organization carried out its activities in Latin America:

x x x To avoid Catholic and anticlerical opposition, Wycliffe went to the field under the name of the Summer Institute of Linguistics (SIL). By claiming to be primarily a scientific research organization, it was able to obtain official contracts and cultivate government authorities, whose support usually protected it from expulsion, but also guaranteed a new controversy within a few years.[1]

***

Army World Service Office...was receiving 44 percent ($3.1 million of $7.1 million). The World Relief Corporation obtained 25 percent of its budget from USAID in 1983-1984 ($3.1 million of $12.5 million). Food for the Hungry 9 percent ($9 million of $10 million) and World Vision on the order of 6 percent ($9.4 of an estimated $150 million). Other evangelical PVOs... MAP International and Mennonite Central Committee, and the Summer Institute of Linguistics—received approximately 1 percent or less of their budget from USAID Programs 1983-84 (U.S. Agency for International Development, supplemented by author's estimate for World Vision). Observers like Jean Pierre Bastian and Ruben Alves believe that Protestantism has failed, co-opted by Latin America's authoritarian tradition.[2]

---

[1] David Stoll, *Is Latin America Turning Protestant?: The Politics of Evangelical Growth* (Los Angeles: University of California Press, 1990), 17.

[2] Ibid., 330.

The tentacles of neo-colonialism extend far beyond merely shaping Philippine education policies. It casts a long shadow over almost all facets of national life as exposed by an article by Volt Contreras in the *Philippine Daily Inquirer* back in 2003:[3]

The pervasiveness of its presence is astounding, which makes the extent of its influence a subject of high suspicion.

And agility—the swift coordination that allows one to do several things almost all at the same time—appears to mark the way AGILE (for Accelerating Growth, Investment and Liberalization with Equity) is helping shape many aspects of Filipino life.

That this is hardly known to the Filipino public, or even to certain lawmakers, is among the reasons the uproar over it has been particularly loud.

---

[3] Contreras, Volt. "The AGILE Factor, Unseen Hand Behind 50 Laws, Executive Orders," *Philippine Daily Inquirer*, March 19-23, 2003.

AGILE, a U.S.-funded program that is unique to the Philippines, has so far engaged close to 20 government agencies here since it was put up in June 1998 under an agreement between the Philippines and the United States.

As a mechanism that pools mostly Filipino experts who provide technical services or advice to departments, bureaus and congressional committees, AGILE's inputs have found their way into many of the Philippines' more recent economic measures and policies.

The bottom line, according to AGILE's objectives as presented on its Web site, is to foster a favorable investment climate and thus spur economic growth, create jobs, and reduce poverty.

From industry regulations to agriculture modernization, from revenue generation to anti-piracy campaigns, from orienting the judiciary on newly passed commercial laws to formulating new bidding procedures for government supply contracts—these are just some of the concerns AGILE has helped the Philippine government address.

AGILE chief of party Dr. Ramon Clarete, an economics professor from the University of the Philippines, said there is a 41.6-million-dollar aid package from the U.S Assistance for International Development (USAID).

Back to the language issue, if Filipino taxpayers were U.S. citizens and Protestants in their vast majority, there would, perhaps, be nothing wrong with the influence that these missionaries, and their local collaborators, bring to bear. But the contrary is true, and this makes all such likely interventions in Philippine educational curricula (particularly in the teaching of the Spanish and the Tagalog languages in college) a totally offensive and brazen act of sectarian neo-colonialism.

In stark opposition to this insolent language neo-colonialism, the early Spanish Catholic *conquistadores* begin to look like saints. Attuned to their times, they had one clear, and transparently simple, objective. And that was to profit from what they thought was the lucrative spice trade then held and controlled by their Iberian rivals, the Portuguese.

The Spanish Catholic missionaries who came to the Philippines also had their own objective, which was simple and clear: to live and work with the indigenous peoples of these islands in order to Christianize them and, in the process, to impart to them the basics of European civilization since these objectives, according to their own considerations, would lead to the salvation of native souls.

Instead of suppressing native languages, the friars learned them to preach the Gospel

In order to do their work of spiritual salvation, the Spanish friars learned the native languages of the islanders to enable them to preach the Catholic Gospel. Replacing the native languages with Spanish was farthest from the friars' minds as the J. Law No. XXX of the *Patronato Real* (Royal Patronage) clearly stated what was expected of them to do when it came to religious education:

> *Que los Clérigos y Religiosos no sean admitidos a doctrinas sin saber lengua general de los indios que han de administrar. Don Felipe II, en El Pardo, a 2 de diciembre de 1578.*[4]

With regard to the idea of teaching the Spanish language to the indigenous people, an earlier law, No. XVIII from the book of the Laws of the Indies (*Leyes de Indias*) issued on July 7 and July 17, 1550 by the Spanish Emperor Don Carlos I (Charles V of Germany), it was clearly decreed that:

> *Que dónde fuere posible se pongan escuelas de la Lengua Castellana para que la aprendan los indios. x x x Y habiendo resuelto que convendrá introducir la Castellana, ordenamos que a los indios se les pongan Maestros que enseñen a los que voluntariamente lo quieran aprender como les sea menos molestia y sin coste...*[5]

---

[4] My translation: That the Clerics and the Religious missionaries may not be allowed to teach the (Christian Catholic) Doctrine without (first) knowing the general language of the indigenous peoples whom they are to serve.

[5] That wherever it may be possible, schools for Spanish be opened so that the same may be learned by the natives... And, having resolved that it is convenient to introduce the Spanish language to them, we order that Teachers be provided to the indigenous peoples who will teach Spanish to the said indigenous peoples who may volunteer to learn the same in a manner that is without burden and cost to them....

An old copy of the Law of the Indies.

With these royal policies, the native islanders, ancestors of the present-day Filipinos, had no language problem as we do today because they were not compelled to learn Spanish. The misguided policy to impose English as the medium of instruction in our schools is also mutedly killing Tagalog, our native language. This is being accomplished through the process of destroying its main phonetic characteristics by cramming into it the English, or Taglish, alphabet and preventing the full use of Filipino as the medium of education in the Philippines.

During the Spanish era, there was no such thing as a language problem in these islands as it is understood today. Neither was there an intention to perpetrate any form of social, economic and cultural genocide with the native Tagalogs as the victims through the understated switch of alphabets—which, in turn, would force an unjust language change from a superior one (Tagalog), because phonetic, to another that is clearly inferior, because complicatedly unphonetic, anarchical and illogical (English), spelling-wise and pronunciation-wise.

PART IV

THE EVOLUTION OF THE NATIVE
FILIPINO ALPHABET

CUADRO PALEOGRÁFICO DE LAS ISLAS FILIPINAS

COMPARADO POR

DON PEDRO ALEJANDRO PATERNO

Alfabeto	A	B	D	EI	G	H	K	L	M	N	NG	OU	P	S	T	V	Y
De Manguanes																	
" Tagabanuas																	
" Tagalog (en general)																	
" Camining (peculiar)																	
" Bulacan y Tondo (id.)																	
" Visaya																	
" Pampanga																	
" Pangasinan																	
" Ilocos																	
" Asaba																	
" Toba																	
" Bugui																	
" Borneo																	
" Java antiguo																	
" Arabia																	
" Hebreo																	

NUMERALES

1 Usa
2 Dua
3 Tuló
4 Upat
5 Limá
6 Unôm

10 Isampulo
100 Sangatu

TAGBANUA

co. — Francisco
sig.
gat — San
Pa.

Aldao { dao (sol) }
Al — S.
Danum { num (agua) }
Da — S.

Bula { la-S. (luna) }
Bu — S.
Inum { num (beber) }
I. — S.

O = ba
O = be
Q = bu

S = do + ka
S = de + ki
S = do + , ku

MANGUIAN

ко mi
nasaías
san to
santa
pag
gastal

hambres
Pedro
Cecilia

kag
san Ye
san Pedro
san Dio
Cecilia

ba ye
mujeres
nge

TAGALOG

Don — a qui
Don Agustin — Tambon
Doña — Elena — de la Cruz
Doña — Elena — de la Cruz

Baybayin is a Filipino pre-Hispanic alphabet.

1. MESSING WITH *ABECEDARIO* LEADS TO THE DUMBING DOWN OF FILIPINOS

When the Spanish missionaries came to the Philippine Islands after the establishment of the first permanent Spanish settlement in Cebú in 1565, they discovered that the native languages, particularly Tagalog, Ilocano and Visayan, had no native alphabet to speak of. What passed off as their alphabet was some kind of a syllabary, called *baybayin* or *alíbatá*, of a vague Arab provenance most likely coming from the Sultanate of Sulú, which was believed to have been a dominant power prior to the coming of the Spaniards.

In time, what was, perhaps, one *baybayin-alíbatá* took many written forms to the extent that the Tagalog *baybayin-alíbatá*, for instance, could no longer be easily read by Ilocanos and Visayans for it had developed independently from those used by non-Tagalogs until it evolved into something totally different.

Over time, the differences presented a challenge to the Tagalogs who could no longer decipher the *baybayin-alíbatá* that emerged in the Ilocos and the Visayas. The changes simply became unrecognizable to the Tagalogs.

When the first typographer and printer of these islands, the *chino cristiano* Tomás Pinpín, was commissioned to print the first *Doctrina Cristiana* booklets for each native language, different typographical sets of the *alíbatás* had to be manufactured. Tomás Pinpín saw that he had to manually create each typographic letter or character from each *baybayin-alíbatá*.

While *Doctrina Cristiana* was the first book ever published in the Philippines—a Roman Catholic catechism written by Juan de Plascencia, a Franciscan friar—the first Tagalog primer, *Arte y Regla de la Lengua Tagala.* came out in 1610, authored by the Augustinian Fray Blancas

Dr. T.H. Pardo de Tavera

de San José. When Tomás Pinpin accepted the commission to print the book, he had to painstakingly fashion by hand the wooden letter chips to form each word to be printed. But he soon realized that the completion of so many sets of *baybayin-alibatá* would take a long time, possibly years.

The printing procedure used by his immediate predecessor, Juan de Vera Ken Yong, consisted of carving out letters or characters from a flat wooden board upon which ink was later sprinkled to reproduce the letters, or characters, on a piece of rice paper laid and pressed over that same board. This printing technique is known as the xylographic method, which originated from the Chinese. Tomás Pinpin faced a real challenge in producing the book in view of the several ancient

ANCIENT PHILIPPINE ALPHABETS.

	A	E-I	O-U	KA	GA	NGA	TA	DA	NA	PA	BA	MA	YA	LA	WA	SA	HA

1. Tagalog, Chirino, 1604.
2. Tagalog, San Augustine, 1698.
3. Tagalog, DeMas, 1842.
4. Tagalog, DeMas (no date)
5. Iloko, DeMas, 1842.
6. Iloko, Languel (no date)
7. Bisaya, Ezguerra, 1747.
8. Bisaya, Mentrida, 1637.
9. Pangasinan, De Mas, 1842.
10. Pampangan, DeMas, 1842.

A chart of pre-Hispanic Philippine alphabets based on the extensive research of T.H. Pardo de Tavera, a Spanish Filipino physician who wrote extensively on Philippine culture.

A relief of Tomás Pinpin in his monument at Plaza de San Lorenzo Ruiz in Binondo, Manila,

alphabets (*baybayin-alíbatás*) that he had to deal with before he could start printing the book. The research on ancient pre-Hispanic alphabets by Dr. Trinidad Hermenegildo Pardo de Tavera. More popularly known as T.H. Pardo de Tavera (1857-1925), he produced the chart in the preceding page based on his extensive research on Philippine life, which gives us a pretty good idea of the difficulty that confronted Tomás Pinpin.

But being of Chinese origin, Tomás Pinpin was well aware of the fact that mainland China also had many languages—except that China has always had one common system of writing. In the case of the pre-Hispanic Philippine native languages, they had no common system of writing since each one of them had its respective *baybayin-alíbatá* as shown by Pardo de Tavera's chart.

A Chinese character may have its particular sound in every Chinese language but the meaning it represented was, at that time, generally the same in all the Chinese languages. And the same rule applied to both Japanese and Korean.

It is clear from historical and linguistic evidence that to save himself the awesome trouble of manually making different sets of *baybayin-alíbatá* for every major language of the islands, Tomás Pinpin decided, with the tacit approval of the Spanish Dominican missionaries who commissioned him for the job, to adopt the Spanish-European alphabet and system of writing.

This is why, those who write in any native Filipino language today use the Spanish-European system, and not any of the several and different ancient and pre-Hispanic *baybayin-alíbatá* syllabary systems.

An unintended consequence of Tomás Pinpin's efforts to resolve the production issues he faced with manufacturing *Doctrina Cristiana* in the native languages was the introduction of the Spanish (Western) alphabet—and the respective sound of each vowel and consonant—to the Ilocanos, the Visayans and the Tagalogs.

But while the native languages only had three vowels (an obvious influence from Arabic which up to now still has only three vowels), the introduction of the Spanish alphabet also brought into Tagalog, Visayan and Ilocano the basic sound of the phonemes "E" and "O," aside from a great number of Spanish words that represented concepts and connotations previously unknown to our pre-Hispanic ancestors, such as the name "Filipinas" and the word "Filipino."

As Tagalog and the other major native languages developed their respective literatures, the following alphabet was standardized and adopted by all the native Filipino languages and dialects, with most of its consonants being read with the Batangueño "eh":

> A (ah), B (be), C (se), Ch (se-atse), D (de), E (eh), F (ephe),
> G (he), H (atse), I (ih), J (hota), K (ka), L (ele), LL (elye),
> M (eme), N (ene), NG (nang), Ñ (enye), ÑG (ñga), O (oh),
> P (pe), Q (ku), R (ere), RR (er-re), S (ese), T (te), U (uh),
> V (ve), W (wa), X (ekis), Ya (o, i griega o ye), Z (seta).

It is then plain to see that both the Spanish and the Tagalog-Visayan-Ilocano letters are clearly represented in the native alphabet, known since the early years of Spanish influence as the 32-letter *abecedario*.

But then, some may ask about the origin of the invented or coined *abakada* that was used in the teaching of *purista* Tagalog in the 1900s.

Since 1935 up to 1973, the old Balagtás 32-letter *abecedario* was also arbitrarily replaced with the *abakada* invention when the *balarila* textbook of Lope K. Santos was imposed for the teaching of the national language subject in all public and private schools in the Philippines.

Abakada is something that was deliberately fabricated and made to look like a literal translation of the obsolete, pre-Hispanic Tagalog

Pre-Hispanic alphabet inscribed in copperplate.

baybayin-alíbatá into the present Spanish-European system of writing now used by Tagalog.

Thus, the Lope K. Santos *balarila*, as presented anew by his own daughter, Paralúman Santos Aspillera, in her own book, mistakenly claims that:

> "The Tagalog alphabet is originally composed of twenty letters. They are: A, Ba, Ka, Da, E, Ga, Ha, I, La, Ma, Na, NG (nang), O, Pa, Ra, Sa, Ta, U, Wa, Ya."[1]

And we say "mistakenly claims" because a look at *Florante at Laura*'s first edition, as published by Francisco Balagtás himself, clearly shows by the letters used in its entire text that it was written based on the 32-letter Tagalog *abecedario* and not on any 20-letter *abakada* or alphabet. Her claim is also belied by the fact that any printed matter in Tagalog before the advent of Lope K. Santos employed the original 32-letter Tagalog alphabet.

The Tagalog alphabet was NOT originally composed of only "twenty letters" but 31 letters because of the omission of a composed letter like Ch or RR.[2] The original Tagalog Balagtás alphabet, which is also the same

---

[1] Paralúman S. Aspillera, *Basic Tagalog for Foreigners and Non-Tagalogs*, 1974 revised ed. (Manila: 1981), 1.

[2] *Abecedariong Tagalog* (Manila: Martinez Publication House, 1917).

one used in Ilocano, Pampango, Bicol, Visaya and all the other languages each spoken by over 50,000 Filipinos, never had "twenty letters only."

Yes, Tagalog may have "originally" used 20 *baybayin* "letters" but that was during the time of Lakandula and Rajá Sulayman (1570s). Therefore, to impose the 20-letter *abakada*, but in Roman letters or script, upon the Tagalog language of the 21st century is definitely wrong because between the 1570s and the 1930s, the Tagalog alphabet, after nearly 400 years of contact with the Spanish language, had acquired more letters in the process of its growth and development. To insist that the Tagalog alphabet has only

20 letters straitjackets the language and is tantamount to tolling the death knell for the real Tagalog language. It is a direct assault upon the real Tagalog language right in its own country of origin, seriously putting in jeopardy its long-term ability to compete with English, or even with Taglish, the latter's bastardized form.

But, then, this is what is being done today to the Tagalog language. And this is why any Tagalog speaker and writer must also begin to understand why Paralúman Aspillera wrote what she wrote.

Her assertion that the Tagalog alphabet was originally composed of only 20 letters is not true. Why she made this claim in her book is plain to see. In that same book, she herself revealed that she had taken courses in linguistics at the University of the Philippines under American professors of the Summer Institute of Linguistics. With this admission, it is clear who influenced her to err on the number of letters in the Tagalog alphabet.[3]

---

[3] Aspillera, *Basic Tagalog*, back cover blurb.

In her foreword to the book,[4] it can be also seen that, like Ponciano B.P. Pineda in his *Diksyunaryo ng Wikang Pilipino*, Aspillera gratefully acknowledged the help of her mentors. Most of them, if not all, appear to exhibit Hispanophobia with their rejection of the Tagalog 32-letter *abecedario*.

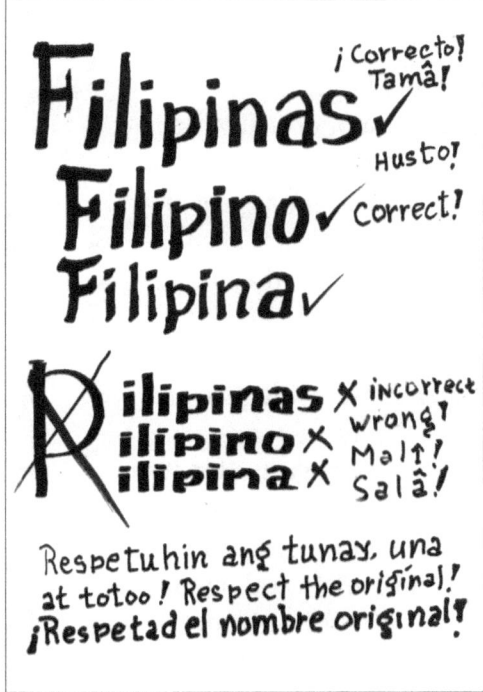

It is clear that the policies pursued by the first Protestant missionaries who came to these shores with the American invasion of 1899 were plain and simple borne out of Hispanophobia or hatred or fear of anything Spanish. It has driven the language policies of our education authorities for over a hundred years. Their anti-Spanish bias has abetted Filipinophobia because it simply cannot be denied that what is truly the Tagalog language and what is truly the Filipino language carries with it a good measure of Spanish influence, the most predominant of which is Roman Catholicism.

Sectarianism in any form is to be condemned. Throughout history, we know what damage its most virulent form has done. It has caused the deaths of millions throughout the world and so much incalculable harm to various cultures.

Think of the past bloodshed in Northern Ireland and the ongoing bloodletting in the Middle East as well as the destruction of the antiquities in Palmyra, Syria by ISIS or the ancient Buddhist statues in Afghanistan blasted by the Taliban just as a couple of examples.

Dr. William A. Donohue, chief executive officer of the Catholic League for Religious and Civil Rights in the United States as of this writing, has

---

[4] Ibid., vii-viii.

noted the anti-Catholic bias pervasive in the U.S. media.[5]

It follows then that the so-called linguists, encouraged and supported by their U.S. WASP mentors and sponsors, "teach" the Tagalog alphabet bereft of any Spanish influence. And in their fierce objective to rid Tagalog of what appears to be Spanish influence, they will go to the extent of even destroying the Tagalog language itself in its own basic phonemes and alphabet, not to mention its possible use as a real official language in its own country and as a better medium of instruction in the school system paid for by Filipino taxpayers themselves.

The controversial "Aves de Rapiña" editorial in the October 30, 1908 issue of *El Renacimiento*.

Hispanophobia and its permutation, Filipinophobia, are undeniably a part of the sectarian WASP neo-colonizers' agenda to control Filipino language policy and basic education.

Some of our so-called linguists have fallen under the influence and sway of this ongoing hidden WASP agenda to undermine, if not destroy, the Tagalog language from its very root—its alphabet.

Notwithstanding the efforts of these so-called linguists to push their agenda, the shortcomings of the *balarila-abakada* have been exposed, effectively rendering it as an anachronism. Not only is it out of sync, it is also useless and even harmful to the Tagalog language itself as the proposed basis of the national language called Filipino.

---

[5] Donahue, William. "Media Passionate about Anti-Catholic Bias." *catholicleague. org.* https://www.catholicleague.org/media-passionate-anti-catholic-bias-3/ (accessed October 20, 2018).

It was actually clearly shown during the National Language Committee hearings of the 1971-73 Philippine Constitutional Convention that the *balarila-abakada* "innovation" surreptitiously introduced into the Tagalog language since 1935 has hamstrung, if not deliberately frustrated, the development of Tagalog as the basis of the national language then called "Pilipino."

There is, of course, the earlier conviction that Dean C. Worcester, who served as a member of the Philippine Commission and later as Philippine secretary of the interior[6] during the American colonial period, ordered Lope K. Santos, a great grammarian in both Spanish and Tagalog, to write the *balarila* textbook and to include in it the use of the *abakada* in line with the sectarian colonizers' agenda to 1) debase Tagalog so that it would not serve, in the long run, as the strong basis, that it should be, of the national language project and 2) to turn it into a pidgin of English by forcing into it the entire unphonetic English alphabet.

It is not far-fetched to conclude that Worcester already saw in Tagalog a future obstacle to the neo-colonial imposition of English in the Philippines. And because of that fear, Tagalog had to be subtly crippled from the start with the imposition of an inadequate pre-Hispanic *abakada* whose consonants

---

[6] In 1908 Secretary of the Interior Dean C. Worcester filed a libel suit against *El Renacimiento*, a newspaper advocating for independence, for its editorial "Aves de Rapiña" (Birds of Prey). Worcester felt alluded to as "the eagle" described by the scathing editorial as the "most rapacious" bird of prey. It also severely criticized American authorities "who, besides being eagles, have the characteristics of the vulture, the owl, and the vampire." Worcester, who conducted zoological studies of the Igorots, believed the editorial crossed the line when it accused certain American officials of conducting these studies as an excuse to search for gold deposits in Northern Luzon. In an article in *The Daily Guardian* (February 26, 2014), University of the Philippines Professor Luis V. Teodoro described the suit as a landmark case during the U.S. colonial period:

"Although the paper did not name him, Worcester filed a libel suit which resulted in the conviction of Fidel Reyes, who wrote the editorial, his co-editor Teodoro M. Kalaw, and publisher Martin Ocampo. Kalaw and Ocampo appealed the decision before the Philippine Supreme Court and later, the U.S. Supreme Court, but their conviction was affirmed in both. Although pardoned by then U.S. Governor-General Francis Burton Harrison in 1914, Ocampo had to pay the then huge amount of P100,000 in fines, which so crippled the paper and its sister newspaper *Muling Pagsilang* [edited by Lope K. Santos] both ceased publication."

are read with a flat "AH" in lieu of its already fully-developed 32-letter Balagtás alphabet whose consonants are read with the Batangueño "EH."

Both the *abakada* and the complicated *balarila* were then engineered to discredit Tagalog by still making it appear as a pre-Hispanic language so that it could never compete, in the future, with English as a medium of instruction, as an official language for law and legislation and as an effective tool and vehicle for development.

Worcester, moreover, knew that Tagalog, with its 32-letter Balagtás alphabet, was structurally superior to English in phonics and spelling (*Mahirap ispilingin ang Inglés*). Luckily, and as we have already pointed out, since the 1971-73 Constitutional Convention, the *abakada* became a thing of the past.

But, to continue with Worcester's obvious plan to destroy Tagalog, the Commission on the Filipino Language under Ponciano B.P. Pineda's long leadership (1971-1999) managed to force into this language the English alphabet which is crippling Tagalog anew, especially with the publication of his misleading *Diksyunaryo*.

PART V
CULTURAL GENOCIDE

A U.S. soldier and a woman survey Spanish-era buildings and churches in Intramuros that were destroyed during the Liberation of Manila.

1. THE CORROSIVE EFFECTS OF CULTURAL GENOCIDE THROUGH HISPHANOPHOBIA UPON OUR NATION

It just so happens that Spanish is also a phonetic language like Tagalog, Visayan and Ilocano. (*Kung ano ang bigkas, siya ang sulat at kung ano ang sulat, siya rin ang bigkas*). In Spanish, words are simply syllabicated and pronounced as they are written. And vice-versa. English words, in contrast, are neither usually written as they are pronounced nor syllabicated and pronounced as they are written. In this case, the basic character of English as a language diametrically runs counter to the basic character of Tagalog, Visayan, Ilocano and the native and phonetic character of all the other native languages and dialects of the Philippines.

To force our grade school students to use the English alphabet in order to misspell Tagalog words is both wrong on its face and tantamount

Manila lies in ruins after being flattened by American bombing and shelling near the end of World War II.

to committing a language and cultural genocide (specifically ethnocide) upon the Tagalog community in particular and the Filipino nation in general. Inflicting ethnocide[1] upon the Tagalog language group in the guise of teaching the Filipino national language is deceitful at the very least.

This unscientific and deceptive practice of sticking the English alphabet into Tagalog may, perhaps, be justified if the Philippines were converted into another U.S. state. But so long as the Philippines is taken as an independent country with its own sovereignty, this kind of linguistic neo-colonial ethnocide is not only an offense against Filipino culture, dignity, sovereignty and national identity but an act of aggression against a weakened people.

Genocide, along with ethnocide, is defined as "the deliberate and systematic extermination of an ethnic or national group." The U.S. White Anglo Saxon Protestants, or WASPs, are a class of people that can be held responsible for the genocide perpetrated against the "Injuns" of North America. And they are the same class of people that invaded the Philippines in 1899.

Cultural genocide against the Spanish-speaking Filipino continues to this day by proxy

The near disappearance of the Spanish language in the Philippines, the destruction of their 1898 *República Filipina* and the extermination of a sixth of the Philippine population of ten million during the Filipino-American

---

[1] According to Barbara Lulunka, a writer from American University, College of Arts and Sciences, Washington D.C., "The concept of ethnocide was created at the same time as the concept of genocide in 1944 in the United States by Raphael Lemkin, a Polish-born lawyer. Ethnocide is a term that is an alternative to genocide according to Lemkin (Lemkin, 1944). The terms were created precisely in regard to the persecution of the Jews by the Nazis in the Second World War.

"In the footnote, to Lemkin's definition of genocide... he wrote that another term for genocide is ethnocide. Ethnocide is a combination of the Greek word ethnos meaning 'nation' and the Latin word *cide* which means 'to kill.' Therefore it can be noted that as the creator of the term ethnocide, Raphael Lemkin did not distinguish between genocide and ethnocide (Semelin, 2005: 373)." "Ethnocide." *sciencespo.fr*. November 3, 2007. https://www.sciencespo.fr/mass-violence-war-massacre-resistance/en/document/ethnocide (accessed October 27, 2018).

Filipino soldiers felled by American bullets during the Filipino-American War.

War are crimes against humanity that can only be attributed to them in their role as Protestant "missionaries" and "English teachers," not to mention their role as military and economic aggressors and colonizers.

The cultural genocide committed against the same Spanish-speaking Filipino nation was successfully repeated during the 1941-45 war against the Japanese through the shelling of Intramuros, Ermita, Malate and several other historic districts in Manila that left the city in shambles. Next to Warsaw, Manila suffered the most in terms of destruction during World War II not because of the Japanese but because of the indiscriminate targeting of buildings and infrastructures by American liberation forces. The unnecessary bombing of almost every old Catholic Church building found in every provincial town outside the capital city made the destruction of our priceless Spanish cultural heritage nearly complete.

The excuse given was the necessity of immediately defeating the fanatical Imperial Japanese Army and quickly ending the war in the Pacific. But the cultural and language genocide did not stop at the end of the American colonial period. It continues to this day against the Spanish-speaking Filipino with the 1987 Cory Aquino Constitution that abolished the teaching of Spanish as a regular subject and as an official language.

In schools this Hispanophobia is evident in circular No. 59, series of 1996, which the Commission on Higher Education (CHED) issued to govern the curriculum in both private and public schools. It totally

Francisco Balágtas' classic *Florante at Laura* uses the 32-letter *abecedario*.

ignores Spanish despite the very obvious Hispanic heritage of the Filipinos in their national identity and in their national culture. It neglects the constitutional provision calling for the teaching of a foreign language as an elective in colleges. In their arrogance, the neo-colonizers and their local toadies smugly claim that the traditions and laws that come with Spanish are now abolished because it is a "dead" language.

The cultural genocide against the Spanish-speaking Filipino became a *fait accompli* with the abolition of the Spanish subjects in Philippine public and private schools. The cultural genocide against the Tagalog ethnic group is now being carried out with the imposition of the English alphabet, and a new Taglish morphology, into the Tagalog language itself through the publication in 1998 of *Diksyunaryo ng Wikang Filipino*, issued by the Commission on the Filipino Language then headed by Ponciano B.P. Pineda.[2]

The same duplicity is also being quietly employed against the Sugbuhanon (Cebuano) and the Ilocano languages. The unnatural injection of the English alphabet into Tagalog has no other aim but to replace the real 32-letter *abecedario* used by Francisco Balágtas, which is the basis of Tagalog and all the other major native languages of these islands.

Changing our alphabet to suit the colonizers' agenda is a form of ethnocide

In summary, this anti-Filipino cultural genocide primarily consists, on one hand, of the direct imposition of the English language through the present school system and, on the other, of the deliberate debasement of Tagalog, which is supposed to be the basis of the national language known as Filipino, into a pidgin popularly known as Taglish.

The promotion, therefore, of Taglish as the Philippine national language appears to be the secret agenda of the authors of this anti-Tagalog,

---

[2] *Diksyunaryo ng Wikang Pilipino* (Manila: Komisyong ng Wikang Pilipino, 1998).

anti-Visaya and anti-Ilocano cultural genocide since the English pidginization of all the major native languages is clearly becoming the goal of the so-called Philippine educational system.

With this deliberate, therefore genocidal, pidginization of the Filipino language, there is moreover the obvious

Cultural genocide involves forcing English on the population and debasing Tagalog

goal of dumbing down the new generations of Filipinos who are increasingly becoming ignorant of their own culture. Their miseducation will forever consign them to a long line of cheap labor for the rich countries to exploit. They become peons of a global economy as domestic helpers, club entertainers and factory workers unable to find decent jobs in their own country as a result of a defective educational system more concerned with kowtowing to the interests of the neo-colonizers rather than in looking after the welfare of Filipinos.

There is, indeed, an undeniably full-scale cultural genocide being committed against the youth of this country through the expensive educational system that does not serve their real welfare. And it is clearly being carried out against the basically Tagalog-speaking Filipino masses by the present Americanized elite. Some of these shameless individuals

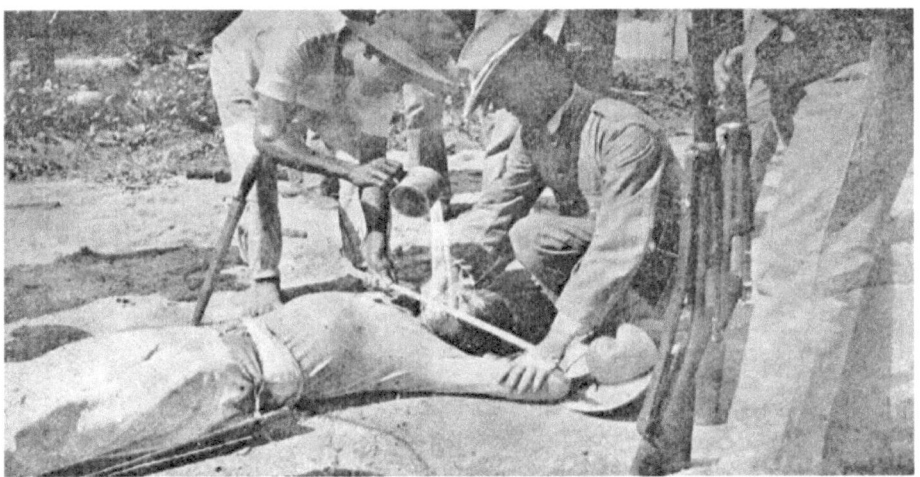

Water boarding is not a new phenomenon. U.S. soldiers used this torture technique against Filipinos during the Filipino-American War as shown in this photo (circa 1902).

are holding positions in the education sector but they are not there to serve the public but their own vested self-interests through the sale of textbooks and other school materials. The same individuals are beholden to U.S. CIA instrumentalities.

One of the features of this full-scale cultural genocide is what looks like the deliberate imposition of functional illiteracy upon the Filipino youth in general as shown by their inability to syllabicate Tagalog words in Tagalog. Syllabication is key to having the ability to spell and read in one's own language. English syllabication drills are hardly done in schools anymore because of its unphonetic words. And the absence of syllabication drills in our classrooms filters down to the Tagalog language itself, thereby condemning the Filipino youth to functional illiteracy.

PART VI

THE IMPORTANCE OF THE TAGALOG
32-LETTER ALPHABET IN EDUCATION

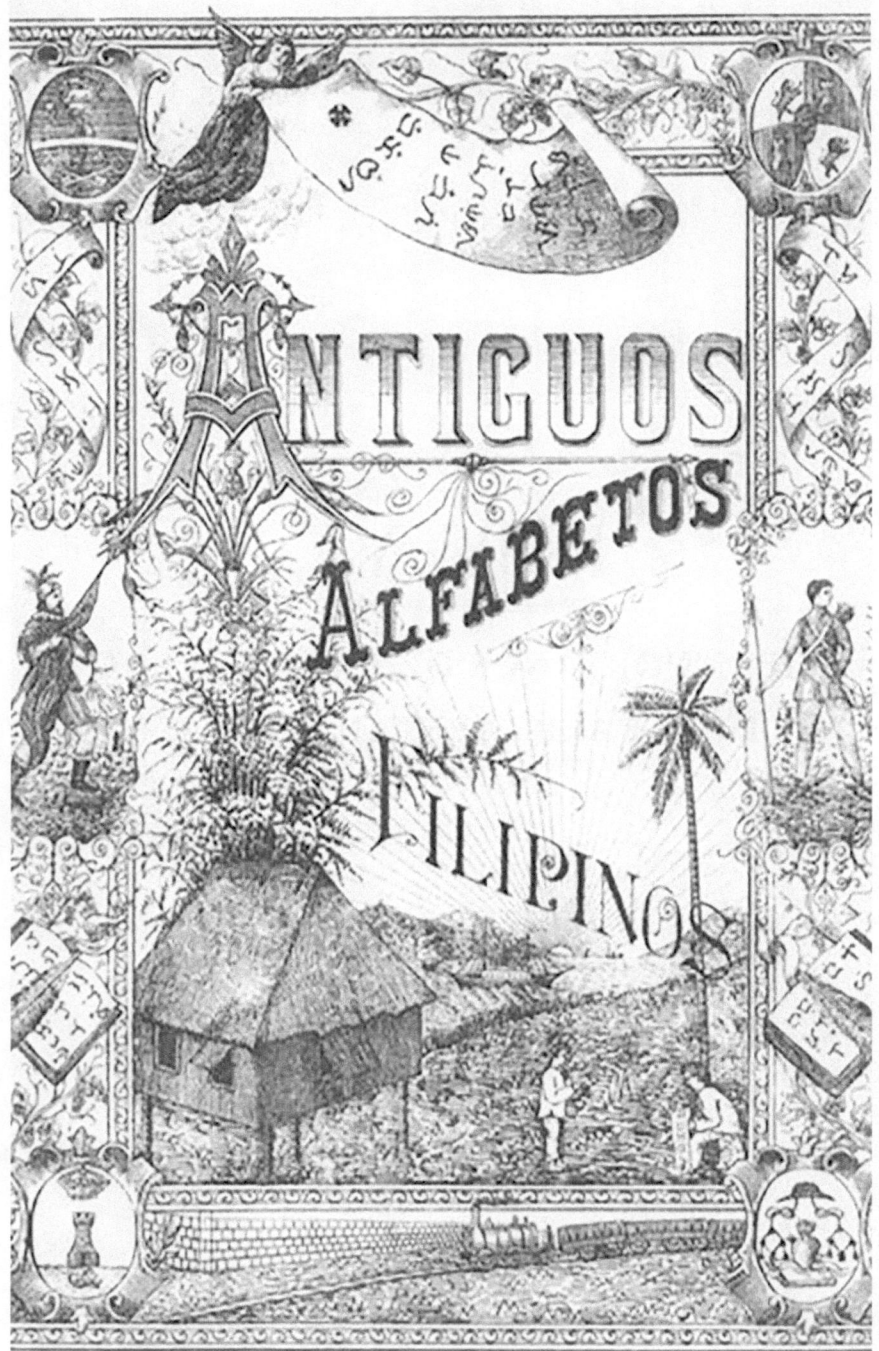

ANTIGUOS ALFABETOS FILIPINOS

A book on pre-Hispanic native alphabets published during the Spanish era.

1. HOW TINKERING WITH OUR TRADITIONAL ALPHABET RUINED EDUCATION IN OUR COUNTRY

What is an alphabet in relation to a language of its own? The answer is simple enough. An alphabet is the beginning of a language. And as such, it serves as the root of the language as a real root is to a living tree. If you poison or cut the root of a living tree, it will wither and die.

The same thing happens when a language is deprived of its own alphabet. It will first be debased into a pidgin or contact vernacular and then die in the long run as a tool for development and communication.

And this is exactly what is being done, if imperceptibly, to the Tagalog language. It is being slowly killed by those who are subverting its phonetic system through the lethal injection of the unphonetically inferior English, or Taglish, alphabet as concocted by Ponciano B.P. Pineda's *Diksyunaryo*.

Another way of killing Tagalog is its non-use as the medium of instruction in all subjects in every school level, in the local courts of justice, in both houses of Congress and in the vast majority of official government communications. This gross neglect, which consigns Tagalog as a second-rate language to English, is a real violation of the constitutional provision on Filipino as the national language.

The greatest irony is that the first to undermine Tagalog, which is the basis of the national language known as Filipino, is the very same government agency tasked to preserve and develop the national language. The Commission on the Filipino Language, which was led by Ponciano B.P. Pineda from 1971 up to the late 1990s, has hijacked the process. Teachers, for example, are told to orally spell in English every Filipino name and surname and every ordinary word while purportedly teaching Filipino, the national language subject.

Our traditional alphabet is being ignored to the detriment of Tagalog

The commission has, in effect, subverted—and continues to subvert—Tagalog when it arbitrarily gave its official nod to the use of the English, or Taglish, alphabet. This imprimatur was effectively given by Ponciano B.P. Pineda when the language commission he headed for close to 30 years published *Diksyunaryo*.[1]

The importance of the 32-letter Balagtás Tagalog alphabet is being deliberately suppressed by the simple act of ignoring its existence. The people responsible for this preclusion are government employees whose salaries are paid for by our taxes.

This assault against the national language and patrimony goes unabated and unpunished because we have politicians and government officials who have entirely surrendered their bodies and their souls to the influence of their foreign masters who use the loans extended to us by their banks as a tool to influence national policies, including those on education.

The suppression of the 32-letter Tagalog Balagtás alphabet is one of the fundamental causes of the miseducation of the Filipino youth at

---

[1] *Diksyunaryo ng Wikang Pilipino*, vii.

a time when knowledge of several languages, including Spanish and their own native tongues, would have tremendously enhanced their competitive advantage in the global arena. Another factor is the official and forced imposition of English as the ONLY medium of instruction in all school levels all over the archipelago.

The ill-effects of imposing English as the only medium of instruction and the unnecessary tinkering with our 32-letter Balagtás Tagalog alphabet are shown in the results of the standardized tests given to both elementary and high school students in the country.

These standardized tests—known invariably as the National Elementary Assessment Tests for Grade Six Pupils or National Elementary Achievement Tests—are mostly administered by the National Educational Testing and Research Center. The dismal performance of Filipino grade school students in these tests all point to a dysfunctional educational system. English as the main medium of instruction has failed our students, except perhaps the students of some elite schools whose obscenely exorbitant tuition makes them inaccessible to poor Filipinos.

The following is an excerpt from a newspaper article on a study assessing the poor performance of our elementary and high school students, which bolsters the view that reliance in English as the sole medium of instruction in our schools obstructs rather than facilitates learning:

> Two main findings have emerged from studies of student achievement in both elementary and secondary schools in the Philippines.

First, mastery level of subject matter by grades in all curricular areas are found to be low, generally between 30 percent and 50 percent, compared to the 75 percent learning norm set by the DEP ED OR DECS (Department of Education, Culture and Sports).

An overall picture can be gleaned from the various results of the National Elementary Achievement Tests (NEAT). For instance, the 1993 results show an overall score of 42.2 percent against a target of 75 percent.

Lowest scores were in Language/Reading/Science/Health and Mathematics.[2]

If students get low scores in English, it is to be expected that they, too, will fare no better in other subjects such as Science, Health and Mathematics since these subjects are taught in English, which, to begin with, they do not fully understand.

For instance, test results in Science administered in English to ten-year-old pupils under a 1983 study show the Philippines with an average score of 9.5 out of a possible 24 compared to 11.2 for the Hong Kong and Singapore students.[3]

The failure to keep children in school and the deteriorating quality of education are old problems. And the main culprit in all this is compulsory English, which threatens the very essence of education in the Philippines.

The reason almost no meaningful education can take place among the Filipino students is the compulsory use of English as the medium of instruction. Discard and replace it with Tagalog and they will be doing better in school and will be sticking it out because they do not have to undergo the same hardships of having to navigate the maze of an unphonetic language. A survey specifically cited the problem of using English as the language of instruction, incompetent teaching staff, insufficient facilities, English (itself) and Science.

How can we expect children to learn when English is an incomprehensible barrier?

---

[2] Pacqueo-Arreza, Elisa. "School Reforms: Mission Impossible?" *Philippine Daily Inquirer*, March 21, 1999. Ms. Pacqueo-Arreza is from the U.P. College of Education, Diliman, Quézon City.

[3] Ibid.

Despite the educational reforms of the '70s and the '80s, the mission of Philippine education remains unaccomplished and inadequate.

At the risk of being repetitious, this glaringly obvious failure of the aims of Philippine education points to the fact that in all school levels (elementary, secondary and tertiary), the language of instruction in majority of the subject areas is still English—a foreign language in most Filipino households. The result is lack of language proficiency, let alone learning efficiency, in both English and Filipino among the students.

The primacy of basic education as a fundamental human right and as an essential factor in personality development cannot be argued. Thus, solid and universal elementary education as an anti-poverty strategy is the best and the most logical strategy. What then shall be its thrust to overcome the adverse conditions surrounding Philippine education and to avert its further decline?

If we want to develop a globally competitive economy, we need to develop a world-class workforce. The way to do it is through quality and relevant education.[4] But how can it be achieved if the transfer of knowledge is being impeded by the very medium of instruction used to teach our children? How can they grasp complicated concepts when they are struggling to comprehend the language being used to transmit ideas?

The answer to these basic questions is to replace English with Tagalog as the medium of instruction so that the transfer of skills and knowledge

---

[4] Ibid.

can be realized. And for Tagalog to be a fitting and adequate medium of instruction, the 32-letter alphabet should be restored and once again made an integral part of the language.

The continued compulsory imposition of the English language as the only medium of instruction in schools has reached a point where it has turned into a huge obstacle to the progress of the Filipino people. This does not bode well for the future of the country. Already, the high number of Filipino children that never attend school or drop out after finishing the elementary or high school level is a cause for alarm. Illiteracy in the Philippines in both its actual and functional levels has really grown by leaps and bounds to the detriment of the country's economic progress.

Of course there is now the K-12 law that adds two more years of education for every Filipino child. Although it includes the use of ten selected major native languages as media of instruction in the elementary grades, it remains to be seen if this is a move in the right direction as far as language is concerned. If the English alphabet is again made the basis of these native languages, as in the case of Tagalog-based Filipino, it will only serve to widen the pidginization of both English and Tagalog to other native languages, worsening the already bleak situation of our basic education in these islands.

On a sad note, all Filipino language subjects were abolished in November 2018 from the required 36-unit college core curriculum, leaving thousands of Tagalog-Filipino teachers jobless. This is a direct result of a Supreme Court decision upholding the constitutionality of the K-12 law and lifting a restraining order on a CHED directive removing Filipino, *Panitikan* and Constitution as required subjects in the tertiary level. To the Spanish language teachers who had lost their job overnight with the removal of Spanish from the college curriculum by the 1987 Constitution, this development is like déjà vu all over again, to use an American expression. The neo-colonial English only policy continues to wreak havoc—unchallenged.

PART VII

THE SLOW DEATH OF TAGALOG-FILIPINO

AS A LANGUAGE

ARTE
DE LA LENGVA TAGALA,
Y MANVAL TAGALOG,
PARA LA ADMINISTRACION
De los Santos Sacramentos,

QVE DE ORDEN
DE SVS SVPERIORES
COMPVSO

FRAY SEBASTIAN DE TOTANES, HIJO
de la Apoſtolica, y Seraphica Provincia de S.
Gregorio Magno, de Religioſos Deſcalzos de
la Regular, y mas eſtrecha Obſervancia de Nu-
eſtro Seraphico Padre San Franciſco
de las Islas Philipinas,

PARA ALIVIO DE LOS RELIGIOSOS DE
la miſma Santa Provincia, que de nuevo ſe de-
dican à aprender eſte Idioma, y ſon Princi-
piantes en la Adminiſtracion Eſpi-
ritual de las Almas.

Impreſſo en la Imprenta del vſo de dicha Santa Provincia, ſita
en el Convento de Nra. Señora de Loreto en el Pueblo de Sá-
paloc Extra-muros de la Ciudad de Manila. Año de 1745.

Spanish fraifes studied Philippine native languages and produced grammar books to educate Filipino children.

1. TAGALOG WAS DEVELOPED AS A MEDIUM OF EDUCATION BY THE SPANISH FRIARS

Immediately after the Philippine Islands became an overseas province of Spain, the Spanish *frailes* went to work in earnest, mastering and developing the Tagalog language. They learned the language mostly for practical reasons and out of sheer necessity. Once deployed to remote mission outposts, they had neither the luxury of time nor enough personnel to impart the Spanish language to the natives as quickly as possible.

It was far easier for the educated friars to learn the local languages themselves rather than impose the teaching of Spanish upon the natives. By learning the local languages, they endeared themselves to the local inhabitants and armed themselves with a powerful tool to educate Filipino children in the latter's own languages. Soon, the children were quickly learning the three R's at convents where they also heard about Roman Catholicism.[1] Along with giving the children basic education, the friars taught them catechism to convert them to Catholicism. It was in line with the Spanish Crown's primary goal of Christianizing the inhabitants of newly discovered lands.

Upon hearing positive stories about the friars from their children, parents themselves became drawn to the convents, making them more receptive to accept Catholicism and get baptized.[2]

The Dominican Fray Francisco Blancas de San José wrote and published in 1610 the first grammar book on Tagalog titled *Arte y Regla de la Lengua Tagala*. It was printed by Tomás Pinpin, a wise and diligent *chino cristiano*.

---

[1] Hernández, OSA, Policarpo, "A Church Built for the Ages," *Search, The Augustinian Journal of Cultural Excellence* 15, no. 2 (2004). 111-113.

[2] Galende, OSA, Pedro, "Catechetic and Religious Instruction," *The 450th Anniversary of the Santo Niño*, typescript, 79-81.

The implication here is that the Spaniards, unlike the invading U.S. soldiers of 1899 and the Protestant missionaries who first came to these shores shortly thereafter, never looked down on Tagalog, Visayan, Ilocano or any other native language as lacking in "any great amount of cultural literature."[3] The Spanish *frailes* did not see any obstacles to the use of the native Filipino languages as a means of religious and educational instruction. In fact, while Fray Francisco Blancas de San José, in his pioneering grammar book, referred to Tagalog as a language (*lengua Tagala*), the American colonizers, through the 1925 Monroe Commission, dismissed Tagalog and all the other native Filipino languages as mere "dialects."

2. DOWNGRADING TAGALOG AS A 'DIALECT' IS ON LANGUAGE AGENDA OF THE NEO-COLONIZERS

IN HER DOCTORAL THESIS,[4] Doña Rosa Sevilla de Alvero, a prominent Filipina educator, sensed the agenda of the American colonizers posing as educators in her country and roundly belied their theory that Tagalog is so inadequate a "dialect" that it can never be used as a medium of instruction.

> *How can we expect children to learn when English is an incomprehensible barrier?*

By labeling Tagalog and all the other Filipino languages as mere 'dialects,' they wanted to convey that since these languages are not widely spoken, they are therefore inadequate vehicles for national development. The American authors of the survey results concluded that our native languages were 'dead languages' and reduced them to mere 'literary curiosities,' along with Spanish.

To further this view, it was the sectarian American colonizers who got Lope K. Santos to rewrite Tagalog grammar with a 20-letter *abakada*, which was resurrected from the long-gone pre-Hispanic *baybayin-alíbatás*,

---

[3] *A Survey of the Educational System of the Philippines* (Manila: Bureau of Printing, 1924), 24-26.

[4] *Crítica del sistema educacional de Filipinas* (Manila: UST Press, 1936).

as they prohibited the continued teaching of the already popularly used 32-letter Tagalog-Balagtás alphabet for both public and private elementary schools.

While they allowed Tagalog to be proclaimed as the basis of the Filipino national language, the WASPs, through their local factotums, were secretly destroying it from within with the imposition of the pre-Hispanic Lope K. Santos purist *abakada*.

In 1973, however, the Marcos Constitution threw out the pre-Hispanic *abakada* when it provided that the national language to be known as Filipino, and no longer as Pilipino, "shall be developed and adopted." [5]

3. WHY TAGALOG IS NOW A DEAD LANGUAGE

WITH THE 1987 CORY CONSTITUTION, the neo-colonizers through their acolytes in the education department and the Commission on the Filipino Language, have succeeded in stuffing into Tagalog the unphonetic English alphabet in order to destroy, if not further downgrade and cripple it. Thus, the quickening descent of Tagalog that they had mislabeled as a mere "dialect" into a vile pidgin of English is safely

Neo-colonizers, through their local acolytes, are responsible for destroying our language

assured. We are told in a published article that it was Lourdes Quisumbing, who headed the education department under Corazon Aquino's presidency, who issued a circular in 1987 requiring the use of the English alphabet in the teaching of a phonetic language like Tagalog or Filipino. At the stroke of a pen, she ruined the chances of Tagalog of ever becoming a true living language of development in education as well as in government.

As it stands now, Tagalog is a dead language, thanks to the neo-colonizers and their Filipino minions.

There are two ways of defining a dead language. First, a dead language is one that is no longer spoken by a single community anywhere in the world. Second, a dead language is one which may still be spoken by a

[5] Vide General Provisions, 1973 Philippine Constitution.

community but, for all intents and purposes, is on life support because it is not being used as a tool either in the education of its young or in the cultural and economic advancement of that same community.

The second definition fits the case of the Tagalog language and all the other languages of the Philippines in relation to the English ONLY policy being currently enforced.

4. TAGALOG IS PURPOSELY NOT USED AS MUCH AS OBLIGATORY ENGLISH

TAGALOG IS, INDEED, GENERALLY SPOKEN by Tagalogs and other ethnic groups in the Philippines. But it is neither used, by and large, as the language of the courts or of the Filipino legislature nor as the primary medium of instruction in the general education of Filipinos in STEM subjects (Science, Technology, Engineering and Mathematics). In short, it has been scrapped as a tool for Filipino development. This official neglect is being carried out to promote English as a neo-colonial tool to condition the hearts and minds of Filipinos to the ways of the neo-colonizers and make them ever more pliant to dictation.

> *Most of our young people end up speaking English in a fractured fashion*

And because of this prevailing situation, neither Tagalog nor any other native Filipino language shall ever fully graduate as a living language of development. If Tagalog *per se*, as well as Tagalog-based Filipino, is not the official and preferred language of the courts, the legislature and the media, it is owing to the fact that even the Tagalogs themselves are NOT fully trained in schools to use their own language in these areas of daily life.

To add insult to injury, most of our young people, despite being forced to learn English in school, end up speaking the language in a fractured fashion, mixing it with Tagalog words and tellingly turning it into a mongrel language known as Taglish but deceptively labeled as "Filipino."

If we continue to allow the devaluation of Tagalog, which is the initial basis of the national language of the Philippines, then there is no hope for it to be ever developed and preserved. It is ironic that the language authorities and educators tasked to preserve and develop it are the very same people who are chipping away at its essence. Unless our bullheaded language policies are changed, neither Tagalog nor Filipino, the

In the Philippines, English is being replaced by Taglish, a pidgin form of the language

aspirational national language, will honorably survive in the long run even in its pidginized form.

With the imposition of the English alphabet and system of spelling and syllabication in Filipino language classrooms, the phonetic soul of Tagalog will get totally debased until the language will just die out after becoming a pidgin, therefore utterly unusable for official and formal communication and formal education. That is to say, as a tool for development in its own cradle.

5. TAGALOG TURNED INTO 'TAGLISH'

TAGALOG IS BEING TURNED into a pidgin called Taglish, a spoken pidgin of English. Taglish will eventually kill off Tagalog aside from English itself in the Philippines if nothing is done to change the present language situation in the country.

NUESTRA HERENCIA HISPANA: TEMOR DEL TRAIDOR

And this is so because while English survival is assured not only because it is widely spoken throughout the world and is the dominant language in its home countries like the United States and the United Kingdom, Tagalog is not used outside the Philippines, its cradle. The same fate awaits Cebuano and all the other major native languages of the Philippines.

In view of the foregoing, it is not difficult to surmise that the present linguistic neo-colonization of the Philippines has clearly programmed the death, the complete disappearance of Tagalog and all the other native languages—something the Spaniards had never attempted to do during their entire direct rule of over three centuries.

For a brief period during the abbreviated presidency of Joseph Estrada (1998-2001), his education secretary—Andrew González—made a big show of trying to make Filipino the medium of instruction in many levels of what is now called "Philippine education." But his move smacked of hypocrisy.

Being a member of the local board of the Summer Institute of Linguistics, his sudden move in favor of using Ilocano and Visayan as a medium of instruction in primary schools only raised some concerns and suspicions. Was it another ploy to

Is there a secret agenda to turn all our native languages into pidgins?

turn our unsuspecting children into pidgin-English speakers of Taglish, Cebuglish and Iluklish—much like the Protestantized stone-age tribes of Papua New Guinea?

6. THE 32-LETTER FILIPINO ALPHABET IS THE SOLUTION

UNLESS THE 32-LETTER TAGALOG Balagtás alphabet, with most of its letters pronounced with the Batangueño *cartilla* "EH," is used to teach Tagalog and other Filipino languages, González' idea would become nothing else but another step to further impose other local variations of English pidgins.

As seen by their track record with regard to the language issue in the Philippines, entities similar to the Summer Institute of Linguistics appear to teach those that come under their sway, like Paralúman S. Aspillera, Ponciano B.P. Pineda, Lourdes Quisumbing and even Andrew González that the best thing for Tagalog, Cebuano and Ilocano is to drill into these languages the English alphabet and to ignore their original and common 32-letter phonetic *abecedario* out of Hispanophobia.

We should not discount the possibility of a finespun implementation, at the expense of Filipino taxpayers, of a secret agenda by groups like the Summer Institute of Linguistics to convert Tagalog, along with Ilocano and Visayan, into English-based pidgins. Once this agenda is accomplished, perhaps it will then become much easier for them and other Protestant missionaries to proselytize using the Bible translated by the anti-Catholic Wycliffe Group.

While the survival of English is assured, that of Tagalog's is in serious jeopardy

7. TAGLISH IS BEING MADE THE BASIS OF THE NATIONAL LANGUAGE CALLED 'FILIPINO'

THE FILIPINO MASSES THAT MAY EITHER HAVE Taglish, Iluklish or Cebuglish as their language can still be counted upon as solid fans of American-made movies, not only in the Philippines but anywhere in the world where there are overseas Filipino workers. The emergence of new generation of Filipinos speaking only in a pidgin of English as their new language will not dent the popularity of American movies. Assured of a captive audience, Hollywood-made movies would be making a killing at the box office while draining our dollar reserves to pay for these expensive foreign films.

Filipino-made movies will never be able to compete against English films, given the fact that even now, many Filipino films already carry English subtitles which in itself speaks volumes about the sad state of affairs of our aspiration to develop a national language understood by every Filipino.

After all, if English-based pidgins like Tok Pisin[6] from Papua Niu[7] Guinea, Bislama from Vanuatu (New Hebrides) and Pijin from the Solomons have been declared the "evangelical" and official languages in those countries, why not further develop Taglish in order to declare and teach it as the official language of the Philippines under the name and guise of "Filipino"?

So-called linguists under the wings of the Summer Institute of Linguistics, who may be decidedly for Taglish, may also forget that whatever little correct English is currently being spoken and written in these islands might also stand to be totally replaced

> *There is outrage against the VFA but none over the destruction of our language*

by its own pidgin as is the proven case of the pidgin-speaking countries we have mentioned.

But while there is an ongoing opposition to the Visiting Forces Agreement (VFA), which practically allows the return of the U.S. Military bases to the Philippines, there is no outrage against the debasement of Tagalog and other native languages by the neo-colonizers and their local underlings.

8. TAGLISH IS MORE DAMAGING THAN THE VFA

THE ENGLISH-TAGLISH ALPHABET in Tagalog is more injurious than any U.S. military bases agreement because it inflicts a permanent psychological impairment upon our collective psyche as a people. Language neo-colonialism is being forced upon every Filipino from his early years until the same becomes, to quote José Rizal, "a cancerous hump on his bent back" and "a shameful mark of subservience" upon his persona.

The removal, therefore, of the English, or Taglish, alphabet from Tagalog with the ridiculous and genocidal classroom practice of spelling Filipino words in English, is of greater urgency and

---

[6] Talk Pidgin?
[7] New?

importance than the rejection of the VFA or any U.S. military exercises in Mindanao or elsewhere.

It is the duty of every Filipino, especially of our elected representatives in Congress, to demand the immediate removal from Tagalog and Filipino of the undesirable English-Taglish alphabet invented by Ponciano B.P. Pineda. Likewise, we should clamor for the immediate restoration, in the national language project, of the 32-letter Balagtás *abecedario*.

Since this 32-letter *abecedario* is also the basis of Cebuano, Ilocano, Ilongo, Kapangpañgan, Bicolano and all the other native languages, it is representative of the phonetic and logical character of all these Filipino native languages.

It is a pity that Filipinos in general still appear unaware of the greater and real danger and damage posed by the contumelious imposition on Tagalog of the unphonetic English alphabet as redesigned by Ponciano B.P. Pineda in his *Diksyunaryo*. Filipinos ought to realize that the survival of their own national language greatly depends on the restoration of the Balagtás 32-letter *abecedario* in the teaching of Tagalog-based Filipino to our youth.

Those who wish to continue using the *abakada* have nothing to lose with the restoration of the 32-letter Balagtás *abecedario* since its letters are already covered by the *abecedario*.

We have to remedy the present situation by immediately correcting the error of using the entire English alphabet in the teaching of the Filipino language in our schools because the continued ascendance of Taglish will, in the long run, destroy both English and Filipino in our country.

PART VIII

EL DIA DE LA HISPANIDAD

Roman Catholicism is one of the greatest legacies Spain has given to the Philippines. Beautiful Spanish-era temples such as the Binondo Church shown above form part of our rich Spanish heritage.

1. BELONGING TO THE HISPANIC WORLD CARRIES ENORMOUS ECONOMIC POTENTIAL

It has been slightly over a generation since the ouster of President Ferdinand E. Marcos from power in 1986, but what a difference 32 years make. Long reviled as a hated dictator by the Yellows who for so long have hoodwinked the Filipino people into believing that the oligarchic Aquino-Cojuangco political dynasty is the paragon of virtues deserving to be elevated to the pantheon of Catholic saints, President Marcos is finally being viewed with fresh eyes by a new generation of Filipinos who have come to know his side of the coin with the advent of social media.

In contrast to the Yellow regimes under whose corruption and incompetence Filipinos had suffered a great deal, the Marcos government easily comes out on top of opinion polls conducted in social media and in traditional surveys nowadays. More and more Filipinos are now becoming nostalgic about the Marcos years. Although many of these people are millenials, they nevertheless look back with appreciation at the many accomplishments of President Marcos.

This longing for the competent and intelligent leadership of President Marcos is inescapable since truth has, in the end, a way of bringing itself out into the bright light of day. Long buried by the black propaganda of the Aquino-Cojuangco Yellow regimes, truth has finally emerged to shine the light upon itself and to reveal for everyone to see the many great social programs and infrastructure projects of President Marcos that Filipinos continue to enjoy up to this day.

As a leader, President Marcos was visionary. For example, he opened full diplomatic relations with China's Mao Zedong in 1975, four years ahead of the United States which took the step only in 1979. In the area of language, he recognized the importance of Spanish and our strong ties with *Madre España* and with other Hispanic nations.

A set of statues depicting the blood compact between *adelantado* Miguel López de Legazpi and Bohol Chieftain Datu Sikatuna.

This keen awareness of the primacy of Spanish and of our Hispanic heritage to our national identity on the part of President Marcos led him in 1973 to declare October 7-13 Hispanic Week.

With our recollection of this inspired executive action by President Marcos, it behooves upon us to articulate what Hispanidad means to our national soul.

Hispanidad, geographically speaking, consists of some 33 or more Hispanic nations with a total population of about 1.5 billion. These nations, whether independent or annexed by certain powers, occupy more than one-fifth of the world's total land area. Their principal language is Castilian or *castellano*. Another widespread Iberian language is Portuguese which, because of its strong similarities with Spanish, is often mistaken as Madrid Spanish. Modern grammarians have narrowed to ten simple rules the basic grammatical differences between these two Hispanic tongues. However, knowledge of either one automatically makes the other perfectly intelligible.

Hispanidad, in the realm of sentiment, is the spiritual and cultural brotherhood of all the nationalities that sprung from what was previously the Spanish and Portuguese empires. Many confuse Hispanidad as plain Españolicidad or Españolismo. This is not accurate. Españolicidad or Españolismo merely and specifically refers to only the culture of peninsular Spain. Hispanidad is much wider in scope and vision for it includes the cultural concepts of Mexico, Cuba, Brazil, Venezuela, Argentina, Mozambique, Timor, Goa, Macao, Sidi Ifni, Morocco, the Philippines, the Caribbean countries, the Israeli Sefarditas, etc.

A common culture, or lifestyle, anchored on the Spanish language, on ecumenical Christian Catholicism, on a colorful past and on a brilliant promise of a common cause in the near future in all aspects of world affairs, is the basic hallmark that unites and makes of Hispanidad the family of living nations that it is.

Hispanidad covers a family of nations that once fell under the Spanish Empire

The salient characters and attributes of Hispanidad are of Iberian, Roman, Arabic and Hellenic origin. Owing to the Roman contribution, all Hispanic countries are Latin. The Arabic influence that ruled and permeated both Spain and Portugal for about 800 years has inevitably given Hispanidad, in spite of its Catholicism, marked Arabic-Muslim features. And if Hispanidad includes Hellenic influences in its concept, a great deal is due to the Arabic influence in the Iberian Peninsula which preserved, in Cordoba, what the Arabs had learned from Greece. This is why Spain today is the only Christian nation that is considered a sister-nation by the great Arabic-Muslim block of countries.

A good portion of the United States of America also forms part of Hispanidad.[1] New York City has over two million Spanish-speakers, for which it is considered one of the biggest Hispanic cities in the world in spite of its Dutch and Anglo origins. The North American Southwest is also Hispanic. The Latino population of the United States of about 58 million, as of 2016, represented 18 percent of the total U.S. population, making it the second largest ethnic group among American citizens.[2] These Hispanic Americans, whether *chicano* or *estadounidense*, according to statistics,

---

[1] The U.S. Census Bureau released in August 2013 an online map pinpointing the vast host of languages (other than English) spoken in homes across the United States. According to the report, the map represented approximately 38 million people *que hablan español*. That makes the U.S. the fifth largest Spanish-speaking country on the planet, behind Mexico, Spain, Colombia and Argentina.

[2] "How the U.S. Hispanic Population Is Changing." *pewresearch.org*. http://www.pewresearch.org/fact-tank/2017/09/18/how-the-u-s-hispanic-population-is-changing/ (accessed November 1, 2018).

The yellow and red colors of the Spanish flag dominate many a religious fiesta throughout the Philippines speaking to the deep Hispanic roots of Filipinos.

"spent 1.5 trillion U.S. dollars in the retail and CPG [consumer packaged goods] market in 2015. The buying power is expected to increase to 1.7 trillion U.S. dollars by 2017."[3] The Spanish language media and advertising are now enjoying a big boom in the United States.

And October 12 is the definite "Día de Hispanidad." To Anglo-Americans, the date is celebrated as "Columbus Day," a holiday. To Italians, in and out of the U.S.A., October 12 is "il día de Italia."

Ideologically and culturally speaking, Hispanidad means "international unity," "enlightenment" (*los ilustrados*), "upliftment and liberation," a "common culture," "the historical meeting and embrace of so many races with the Spanish and Portuguese peoples."

In short, Hispanidad is *mestizaje*, a word that can mean the biological interbreeding of races and cultures into a specific homogeneous group to the spiritual acculturation of contrasting tribes into an Iberian pattern toward a particular national awakening.

Hispanidad in Mexico is the marriage, the *mariachi*, between the Aztec-Tinochticlán and the Spanish cultures. In Guatemala and

---

[3] "Buying Power of Hispanic Consumers in the United States from 1990 to 2017." *statista.com*. https://www.statista.com/statistics/251438/hispanics-buying-power-in-the-us/ (accessed November 1, 2018).

other Central American countries, it is the blending of what is Spanish with the Mayans.

In Peru, Ecuador and Bolivia, it is the mixture between the Inca and the Spanish cultures.

In Cuba, the Dominican Republic, and Puerto Rico, it is Spain with Africa, the Siboneyes and the Borrinquenes.

In Chile it is Spain with the Araucans.

And in Argentina as well as in Paraguay, it is the Guaranis with Spain sprinkled over with other European influences, notably Italian and German.

In the Congo it is Spanish culture inherited by the tribes that now form the Republics of Santa Isabel and Fernando Po, now called Bioko, in the Equatorial Guinea.

In Morocco it is Melilla, Ceuta and Tetuan.

In West Africa it is Spain and the Sahara among the Rioesenses and the Sidifnises, now the Arab-Hispanic Saharawis.

In South Africa it is Portugal with Angola and Mozambique.

In India it is Goa, Damau and Diu.

In Sri Lanka, Timor and to a degree, Macau, it is still Portugal infused with some Indian, Indonesian, Malayan and Chinese groups.

In the Middle East it is Israel with its Sefardies, the Hispanic Jews, Ladinos.

In the Philippines, Hispanidad is the result of simultaneous inter-fusion of the Spanish language and culture with that of ancient Malays, the *chinos cristianos criollos* and the Japanese; aside from almost all the basic ethnic groups of our islands classified as Tagalogs, Cebuanos, Hiligaynos, Bicolanos, Ilocanos, Pampangos, Maguindanaos and others whose languages are basically Hispanized.

Hispanics are projected to make up a quarter of the U.S. population by 2045

Hence, while the official language, the laws, the social conduct, the economies, the ethics, the nationalistic concept of the Filipino, the literature of Burgos, Rizal, Mabini and Recto and the spiritual values are basically Spanish-inspired, the diverse racial extractions making up the Filipino people are the perfect ground upon which Hispanidad, as a lifestyle did, and still does, thrive.

Hispanidad is a unitive, homogenizing factor in Filipinism, whether *indio* or *ilustrado*. The most distant, and contrary, groups, through its process of *mestizaje* and *aculturación católica,* have ended up as a single national unit.

Spain converted our ancient *barangays* into *barrios.* From several *barrios,* Spain instituted the concept of the *municipio,* or the *pueblo* with its *poblaciones.* Through a centralized form of government established in Manila, these *municipios* were strung together to form the national Filipino unit after a tutelage of nearly four centuries.

Tomás Pinpin, a Hispanized, therefore Filipinized, Chinese was instrumental in supplanting the different systems of writing, which our native dialects had, with the universal Spanish *abecedario.* A century or more later, Francisco Balagtás wrote his immortal *Florante at Laura,* according to the tenets of the Spanish *abecedario, gramática* and *métrica,* thus fathering literary Tagalog. This Balagtás, Hispanized Tagalog, was, however, saddled with the backward Lope K. Santos *balarila* and *abakada* of 20 syllables, thereby limiting its true potentialities as a more assimilable national language in fact by the non-Tagalog majority of the country.

A forward-looking foreign policy should place importance to our Hispanic ties

For Filipinism to triumph, Hispanidad is indispensable. This is why the "Día de Hispanidad" was always celebrated in the Philippines before the Second World War as something like "Filipino Identity Day." And Filipinos then, regardless of ethnic and dialectical origins, were faster drawn together as brothers, as one people, by speaking the same prestigious international language, Spanish; by professing the same creed in churches built along the same architectural baroque lines, dotting every Philippine *barrio* or *pueblo;* and by dancing, eating, playing, singing and living in Vigan-like houses, plazas and streets that reaffirm the integrity of the Filipino national spirit and identity. After all, Hispanidad is the human crucible through which Filipinism, in its authentic manifestations, was truly fashioned.

But Hispanidad cannot, and should not, be confined in nostalgia alone. For the revival of the "Día de la Hispanidad" commemoration by President Marcos back then was possibly one of the greatest positive investments made by the Philippine government and people for their future progress.

We say investment because the moment the Philippines becomes fully industrialized, like Japan is today, the need to open newer and wider markets for our export products and services will inevitably arise. And, at the rate of about four Filipino babies being born a minute today, further overpopulation will imperatively demand that we produce more food, open more foreign markets for our products, provide adequate public services and generate many more livelihood opportunities for our people if we are to continue surviving as a free nation.

We shall then have to set our eyes on the Hispanic countries across the Pacific Ocean as possible markets for our products and as the possible destination of future demographic necessities. And we shall only be able

A *mestiza terciada* is featured in a tourism poster.

to do this if we maintain today our Hispanic heritage, which is the bond that will make us acceptable to the Latin Americans as their future trading partners and brothers. While the Asiatic nations shall have been overpopulated and, perhaps, beleaguered by socio-economic upheavals, the huge Latin American continent, with all its unexploited natural resources and wealth, shall still be underpopulated.

Japan, without being a Hispanic nation, has already managed to gain a strong demographic and economic foothold in South America through what we can safely label as a "Japanese Hispanizing Program."

It was then a very wise move, on the part of President Marcos, to restore the official status of Spanish in the 1973 Constitution and to declare October 7-13 as "Philippine Hispanic Week."

The next best thing to do is not only to restore Spanish as a 12-unit language course in college but to upgrade its teaching there and to also introduce it as a subject in the elementary and high school levels.

With the proper teaching plan and aids, any Filipino teacher can teach Spanish even if he or she did not know the whole language.

Hispanidad also means many positive acquisitions which help the Filipinos, as individuals, as families, as interrelated communities and as a whole nation, to survive the daily struggle. To cite but the most immediate examples, the present food shortage in many parts of the world has literally caused us to turn to something we owe Hispanidad: corn.

Corn was brought to us from the American continent by the early Spanish missionaries of Hispanidad without ever thinking that somewhere in the future we would need it as a food staple. Along with corn, Hispanidad also gave us a variety of fruits, vegetables, root crops and agricultural plants: tomato, onion, *camote*, cassava, *sincamas, tamiz, ube, nanca*, chili (*sili*), papaya, *guayaba, ciruela*, avocado, *guayabano, tamarindo, camachile, santol, chico* and *atis*.

For Filipinism to triumph, Hispanidad is indispensable as it is the tie that binds us

It provided agricultural products like coffee, cacao, sugar (*tubos de caña dulce*), *mani* and *pili* nuts. It introduced public services like electricity, telephone and telegram, potable water, wheel transportation, irrigation system, public hygiene and popular education.

It established the printing press which introduced Filipinos to new ideas through books, magazines, pamphlets and newspapers. It imported domesticated animals like the *cabayo*, the *vaca*, the *pavo*, the *ganza*, the *carnero* and a variety of *patos*. It launched industries like those spawned by abaca, tobacco, jute and palm. It built infrastructures like roads, plazas, bridges, ports, public town and city buildings, dams and canals. The way the Spaniards constructed our towns and cities still serves as our template today in our drive toward urbanization. The Hispanic heritage of the Filipino is so great, so common a thing, that many of us fail to fully discern it.

> *Hispanidad also means many positive acquisitions which help the Filipinos*

According to a news report carried by *El País* in 2011, "by 2050 10 percent of the world population will speak Spanish and the United States will be the biggest Spanish-speaking country." The report quoted the general-secretary of the Association of Spanish Language Academies as making this prediction:

> Cuban writer and academic Humberto López Morales made this prediction during his speech when he was awarded an honorary doctorate by the University of Valencia at a ceremony presided over by Spanish Education Minister Angel Gabilondo.

He noted that the current situation of Hispanics in the United States is the result of a confluence of historical processes headed by Mexico at the beginning of the 20th century, followed by Puerto Rico, Cuba, the Dominican Republic and, more recently, Venezuela and Argentina.

'Knowing Spanish is ... among other things, a business,' and in some states, like Florida, 'Spanish is a good passport for obtaining a job,' he said.
According to another study cited by López Morales, 'every minute that goes by, 2.5 Hispanics enter the stream of immigrants to the country, that is to say, 3,700 per day.'

If the forecast is borne out, the United States by 2050 will become the largest Spanish-speaking country in the world and Spanish will be the second-most-spoken language on the planet, surpassed only by Chinese.[4]

The Philippine flag occupies a prominent place in the logo of the Iberoamericana 2018 summit.

---

[4] *newamericamedia.org.*

PART IX

BAYANIHAN: A REPOSITORY
OF CULTURAL TREASURES

The Bayanihan Philippine Folk Dance Company is a truly national treasure, preserving our folk dances for future generations through meticulous research and creative choreography that projects the best of the Filipino people in the Philippines and abroad.

1. *DANCE ICON*: TREASURED DANCE PIECES

IN 2014, THE BAYANIHAN Philippine Folk Dance Company mounted a new show it dubbed *Dance Icon*. Conceptualized by Dr. Suzie Moya Benítez, *Dance Icon* is "a collection of treasured dance pieces" which, as expected, were masterfully translated for the grand stage by multi-awarded choreographer Ferdinand José with musical arrangements provided by Melito Vale Cruz.

With *Dance Icon,* the Bayanihan Philippine Folk Dance Company proves once again that, like vintage wine, it is getting better and better with the years. Simply put, Bayanihan is the best vehicle to preserve and embellish what is Filipino in dance, music, native costumes, song, stage technology and poetry.

> *Bayanihan is the repository of what is Filipino in dance, music and poetry*

Dance Icon begins with the "Filipino Hispanic Suite" under the subtitle of "Parian de Intramuros." The dance numbers consisting of *cuadrilleros, alegría, en recreación, canción, luna verde, torneo* and *malagueñas de Pila* (Laguna) belie the mistaken view that a Philippine *parian* was a "Chinese ghetto where crime and misery were the standard."

The *parian*, particularly that of *Intramuros de Manila*, was a Spanish and *chino cristiano* community of trade, opulence, grace, beauty, dignity, culture and progress. The architectural restoration of the Walled City of Intramuros has recreated a *puerta* (gate) *de parian*, a *calle del parian* and a *mercado del parian* giving us a sense of that thriving community that now belongs to the past. There were two *parianes*, one inside the walls (Intramuros) and the other outside the walls (Extramuros) where Spanish-speaking *chinos cristianos* engaged in commerce became an important part of the Manila-México galleon trade that lasted for 250 years.

In almost every provincial capital of this archipelago, one can find architectural and cultural traces of a Spanish-speaking *parian*, a *pariancillo* or a *sector de mestizos*, the former home of the Spanish-speaking *chino cristiano* being referred to as *el mestizo* since the Spanish settler was known as *el criollo*, the creole. Both the Spanish creole and the *chino cristiano* were regarded as Filipinos—*los primeros filipinos*, followers and taxpayers of King Felipe II of Spain. And they were *residentes del parian*. The *parian* residents, being *ilustrados*, were slightly distinguished from their *indio* compatriots but both enjoyed the same Filipino and Spanish citizenships after having accepted Felipe II of Spain as their "natural sovereign."[1]

"The Moro Suite" of *Dance Icon* is a gem since it has integrated into a single, fast-paced dance number all the delightful sparklers of the Moro dance that only Bayanihan can deliver with authentic grace and spirit.

> *Bayanihan researchers have discovered that the lumads are the majority in Mindanao*

Then there is the "Fernando Amorsolo Suite" that celebrates the immortal works, the paintings of this great national artist, glorifying the Filipina and the richly impressive native Filipino ambiance and culture, brightened by the golden Philippine sun, like no other artist ever did. With Bayanihan's mastery of Filipino dance, dress and song, the rich Amorsolo vignettes come to life for the present generation to enjoy with overwhelming satisfaction.

And the *lumad* cultural minorities of Mindanao are given a voice in *Dance Icon*. As students we had been always taught that Mindanao is predominantly Muslim. But a Bayanihan research on Mindanao native songs and dances, spearheaded by Suzie Moya Benitez, Ferdinand José and Melito

Suzie Moya has risen from the ranks of dancers to become today's Bayanihan executive director.

---

[1] All Spanish overseas possessions were called *Indias*, ruled by a *Consejo de Indias* and a set of laws called *Leyes de Indias*. Thus, the name *indio* was given to its indigenous or aboriginal population since both the Spanish *criollo* and the *chino cristiano* did not have native or aboriginal roots. But then, all ended up as Filipinos.

Vale Cruz, found otherwise. While discovering the rich *lumad* culture and that of other non-Muslim minorities like the Manobos, they also found that these non-Muslim groups actually form the majority population of Mindanao, not the Moros. And the rich and original non-Muslim materials emanating from the culture of Mindanao's *lumads* can now be enjoyed as one of the principal suites of *Dance Icon* under the subtitle of "Kadabawan."

Mariele Benitez, one of Bayanihan's principal dancers.

As grand finale, the "Philippine Countryscape Suite" is presented with a masterful combination of the "Kawayanan" dance followed by "Las Mayas" and by that lilting stick dance, "Sakuting," a blend of Chinese and Spanish Basque energies. It culminated in the breathtaking and acrobatic "Sayaw Sa Bangkô," ending with a parade of colorful dresses of Andalusian inspiration that glorifies both the *baro't saya* and the *traje de mestiza de Maria Clara*.

2. BAYANIHAN'S GREAT CULTURAL CONTRIBUTION

AN ALMOST BARREN PHILIPPINE CULTURAL LANDSCAPE of the 1950s stirred to life when the Bayanihan Philippine Folk Dance Company was formed in 1956. Since then, this national treasure has danced its way to become *the* ultimate Filipino dance troop in the eyes of every Filipino, representing the best of our culture anywhere it performs around the globe. Since its birth over half a century ago, it is now the undisputed repository of almost all Filipino native dances, traditional dresses and songs.

In the 1960s, Lucrecia Úrtula, later declared as Philippine National Artist for Dance, scoured Mindanao, the Cordilleras and almost every island of the country in search of *katutubô* Filipinos. Whenever she found them, she asked them to perform before her their own ancestral ethnic or tribal dances. She diligently noted down every nuanced movement of their dances until she had enough knowledge of these dances to bring home to the Bayanihan dancers in Manila, where these dances were properly choreographed and performed on the grand stage. Thanks to her efforts, these dances will be there for the dance company to revive, to interpret and to preserve for posterity.

Bayanihan not only performs ethnic dances but preserves them for posterity too

Today, the descendants of those *katutubô* dancers of more than 50 years ago literally have lost their indigenous roots, along with their vernacular languages, dances and songs. The loss may be traced to their assimilation into our highly Americanized pop culture either through education in compulsory English or the pervasive media. As these new generations of *katutubô* leave behind the collective memories of their roots to embrace pop culture, it has become nearly impossible for any new dance company to go directly to the source when researching on folk dances. This is where Bayanihan's importance lies: imparting while safeguarding those dances compiled and rendered for the stage by Lucrecia Úrtula many years ago.

Bayanihan has lived up to that big challenge. Aside from its ongoing shows and performances, it has produced tutorial videos and organized

Dancers showcase the best in traditional Filipina costumes in their performances.

many dance seminars and workshops to share with all those interested in what it has accumulated through the years.

Both Lucrecia Úrtula and Lucrecia Kasilag, also a National Artist for Music, conducted research on Filipino lowland or Christian folk dances and songs to preserve them for future generations.

These dances and songs are classified into three level groups: (1) urban or creole (*kriolyo*) (2) *baile popular* and (3) *baile rural o provincial.*

The *kriolyo* dances and songs are those brought to these islands when *Filipinas* was still an overseas province of Spain. Thus, the music is purely Spanish. But their *jota, fandango* and *sevillana* steps when executed by Filipinos end up reflecting the native expression and temperament,

One of Bayanihan's principal dancers.

Bayanihan has lived up to the challenge of carefully documenting Filipino folk dances

thereby becoming purely Filipino in soul.

The *baile popular* folk dances are still Hispanic in their steps and motif, but their music, even if still based on the Spanish *seguidilla* chord, is composed by Filipino musicians thus rooting them further into the Philippine soil.

The *baile* rural folk dances, as compiled by Francisca Reyes Aquino, are also Hispanic but they also betray a greater native expression and

soul even if sung either in Spanish, Tagalog or Visayan with words spelled and syllabicated with the 32-letter Balagtás alphabet.

While the reservoir of the *katutubô* or tribal dances has almost dried up, the Hispanic or Christian Filipino native dances still remain to be fully rediscovered and retrieved. A source of these native dances and songs is the *moro-moro*. Another is the *zarzuela* and the *revista* (stage shows), now long forgotten, that popularized the *pasadoble*, the *pasacalle*, the *habanera*, the *kundiman*, the *kuratsa*, the *pandanggo*, the *valse*, the *danza*, the *chótis*, the *kumintang*, the *marcha*, the *balitao*, and the *mazurka*.

The thing to do now is to turn to historical events and places to bring back, string together and coordinate all these rich *zarzuela* and

A string musician plays a Filipino folk song on his instrument as performers in a colorful native costume go through their dance routine.

revista materials into purely Filipino choreography and dance suites. In this regard, the competent staff of the Bayanihan Philippine Folk Dance Company have really got their work cut out for them.

Poster announcing shows of the dance company presented by the Cultural Center of the Philippines in 2017.

PART X

VESTIGES OF OUR SPANISH PAST REMAIN IN
LA MUY LEAL Y NOBLE CIUDAD

The Augustinian-run San Jose Placer Parish Church in front of Plaza Libertad in Iloilo City is the focal point of the world-famous Dinagyang Festival every January.

1. ILOILO AND ITS TWO *PARIANES*

THE WORD *PARIAN* (plural: *parianes*) is commonly called today a Chinatown, to which some of our compatriots have attached a negative connotation, especially the highly-Americanized Filipinos among us who dismiss this neighborhood as a mere "Chinese ghetto." But in the context of a deeper Filipino history, a *parian* is never a ghetto where crime and misery abounded, but a Christian Chinese-Hispanic community of trade and opulence. It enjoyed wealth and frenetic business activities because the Filipino *parian* of the Spanish era was an offspring of the China-Manila-Mexico-Spain galleon trade.

Beautiful Chinese silk and ceramics were the principal products of the old galleon trade that started in *Intramuros de Manila* on the same day of its founding (June 24, 1571) as the capital, or *cabecera*, of the *Estado Filipino* then headed by Spain's Miguel López de Legazpi.

Since Intramuros with its *aduana* (customs house) is the birthplace of the galleon trade, it was but natural that the first *parian* was organized next to the Dominican church of Santo Domingo inside Intramuros. In time, it was relocated as a *chino cristiano* neighborhood to what we know today as the *Puerta del Parian* and the *Calle del Parian* (*Calle Real*) still inside Spanish Intramuros.

The *chinos cristianos*, having accepted the King of Spain as their natural sovereign, became Spanish citizens, therefore Spaniards, and with their own Chinese *fuquienhua*, adopted Spanish as also their own language.

Spanish Dominican Bishop Fray Domingo de Salazar wrote in 1591 how both the Spanish friars and *conquistadores* highly appreciated their principal Chinese business partners in the galleon trade who took care of supplying their local walled city community with the daily basics of food, clothing and other amenities. The conduct of the Chinese made a very positive impression upon Fray Domingo de Salazar, the first bishop of the Philippines (1579-94), who viewed them with admiration. In his report to King Philip II of Spain, he described the Chinese as "a white-skinned people like us, Castilians" and "are the smartest people on earth (*los más ingeniosos que debe haber en el mundo*)."

The scope of the galleon trade, of course, was not solely limited to Manila because to further strengthen the capital city with greater services and raw materials for export, more *parianes* were established for the Chinese merchants whose trade activities were directly related to the procurement of the necessary export products from China and from many places across these islands destined to the markets of Mexico, Central and South America and Spain in far away Europe.

A big *parian* was founded in Cebú and two others in Molo and in Jaro were also started in the environs of what was the Spanish *ciudad de Iloilo*.[1]

Iloilo City proper, later labeled *la muy noble y leal ciudad de Yloilo*, had to be fortified with *Fuerte de San Pedro* (later *La Cotta*), which jutted out to the Iloilo Straight fronting Guimarás Island. From it, two roads were built. The first one was *Calle del Santo Rosario* leading to Plaza Libertad (formerly *Plaza de Alfonso XII*) and to the main street known up to now as *Calle Real*. And the second road from the same fort goes toward the mouth of the salt water Iloilo river, an estuary called

Parianes were centers of culture and business, not crime-ridden ghettos

Farola because of a lighthouse facing the sea, winding up the dock where a majestic *aduana*, or customs house, is situated. Tabúcan is to the left reaching the old and smaller wooden dock of the Molo *parian* as it further continues onward to its other mouth somewhere between *Villa de Arévalo* and old Otón town. This estuary was called *Ria*,[2] Spanish for salt water river, and was frequented by galleons and *falúas*, or ships of every tonnage from Manila, and the sturdy Chinese junks (*juncos*) from China.

---

[1] In northern Luzon, the *parian* was officially called *sector de mestizos* as in the case of Vigan, Ilocos Sur and Malolos, Bulacán. The same Chinese trade enclave was also called *pariancillo* as in the cases of the old town of Pasig, Calamba, Lipá and Cavite's Puerto Punta Sangley.

[2] Rio, on the other hand, is Spanish for fresh water river.

A cluster of houses owned by Iloilo's elite families in Molo, one of the city's *parianes* during Spanish colonial times (circa 1900).

As earlier mentioned, Iloilo had two *parianes*. The first one was *El Parian de Santa Ana de Molo*, whose original Chinese Christian residents were transferred from the older *Villa de Arévalo* town after the Augustinians had won a dispute against the Jesuits who insisted that the Chinese settlers had to be placed under their pastoral jurisdiction and care. The second Iloilo *parian* was established in the elegant and opulent *municipio de Jaro* where the Metropolitan Cathedral of *Nuestra Señora de la Candelaria* is the cultural and infrastructural centerpiece of the proud *jareño ilustrados*.

But the Spanish *ciudad de Yloilo* became economically stagnant for a time since Spanish immigration only came in trickles. On the other hand, both Molo and Jaro became fast-growing centers of industry and agriculture. Their growth was fueled by the numerous Chinese Christian families who cultivated the nearby provincial farm lands owned by the Iloilo provincial *municipio* that the Spanish administration had distributed to them. These lands were developed either into rich rice lands, sugarcane *haciendas* or fruit and vegetable *granjas*. The wealth of these

Nelly's Garden Mansion in Jaro, another district of Iloilo where a *parian* was established.

old Spanish and Chinese Christian families[3] was further augmented when the nearby island of Negros was parceled out, at very low Spanish government prices, into the *haciendas* and *centrales azucareras* that we know up to the present time.

The China-Manila-Mexico Spanish galleon trade, aside from silk and ceramics, also brought to these islands corn, onion, tomato, potato, *camote*, *sincamas*, sugarcane, tobacco, coffee bean, cacao, papaya, and guava to enrich the land and improve the ancient native diet with cottage industries like the manufacturing of local preserved foods and candies.

---

[3] Among the most prominent of these families are the Lópezes, Villanuevas, Locsins, Sians, Ledesmas, Lacsons, Lizareses, Gamboas, Aranetas, Benedictos, Jisons, Consings, Dichings, De la Ramas, Gómezes, Arroyos, Coscolluelas, Avanceñas, Mapas, Jalbuenas, Jalandonis, Javellanas, Montinolas, Garcías, Tioncos, Quilaycos, Uriartes, Yusays, etc.

To develop farming and local transportation, the Spanish galleons also introduced into the country draft animals like the carabao from Vietnam, the horse and the mule from far away Spain, together with the plow (*arado, araro*) and the hoe (*asarol, sadul* or *azadón*) from Mexico..

These tremendous economic movements greatly changed for the better the local lifestyle of both the *parian* communities and the native *indio principalía*. Owing to its residents' refined culture, the town of Molo was dubbed "the Athens of Western Visayas." It lived up to that moniker with several centers of learning such as the *Colegio de Santa Ana* owned and run by the highly praised Avanceña sisters, the *Liceo de Molo* of Don Manuel Locsin and the *Centro Escolar de Molo* of the Salas brothers.

Molo's pioneering tycoon was Don Eusebio Villanueva, a pure *chino cristiano*, who started a progressive construction company that served both Molo and Jaro aside from the *ciudad de Yloilo*. He imported logs and lumber from a rich Spanish *mestizo* Bicolano family, ultimately marrying a daughter of this Bicolano family, Maria Felipe who, upon transferring to Molo, developed a *jusi* and *sinamay* manufacturing industry.

Don Eusebio and Doña Maria begot 22 children and two of their daughters married scions of the *jareño* López family. Many of the Molo and Jaro grand old houses were reportedly constructed by Don Eusebio's *compañía constructora*.

Chinos cristianos living in its two parianes made Iloilo a very progressive city

Doña Maria Felipe de Villanueva is remembered in Iloilo as the founder and faithful sponsor of the "Abre Salón" dance soirees in her grand mansion (*balay ñga bató* or *caserona de cal y canto*[4]) next to both the *Colegio de Santa Ana* and the famous orphanage *Asilo de Molo* of the Spanish Sisters of Charity (*Hermanas de la Caridad*) known for the exquisite embroidery of their wards.

---

[4] A house made of limestone.

Another mansion in Jaro owned by the Benedicto clan.

The monthly "Abre Salón" fiesta was a dinner *tertulia y velada,*[5] held after an afternoon *panguingue*[6] and *madióng*[7] sessions, that featured Spanish dances, songs, poetry declamations and oratory in Spanish, performed by her own numerous children with the sons and daughters of almost all of the Chinese Christian *moleño* and *jareño* families who impressed even Sir John Bowring, Hongkong's governor-general from 1854-60, when he visited Molo in the late 1850s.[8]

From the two López-Villanueva couples came the *hacendero*-industrialist Don Eugenio López and the politician Don Fernando López, who served as vice president of the country three times.[9] Also from the same marriage came Don Vicente López who continued, after the Second

---

[5] An after-dinner party or gathering, typically in a private house, for conversation or music.

[6] A 19th-century card game believed to be of Filipino origin, which also spread to the American Southwest and even found its way to Las Vegas casinos.

[7] Filipino spelling of mahjong.

[8] John Bowring, "Iloilo and Panay," *Visit to the Philippine Islands* (London: 3mith, Elder & Co.,1859), 359.

[9] López served as vice president of the Philippines three times. He first was elected with Elpidio Quirino (1949–53) under the banner of the Liberal Party and later with Ferdinand Marcos (1965–69), also under the Liberty Party. He won reelection in 1969, this time as a running mate of President Marcos under the Nacionalista Party but his four-year term was cut short in 1972 with the declaration of martial law.

World War, the "Abre Salón" tradition of his grandmother, Doña Maria, in his famous Nelly's Garden Mansion in Jaro, that featured the *parian* Spanish dances of Chloe Cruz Rómulo Periquet, with Rubén Nieto from Manila and her friends from neighboring Negros Occidental, Mini del Rosario y Lizares, Maria Vicenta Gamboa-Bonin, Anita Arregui and Baby Feria, who all hail from present-day Silay City, which was the *parian* of Bacolod City.

Another descendant is Don Serafin Villanueva, whose several "S. Villanueva" heritage and Old World buildings still stand along the main streets of present-day Iloilo City.

The 1920s and the 1930s brought to Iloilo more Chinese immigrants from Minnan, Xiamen and Canton who founded many businesses and department stores that contributed to the city's economic progress even if, since the early Spanish times, such Chinese Christian families like the Marques-Lims had already opened famous *bazares* on the *Calle Real de la ciudad*, which are still remembered for their textile goods and many other products called *chucherias*. And most of these Chinese *bazares* of Iloilo still have Spanish names such as *La Pepita de Oro de Don José Chin*

Until recently, many of Iloilo's elite families who come from Jaro and Molo districts, which were established as *parianes* during Spanish times, try to relive the glory of their ancestors' past with ballroom dancing at local hotels.

Lam Chu Suey, La Virtud, Las Tres Estrellas, La Belleza, El Noval del Señor Sua Boc San, etc. Today, Iloilo has Chinese schools like Sun Yat Sen, Chiang Kay Shek and the Chinese Commercial College that greatly contribute to the education and culture of our young people.

It is from this solid foundation, beginning from the now historic Manila-Acapúlco galleon trade (a global galleon trade, really)—an almost forgotten, long-time partnership between the Spanish *conquistadores* and the Chinese Christian traders, on the

An elegant couple—Don Serafin Villanueva and his wife Doña Anita—from one of the old families of Iloilo's *parianes.*

missionaries, on one hand, and the Chinese Christian traders, on the other—that Iloilo today has the inspiration and the experience to become a modern city worthy of reclaiming its old glorious title of "Queen City of the South."

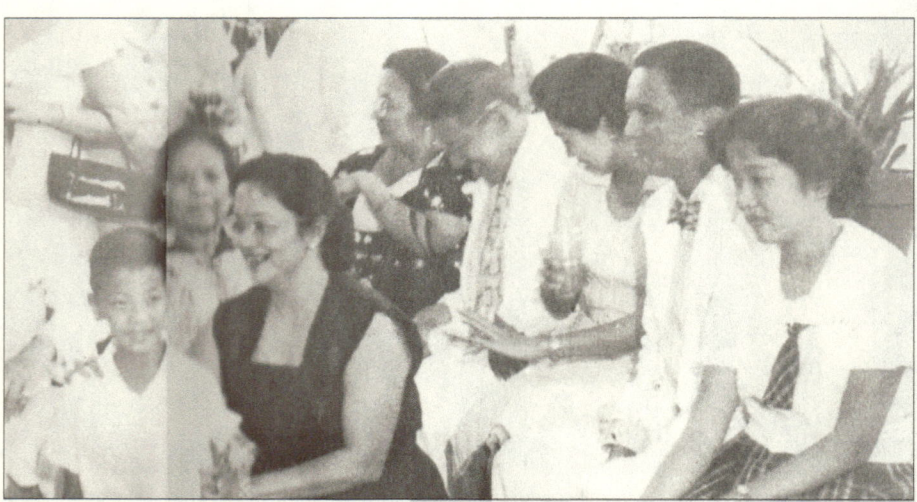

A gathering of the Lopez-Villanueva clans of both Jaro and Molo. Second from right is Don Vicente Lopez who continued the "Abre Salón" tradition of his grandmother, Doña Maria Felipe de Villanueva.

PART XI

THE STRANGE HISTORY
OF HOW CALINOG TOWN WAS FORMED

POR DIOS Y POR ESPAÑA
(novela filipina)

LA EXTRAORDINARIA AVENTURA DE UN MISIONERO ESPAÑOL EN FILIPINAS

POR

GUILLERMO GÓMEZ RIVERA

DE LA ACADEMIA FILIPINA DE LA LENGUA
CORRESPONDIENTE DE LA R.A.E.
Manila, Filipinas, 2015

Por Dios y por España is a historical novel about the strange founding of the town of Calinog in Iloilo.

1. FELIX LAUREANO, FIRST FILIPINO PHOTOGRAPHER

Recently invited to talk before the faculty of the University of the Philippines in the Visayas at the school's Iloilo City campus, I was asked to deliver a lecture around the theme of "From Bugasong to Barcelona." The symposium was organized to celebrate the life of Felix Laureano, considered the first Filipino photographer. While mainly delving into his achievements, the greater aim of the gathering was to gain a better understanding of our Visayan and Hispanic past and of ourselves as a people. Below is the full text of my lecture:

Since our friend Frank Villanueva assigned me to develop the topic on our Hispano-Filipino legacy, I will start by touching on a subject

A Spanish friar fending off an attack by the natives, one of the many dangers Catholic missionaries faced in remote mission outposts throughout the Philippines during Spanish colonial times.

Calinog is situated in Central Panay in the province of Iloilo.

which was considered taboo in my younger days. And that subject is about Filipinos who happen to be descendants of a friar, a Spanish Catholic missionary.

This topic becomes relevant to, and even appropriate in, this symposium. And this same topic has to be discussed frankly since Felix Laureano, according to his biography, is the son of a Spanish friar with a *china cristiana mestiza india*[1] from Bugasong, Antique.

It so happens that I am completing a novel[2] about the Spanish friar who founded the town of Calinog, Iloilo. In my research while writing the novel, I learned that it was the Mundó-Calibuganes women of Central Panay who seduced him to father a hundred or so children with them. By

---

[1] The term *india* or *indio* has not always carried pejorative connotations. The term is derived from Spanish documents issued from Spain's overseas provinces which were then called *Indias* (Indies) and ruled by a *Consejo de Indias* and a set of *Leyes de Indias*. In the context of Philippine history, the meaning of *indio* is, in fact, native *provinciano* citizen. The word *indio* only became somewhat offensive when it was used as a propaganda item against the Spanish friars and the Spanish *conquistadores* by those who wanted to grab from Spain its overseas provinces, Cuba, Puerto Rico and *Filipinas*. For sure, the term dates back to Christopher Columbus' discovery of the New World in 1492. When he landed in the Carribean, he thought he was in the East Indies. In his letters, he mistakenly referred to the natives there as *indios* after the country India, which he had thought to be the place his expedition encountered. A much later and controversial assertion as to the origin of the term was made by author Edward Abbey in his book *The Fool's Progress* (1988). In the November 3, 1991 issue of *The Los Angeles Times*, letter-writer James A. Campbell summarized Abbey's claim thus: "Abbey writes that 'Columbus knew he was nowhere near India' and that he was so charmed by the people he found in the Caribbean—so sweet, happy, blessed—he called them *Los Gentes en* (or in) *Dios*, meaning 'the people in God.' This is what Columbus wrote to Ferdinand and Isabella, Abbey reports, and the name *Indios* stuck, becoming changed by usage to Indians."

[2] That novel of mine is called *Por Dios y por España (For God and for Spain)*.

Fray Felix Castroviejo is offered a love potion by tribeswomen in this artist's rendition of events that led to the founding of Calinog.

ensnaring the friar, they wanted to achieve two important goals: to ensure their survival through the support of the priest and to have children for they could no longer rely upon their menfolk for sex as the latter were so hooked on *apian* or opium that they were rendered totally useless to do anything.

What we would label today as criminal seduction was accepted as part of the tradition known as *lumay*,[3] a practice which was prevalent among our pre-Hispanic ancestors here in Panay who had no notion whatsoever about the sacred status of a Spanish Catholic priest.

Mundó in our vernacular means "wild" and Calibuganes refers to a tribe, or tribes, whose components are offsprings of the encounter and eventual union between the aboriginal Ati, or Aetas, and the Malay-Bornean settlers as suggested by the *Maragtás sang Panay* or *Kinaragto*.

Maragtás, as you know, is our oral pre-Hispanic history as repeated to us by our elders. In my particular case, it was told by my own *yaya*[4] who left her hometown of Calinog 20 kilometers away to work for my family as a live-in nanny in Barrio Tabugón, *municipio de Dingle*.

---

[3] Seduction with the use of love potion, which comes in the form of a drink, is said to have the magical power of making a woman fall in love with a man or vice-versa once it is imbibed by the intended lover.

[4] Nanny.

Lumay or seduction is carried out by giving the male or female victim an alcoholic drink called *tubalina*, an unfermented wine produced from the nipa palm, which carries natural aphrodisiac.

Padre Felix Castroviejo was a missionary in his late '20s when he fell victim to the Mundó-Calibuganes women. They offered him a *tubalina* drink mixed with fine powder from a flower called *nipay*. The drink caused him to be heavily drunk and sleepwalking as somnambulism was one of its side effects. While the priest was in a state of stupor, the women had sex with him without him being fully aware of what was going on around him.

> **Tribeswomen used a love potion to keep a missionary captive to their wiles**

The act of seduction or *lumay* (*gayuma* in Tagalog) was part of the Mundó-Calibuganes culture. We should take into account the fact that the Mundós were nomads who did not practice agriculture. They survived by traditional subsistence activities such as fishing and hunting and scavenging for wild berries and anything edible they could find in the rich forests of Simsiman, which later became the municipality of Calinog.

The Mundó women depended almost totally on their men for sustenance. The male Mundó who could provide was approached by the female Mundós who offered themselves as his wives in exchange for food and protection. Reluctant male Mundós would be offered *tubalina* to arouse their libido for sex and procreation purposes.

Tribeswomen trying to seduce Father Felix after spiking his drink with a love potion.

Since Fray Felix Castroviejo, with the assistance of his *chino cristiano* sacristan Mónico Sinlo, had developed a prosperous *hacienda* near the areas where the Mundós lived, it did not take long for the Mundó women to cast their eyes toward both men as potential husbands and good providers. Since Padre Castroviejo strongly refused their

> *A friar sired a hundred or so children with different women, giving birth to a town*

sexual advances, the Múndo women subjected the priest to the *lumay* ritual. They spiked his drink with *tubalina* and temporarily blinded him with powder derived from a certain variety of the *nipay* plant.

In his constant state of induced drunkenness, the poor Fray Felix Castroviejo ended up siring so many children with scores of Mundó women who all moved into his *hacienda* to the consternation of the elder Mundó males who were left abandoned not only by the women but by the younger tribesmen who joined the women in the *hacienda* where food was plentiful. Since the priest and his sacristan were poultry and pig farmers, there was enough food for everyone. The younger men made themselves available as servants to Fray Castroviejo's loyal sacristan, who managed the *hacienda* while the priest was being practically held a sex captive by the Múndo women. Mónico himself never drank the *tubalina*. He befriended the Múndo princess and housed all the womenfolk inside a big bamboo and nipa camarin, which was constructed like a spacious military barracks.

The Múndo princess would eventually become Mónico's wife. In the meantime, he allowed the Múndo women to do as they pleased with Fray Felix. The women tied Fray Felix either to a bamboo bed or chair to perform their ritual but they also made sure he was well-fed and kept clean by washing and bathing him. They venerated and loved him like a living *anito*.

Mónico enlisted the help of the women and the young Múndo males to help him in farm work at the *hacienda*. In the process, they learned farming under his direction. They also helped in raising the poultry and in tending to the herd of cattle and horses, pigs and other farm animals.

After some two or so years had elapsed, the Múndo women finally agreed it was time to set Fray Felix free. They weaned him off the *tubalina* and allowed him to stay in separate quarters. As Fray Castroviejo regained

Fray Felix Castroviejo's faithful sacristan, Mónico Sinlo, a *chino cristiano*, is depicted as a loyal assistant in this illustration.

his senses and recovered his sight, Mónico told him everything that had happened to him in the hands of the Múndo women. He was naturally horrified, but in due time, he accepted everything as the will of God.

Making the most out of his situation, Fray Felix set out to Christianize the Múndos. He taught his children and their mothers catechism to prepare them for baptism, along with the wives and children of Mónico. He got them to help him build his parish church. At this point, the Múndo women had come to understand his vow of celibacy and to respect his priesthood. Soon, the town of Calinog was formed.

He and Mónico designed the *pueblo* of Calinog. A stone church was built in front of a spacious plaza. Across the town square rose the *Casa Real y Tribunal con escuela y carcel* while a *mercado* was erected at the right side of the same plaza. A road network was constructed, giving rise to *pueblo* streets along which housing lots were assigned for the innumerable children of Fray Felix and those of Mónico Celo (Sinlo/Locsin). The farm lands developed around the *pueblo* proper were also equitably distributed among their children.

Fifteen years later, the numerous children of Fray Castroviejo had reached puberty together with those of his loyal sacristan. Attracted to the daughters of the priest and his sacristan, Múndo-Calibuganes males started seeking baptism for they knew that it was needed before they could be permitted to marry the women. What started out as a desperate move of the Múndo women to ensure their survival from hunger evolved into

The town of Calinog is designed *a cordel* which means government and church buildings are constructed around the plaza with the town hall (above) at one end and the Roman Catholic church (below) at the other.

a community of Catholic believers, with the offsprings of the friar and his assistant forming its core.

As we said, Fray Felix Castroviejo designed the municipality of Calinog *a cordel*. Towns that missionaries built throughout most of the Spanish colonies followed the pattern of constructing the church and the government offices around the town plaza and in a straight line (*a cordel*)

Father Felix with his numerous children.

tracing the plaza's contour. It places the church at one end of the plaza and the tribunal building at the other. The town market or *palenque* was built on a side street called *Calle Real*. The whole town was divided into residential lot parcels while lands outside the *pueblo* proper were divided into small farms for rice and sugarcane cultivation. These lands were given to the male children of both Fray Felix and Mónico.

They also took Spanish surnames that began with the letter "C" like Celo, instead of Sinlo, Celosía, Catalán, Celestial, Celeste, Centena, Centina, Casas, Castigador, Católico, Concepción, Cataluña, Castillo, Castronuevo, Chavez, etc. In the end, almost all the Calinognons became *mestizos terciados,* a mixture of the native blood of the Múndo-Calibuganes, on one hand, and the blood of both the Spanish Fray Castroviejo and the Chinese Mónico, on the other.

Now, the question that has to be asked is this: Did the same odd process of racial mixing happen in Bugasong, Antique between the parents of Don Felix Laureano? And if so, was it an isolated case or was it repeated in other places throughout Iloilo, Capiz and Antique?

PART XII

A SECOND CRITICAL LOOK
AT LAPU-LAPU AS HERO

New research suggests that Lapuklapuk was not a virile young man but was in his '70s, debunking the myth that he personally faced Magellan in a hand-to-hand combat during the Battle of Mactán.

1. CURRENT EVENTS AND A SECTARIAN PROVOCATION

The vast majority of Filipinos were euphoric when, in October 2012, Pedro Calungsod was canonized. Before they could fully recover from the joy and pride they felt over the canonization of the second Filipino saint, another piece of good news came when in November of the same year, Antonio Tagle y Gokim, archbishop of Manila, was named a cardinal by Pope Benedict XVI.

San Pedro Calungsod was killed in 1672, along with Spanish Jesuit missionary Padre Diego Luis de San Vitores, while doing missionary work in Guam. Both were hacked to death by a pagan islander.

Since the martyrdom of San Pedro Calungsod was hailed as a national event, it prompted a *Philippine Daily Inquirer* columnist to write: "And I couldn't help thinking then: What if the Vatican canonized Magellan or some zealous Spanish friars who, as we were taught in school, brought the Sword and the Cross in the name of Spain and God and made Christians of almost all of us? What would that make of our Lapu-lapu and his bare-breasted braves who fought and killed some of the invaders? Villains? Would we protest? I, a Christian and Catholic, would."

Now, that is a provocative reaction with regard to Magellan from an obviously misled writer who professes to be a Catholic. In answer to this provocation, we can also ask the following question: And why should Magellan not be canonized a saint when it was he who brought to Cebú the first Catholic Mass, the first Catholic Cross which he planted there, the first image of Mama Mary and the first Santo Niño for the city and the island of Cebú?

It is obvious that the *Inquirer* columnist was only echoing the sectarian demonization of Ferdinand Magellan which is being perpetrated by the neo-colonizers. The demonization of Magellan and the Spaniards, which the columnist uncritically parroted, continues to this day through history textbooks used in both our public and private schools under U.S. neo-colonial policy.

2. WHY IS THERE AN OFFICIAL DEMONIZATION OF FERDINAND MAGELLAN?

WHY IS THERE, INDEED, a sectarian, and now official demonization of Ferdinand Magellan in the teaching of Philippine history? The answer is simple but hard to say because we will have to bring out the matter of American colonization of this country which is a topic that is inconvenient to some present-day Filipinos, especially those who have received training only in English and occupy a lofty perch in the social totem pole. Discussing this subject runs the risk of being labeled as being politically incorrect. But the time has surely come when the truth must be told for the Filipino's own interest as a "free and democratic people."

Ferdinand Magellan has to be demonized up to now because he discovered in 1521 the Philippine archipelago for himself, for the Spanish King and people, for the world and for the Filipinos themselves. And with his discovery, Magellan started and caused the eventual Catholic evangelization of the original inhabitants of these islands—something which traditional anti-Catholics, like the White Anglo Saxon Protestants who invaded our country in 1899, frown upon. Among the neo-colonizers, we still can find the traditional bias against Catholics, a bias

The demonization of Magellan is part of anti-Catholic propaganda

which has not escaped the notice of Mr. William Donohue of the American Catholic League who calls it "the greatest bias in the U.S.A."[1]

To suit their narrative, they have demoted Magellan, a Portuguese, as a "rediscoverer" of the Philippines and have always depicted him as "an invader" which he was not. He was a merchant explorer in search of the fabled Spice Islands who accidentally stumbled upon this archipelago, whose geographic location was then the subject of a dispute between Spain and Portugal. The disagreement stemmed from differing interpretations regarding the demarcation line drawn over the world map by Pope Alexander VI in Rome.

In 1493 Pope Alexander VI issued a papal bull, *Inter caetera*, which divided newly discovered lands between Spain and Portugal, fierce rivals for world supremacy during the Age of Discovery. "It decreed that all lands west and south of a meridian line 100 leagues west of the Azores and Cape Verde islands rightfully belonged to Spain. However, it did not solve the tensions between the two colonizing nations, partly since it failed to specify the lands on the other side of this line as Portuguese possessions. This led to Spain and Portugal clarifying matters in the 1494 Treaty of Tordesillas."[2]

Upon arrival at Cebú, then Sugbu, Magellan claimed it as a zone belonging to the Spanish Crown asking the local *reyezuelo* (kinglet) in the person of Rajah Hamabar (also called Humabon) to accept the Catholic King of Spain as his natural sovereign in exchange for commerce and military protection. A blood compact, as was the custom of the time,

---

[1] Donahue, William, *Catalyst, catholicleague.org*.

[2] "Pope Alexander VI Divides New World Between Spain and Portugal." *litencyc. com*. https://www.litencyc.com/php/stopics.php?rec=true&UID=13912 (accessed November 2, 2018).

LA PRIMERA ESPOSA DE HUMABON SE SINTIÓ ATRAIDA POR LA IMÁGEN DE LA VÍRGEN MARÍA, ERA LA PRIMERA VEZ EN QUE VEÍA Á UN "ANITO" DE SU SEXO. EL PADRE PEDRO VALDERRAMA, ENTENDIENDO SU CURIOSIDAD, SE LO REGALÓ EXPLICÁNDOLA EL ALTO ESTADO SOCIAL DE LA MUJER CRISTIANA GRACIAS AL EJEMPLO QUE DABA LA MADRE DE CRISTO...

Naakit ang pangunahing asawa ni Humabon sa imagen ng Virgen María. Nuon lang siya nakakita ng isang "anitong babae". Ng maintindihan ni Padre Valderrama ang kaniyang pagkamausisa, ipinagkaloob niya agad ang imagen sa Reina.

was celebrated between Magellan and Humabon. But Humabon had internal problems with his own lieutenants over supremacy in the neighboring island of Upon, now Mactán, then divided between his two sub-chiefs, Sula and Pulaco.

Pulaco, for some reason, refused to pay tribute to Humabon, prompting the latter to declare the defiant sub-leader a tax delinquent. Pulaco had previously given his own sister as a concubine for Humabon, but after tiring of her, Humabon demanded that Pulaco must finally settle the payment of the taxes (tribute) due him.[3]

By not paying his taxes, Pulaco was in a state of rebellion against Humabon. To discipline the tribute evader, Humabon had sent Sula to capture Pulaco, but Sula failed. That is why, when Magellan came along as an ally, Humabon got Magellan, on the strength of the blood compact they had, to run after Pulaco in Mactán. Unfortunately, Pulaco's men outnumbered the Spanish contingent and succeeded in killing Magellan "after sand was thrown on his face and 200 men" armed with spears and swords felled him while Pulaco was watching from a distance.

This account comes from Antonio Pigafetta himself, the Italian scholar and navigator who chronicled Magellan's voyage as a member of the expedition. Even Rizal did not deviate from the account of Pigafetta. In his pertinent annotation of Antonio de Morga's *Sucesos de las Islas Filipinas*, he did not question the account but rather took it as the truth from someone (Pigafetta) who was there when it happened. What is even more interesting is an older account in verse of the Magellan-Pulaco encounter because it gives us a sense of how Filipinos, prior to the American invasion in 1899, saw the Magellan-Pulaco encounter in an entirely different light.

---

[3] Molina, Antonio M., *The Philippines Through the Centuries* (Manila: U.S.T. Cooperative, 1960-61), 41-46.

A *chino cristiano* principal of Binondo by the name of Don Carlos Calao wrote in 1614 a poem in Spanish which hews to the written history of the event as told by Pigafetta. But he portrayed

Early Filipinos had a different view of the man known today as Lapu-lapu

Pulaco not as a hero but as an agent of Satan for the death of Magellan:

Que Dios le perdone al salvaje,/al pagano de Mactán/que no entendió la palabra/ de Dios en el Capitán,/Magallanes, a quien muerte/dió por orden de Satán,/el enemigo de Cristo,/el punsuñoso alacrán.

A dos cientos cobardes/Cali Pulaco mandó/que se le tire arena,/en los ojos a traición,/y que con pedradas y palos,/se le cayera el toisón:/¡un hombre contra dos cientos/salvajes sin corazón!

El Capitán Magallanes/los invitó a servir/al verdadero Dios nuestro;/mas, aquel régulo vil /llamado Cali Pulaco/no quiso ver ni sentir /la dádiva de la Fe/y nos lo hizo morir.

Mas, no fue en vano la muerte/del noble conquistador,/el Niño Jesús que se entrona/en Cebú es hoy la flor /que a su martirio perfuma./Nadie recuerda al traidor/que a Magallanes dio muerte,/tal vez, otro vil traidor.[4]

Don Carlos' poetic rendition of the skirmish not only reveals his contempt for Pulaco but also reflects the general sentiment of the early *chinos cristianos* and the early Catholic natives as far as Pulaco was concerned. But the U.S.WASP propaganda machine has created a fictionalized account of that fateful event and succeeded in making us

---

[4] My translation: May God forgive the savage,/the pagan from Opon/who did not understand the word/of God in Captain Magellan, whom death/he gave by order of Satan,/the enemy of Christ,/the poisonous scorpion.

Two hundred cowards, Cali Pulaco commanded/to throw sand with treachery/ upon his eyes /and with stones and sticks/cause his insignia to fall:/one man against two hundred/heartless savages!

Captain Magellan,/had invited them to serve/the true God of ours/but that vile chieftain/called Cali Pulaco/did not want to see nor feel,/the gift of Faith/and he had him put to death.

But the death/of the noble *conquistador* was not in vain,/the Child Jesus that is now enthroned/in Cebú is now the flower/that perfumes his martyrdom./Nobody remembers the betrayer/that gave death to Magellan,/perhaps, but another betrayer.

falsely believe that there was a hand-to-hand combat between the so-called Lapu-lapu and Magellan. Their false narrative is being aided by the compulsory history subjects taught to us in school by an educational system devised to suit the purposes of the neo-colonizers.

3. WHY WAS LAPU-LAPU TURNED INTO A HERO BY THE U.S. WASP INVADERS?

THE DEMONIZATION OF MAGELLAN—and by extension of the Spanish friars and the Spanish administration of these islands—was greatly needed by the 1899 U.S. WASP invaders in order to justify, and if possible to hide, the very bloody war they launched against the First Filipino Republic. During the Filipino-American War, they killed as many as—according to some estimates—a sixth out of the nearly 10 million Filipinos counted by the 1890 census. Not only did they slaughter millions of lives in their scorched-earth policy against Filipino defenders, they also stole the gold and silver reserves of the *República Filipina* worth over a hundred billion U.S. dollars, according to no less than Presidente Don Emilio Aguinaldo in an interview in 1958.[5]

With this hideous atrocity for a historical backdrop, the surviving Filipino people of the 1900s naturally despised the American invaders. To subjugate the recalcitrant Filipinos, the U.S. colonial and military government in the Philippines had to launch a propaganda campaign to change the minds of the Filipinos. They started with the Filipino children whom, in the guise of free public instruction in English, they taught that the U.S. invaders were liberators from "the tyrannical, inhumane and cruel Spanish friars, *encomenderos*, *guardias civiles* and corrupt government officials."

Even as they blackened the Spanish record, the U.S. WASP "liberators" stroked the Filipino ego. To prop up native pride, the colonial American government invented several native heroes. It was the Philippine Commission, which was created by U.S. President William Mckinley in 1900 to help govern the Philippines, that legislated and proclaimed Pulaco,

---

[5] See the full transcript of my Aguinaldo interview on page 195.

whom they called Lapu-lapu, a "national Filipino hero." From then on, the demonization of Magellan and of Spain as "the invaders" of the Philippine Islands went into high gear.

To be sure, it was not the first time that the U.S. government had resorted to this type of propaganda technique of rewriting history to suit its purposes—or would it be the last. According to writer Edwin Burmila, the Americans have done the same thing in burnishing the image of Columbus at the expense of historical facts:[6]

Colonial Americans adopted Columbus as a cultural icon because of the practical need to construct a national historical identity that excluded Britain. Celebrating Columbus, for much of American history, has been an exercise in projecting onto him the virtues we would like to see in ourselves and our country.

Today, in an America learning to accept the Columbus legend as a hagiography, using Columbus as a national metaphor feels dated and naive. Only willful ignorance of the historical record can preserve him today as the enlightened voyager who discovered and brought blessings upon an unknown land.

Between 1916 and 1917 an American committee was formed in Cebú City to draw up a resolution for the erection of a "monument to Lapu-lapu in Mactán." There were

TODOS SOMOS DESCENDIENTES DE ADAN Y EVA Y FUIMOS REDIMIDOS POR JESUCRISTO. Lahat tayo'y magkakapatid sapagkat iisang ama at ina, si Adan at si Eva, ang ating pinan-galifigan. At tayo'y binawi ni Jesús sa Kasalanan...

POR MEDIO DEL INTÉRPRETE, ENRIQUE, TODOS ENTENDIERON Y ADMIRARON EL EVANGELIO DE LA HERMANDAD HUMANA. EL PUEBLO SENCILLO SE EMOCIONÓ A TAL GRADO QUE DEMANDÓ SER BAUTIZADO POR EL SACERDOTE. TODOS RECIBIERON EL BAUTIZO. Sa pamaguitan ng intérpreteng si Enrique, nakaentendi at humañga ang lahat sa katotohanan ng pagkakapatid ng sangkatauhan. Nagpabinyag sila.

[6] Burmila, Edwin. "The Invention of Christopher Columbus, American Hero: How the Founding Fathers Turned Christopher Columbus, a Mediocre Italian Sailor and Mass Murderer, Into a Historical Icon." *thenation.com*. https://www.thenation.com/article/the-invention-of-christopher-columbus-american-hero/ (accessed November 2, 2018).

As executive secretary of the National Language Committee of the Constitutional Convention of the Republic of the Philippines (1971-73), the author (extreme right) attends a public hearing of the committee in Manila. Also in photo are members of the committee (left to right) Delegate José Romualdo (Leyte), Delegate Francisco Albano (Isabela) and Delegate Gerardo M.S. Pepito (Cebú), committee chair.

many prominent Cebuanos who objected to such a monument. Among the oppositors were Bishop Juan Gorordo y Garcés and *el jurisconsulto* Don Mariano Cuenco Abao who resided in Cebú's *parian*. Years later, Rep. Miguel Cuenco y López from Cebú, with whom I had worked for a period of 20 years, directed his staff to read the book that contained that questionable resolution and to familiarize themselves with it.

During discussions on a new Constitution by the Philippine Constitutional Convention (1971-73), the controversial issue came up again. For example, Cebú delegates like Judge Gerardo M.S. Pepito and radio commentator and Cebuano movie producer Natalio Bacalso, Rep. Miguel Cuenco and his brother Jaro Archbishop José Maria Cuenco, D.D. asserted that the name Lapu-lapu given to the "hero" declared by the Americans was not faithful to historical records. The name of the Mactán leader, as provided by Rajah Humabon to Pigafetta, is Cilapuklapuk (Humabon most probably said "Si Lapuklapuk"). "Lapuklapuk" in Cebuano means "dirty mud," which is clearly a depracatory phrase used by an angry Raja Humabon to describe his nemesis.

Over time, Lapuklapuk was Americanized to Lapu-lapu, which unintentionally rechristened the invented hero with the same exact name as a popular fish. How that evolution came to be is a head-scratcher, considering that many writings in Spanish refer to the Mactán sub-chieftain as Cali Pulaco or the *abakadized* Kalipulako.

Up to now there is a street in old Lipa City called Kalipulako, which goes to show that the name Lapu-lapu is dubious at best. But what can we expect? It was given by a careless committee composed of sectarian anti-Catholic colonizers who probably did not even know any Cebuano or Sugbuhanon.

Parts of the Lapu-lapu monument resolution as reproduced in the book *Crónicas Visayas* read:

(1) Que los propósitos que informan a dicho Comité de monumento a Lapu-lapu, son idénticos a los de los habitantes...

(2) Que por deuda de gratitud a la veneranda memoria de aquel que se llamó Lapu-lapu, el que siendo régulo de la isla de Mactán resistió contra los españoles y los frailes (*¿frailes?*) en 1521..., estos Consejos solemnemente ratifican y aprueban lo actuado por Lapu-lapu.

(3) Porque por aquella resistencia, el pueblo filipino disfrutó de su independencia (*selvática*) durante cuarenta y cuatro años, o sea desde la llegada (*y asesinato*) de Magallanes a 1565 de la vuelta de Legazpi.

(4) Que los Consejos, no olvidando a los que cayeron durante la noche y considerando a Lapu-lapu el padre de los que cayeron, es y debe ser indiscutiblemente acreedor al homenaje...[7]

The italicized comments in parentheses were made by columnist Esteban Y. Lanza. The reasons given for the erection of the Lapu-lapu monument in Mactán were refuted not only by Lanza but by lawyer Don Mariano Cuenco Abao as recounted to us by his own son, Rep. Miguel Cuenco, a distinguished historian and writer. Bolstering his recollection was his brother, Jaro Archbishop José Maria Cuenco, who was also a former editor of the Catholic weekly *Véritas*.

---

[7] Esteban Y. Lanza, *Cronicas Visayas*, (Manila: UST Press, 1917), 296.

The rationale listed by the resolution to justify the construction of the Lapu-lapu monument was rebutted point by point by both the ecclesiastical and Catholic lay leaders of Cebú in the following manner:

(1) That the purpose that informs the said Committee for the Monument to Lapu-lapu are the same as that of the people...

YO TE BAUTIZO, CARLOS, EN EL NOMBRE DEL PADRE, DEL HIJO Y DEL ESPÍRITU SANTO... YO TE BAUTIZO, JUANA, EN EL NOMBRE DEL PADRE, DEL HIJO Y DEL ESPÍRITU SANTO...

DESPUÉS DEL BAUTISO DE TODOS LOS SÚBDITOS DE HUMÁBON, EL PADRE PEDRO DE VALDERRAMA DIJO MISA. EL REY CARLOS (HUMABON) SE CASÓ CON LA REINA JUANA, PROMETIÓ ABANDONAR A SUS CONCUBINAS Y AMAR A SÓLO SU MUJER Y REINA. MAGALLANES QUEDÓ MUY CONTENTO. Pagkatapos ng pagpabinyag ng lahat, nagmisa si Padre Valderrama. Nagpakasal ang bagong si Haring Carlos ng Cebú sa kaniyang si Reina Juana. Labis ang pagka-contento ni Magallanes.

Those opposing the resolution denounced this as a "a great lie" (*una gran mentira*). They pointed out that this was not possible since the people of Cebú, being Catholic in general, vehemently disliked Lapuklapuk for killing Magellan who brought them the first Mass, the first Cross and the Santo Niño.

But then, who could stop the American colonial authorities at that time? Together with their local collaborators, they went full steam ahead with their scheme to play fast and loose with historical facts to achieve their propaganda aim and proceeded to erect the Lapu-lapu monument in Punta Engaño, notwithstanding the vast majority of Cebuanos who saw it as an affront to their Roman Catholicism.

(2) That out of a debt of gratitude to the venerated memory of the one called Lapu-lapu, who as chieftain of Mactán resisted against the Spaniards and the Friars in 1521...these Councilmen solemnly ratify and approve the actions of Lapu-lapu...

The opponents of the resolution disputed the claim that Lapuklapuk ever exercised leadership supremacy as he was never a chieftain since the true chieftain of Cebú, including Mactán, was Humabon, and not "Si Lapuklapuk," which is how Rajah Humabon called the individual now being called with the name of a fish.

Lapuklapuk, they added, was in fact a traitor not only to the duly constituted authority of Cebú and Mactán but to all Cebuanos for defying Rajah Humabon. That if ever a monument was to be raised, it should be instead in honor of Rajah Humabon, who drove away from Cebú the remnants of Magellan's ill-fated expedition.[8]

Moreover, it was also pointed out that no Spanish friar ever went to Mactán to fight Lapuklapuk. That the addition of the word "friar" in the resolution simply revealed the anti-Catholic prejudice of those who wanted a monument for Lapuklapuk to confuse, mislead and divide the Cebuano people in order to peel them away from the Catholic religion of their ancestors.

> (3) Because owing to that resistance, the Filipino people enjoyed their independence during forty four years, or since the arrival of Magellan [until] 1565 when Legazpi returned....

This reason was completely false, according to the opponents of the resolution. Quite simply, between the arrival of Magellan in 1521 and that of Legazpi in 1565, there was no such thing as "an independent Philippines" since the concept of the country now known as *Filipinas* started only with the founding of both the Filipino State and Manila as its capital city by Legazpi on June 24, 1571. That if any independence was lost by all Filipinos, this was a result of the American invasion of these islands at the end of the 19th century and the plunder and destruction

Cebuanos objected to the construction of the Lapu-lapu monument in Mactán

---

[8] After the death of Magellan, the remaining crew voted for a joint leadership of Duarte Barbosa and João Serrão to lead them, but the two newly elected commanders were killed by Humabon during a feast within days after the death of Magellan. The Spaniards barely escaped with the skin of their teeth, fleeing aboard the ships *Concepción, Trinidad* and *Victoria*, under Juan Carvalho. At sea, the crew grew disillusioned with Carvalho and he was replaced by Elcano who steered the crew back to Spain after much hardship. On September 6, 1522, they arrived in Spain with Elcano aboard the command ship *Victoria* with the others sailing aboard *Trinidad*—after ditching *Concepción*. For becoming the first circumnavigator of the globe, Elcano was presented by Charles I with a coat of arms and a globe inscribed with the Latin words *Primus circumdedisti me* ("You Went Around Me First").

of the 1898 *República de Filipinas* under Presidente Emilio Aguinaldo by the same invaders.

(4) That the Councils, not forgetting those who fell during the night and considering Lapu-lapu the father of those who fell [he] is and must be unquestionably worthy of the homage...[9]

The same Cebuano intellectuals, historians and writers labeled this appeal to emotion as manipulative and asserted that it was included in the resolution to distract Filipinos from the unconscionable deaths and destruction caused by the U.S. invading forces after they took over the country from Spain. They reminded Filipinos of the countless men, women and children killed by U.S. military forces under Gen. Elwell Stephen Otis and Gen. Arthur MacArthur for defending the independence and sovereignty of their *República de Filipinas* born in 1896 and declared independent in 1898. They added that the *República de Filipinas* was the culmination of the struggle and the work of Rizal but it was destroyed by the American invasion of 1899. They insisted that in view of the then existing political reality which placed Filipinos under American rule, their children should be given a better role model to follow than a tax-evader like Lapuklapuk.

> **Cebuanos asked the Americans for a better role model than a 'tax evader'**

But as we said, nobody could stop the colonizers from claiming that they invaded and stayed in the Philippines for the reasons spelled out by the sectarian and MacKinleyan agenda to "christianize, civilize and uplift" an already Christian Catholic Filipino people. Couching their imperialistic intent in these otherwise noble terms was meant to hide the atrocities, both actual and economic, that came with their unwanted presence, not to mention the need to gratify their vanity.

Present-day Filipinos, the Catholic Cebuanos in particular, have no alternative but to tolerate the idea of an American imposed so-called hero like Lapu-lapu with a monument in Mactán and even in

---

[9] Lanza, "Ysla de Panay," *Crónicas Visayas,* 296.

Manila. But once the truth is known by the thinking new generations of Filipinos, those monuments to Lapu-lapu will become meaningless, as they are indeed meaningless to a vast majority of present-day Filipinos.

Recent information about Mactán's "Si Lapuklapuk" emerging from a research in Portugal suggests that this Mactán sub-chieftain was already over 70 years old when Magellan landed in Mactán.

While Magellan was in his '30s or '40s, historical revisionists on this particular chapter in our country's history still insist on lying by depicting a virile Lapu-lapu having a hand-to-hand combat with an armored Magellan.

We are by no means a lone voice in the wilderness calling for a stop to this egregious and unconscionable historical revisionism. For, to paraphrase the great New York Sen. Daniel Patrick Moynihan, *these revisionists are entitled to their opinion but they are not entitled to their own facts*. Reproduced below are relevant excerpts from

'People are entitled to their own opinion but not to their own facts.'

a newspaper article[10] citing the opinion of a Filipino scholar who is a member of a research group involved in the preparation for the fifth centenary of Magellan's voyage to the Philippines:

New research suggests Lapu-lapu versus Magellan combat is a myth

A prominent Bicolano historian and author suggests taking a second look at the heroism of Lapu-Lapu.

Dr. Danilo Madrid Gerona, a member of Sevilla 2019-2022 that is leading and coordinating the global celebration of the 500th anniversary of Ferdinand Magellan's circumnavigation of the world, said declaring Lapu-lapu a national hero would be premature.

Gerona, who specializes in pre – and Spanish colonial period accounts, is the only non-Spanish member of the multi-sectoral committee based in Seville, Spain.

The committee published the book *Ferdinand Magellan, The Armada de Maluco and the European Discovery of the Philippines,* using sources from archives in Seville.

Some history books describe Lapu-Lapu as the first native Filipino who fought Spanish colonizers, but Gerona contended that Lapu-Lapu's heroism was based on the wrong belief that he killed Magellan, a Portuguese explorer who sailed under the Spanish flag.

'Fakelore'
He said there was a dearth of information on Lapu-lapu's actual participation in the Battle of Mactán in 1521. 'The story of Lapu-Lapu, depicted with bulging biceps rushing toward Magellan to kill him with a swift stroke of his weapon, is a folklore or 'fakelore' that had been repeated for five centuries,' he said.

Gerona said it was not even Lapu-lapu who killed Magellan. It could be any one of about 1,500 warriors the chieftain sent to fight the foreign troops in the Battle of Mactán.

---

[10] Escandor, Juan Jr. "Lapu-lapu As National Hero? Not So Fast." *inquirer.net.* https://newsinfo.inquirer.net/790091/lapu-lapu-as-national-hero-not-so-fast (accessed November 3, 2018).

The historian pieced together the story of the battle from different sources in the original Spanish and Portuguese manuscripts and the accounts of Portuguese chronicler Gaspar Correa, who came to the Philippines with another Spanish expedition four years after Magellan died.

He found Lapu-lapu mentioned in the chronicles of Antonio Pigafetta, a Venetian who was not even the official chronicler of Magellan's voyage. Gerona said primary accounts that Correa obtained showed the battle was not a 'one-shot' deal but a complicated story.

Testimonies

Testimonies of 18 of 27 members of the Spanish forces who survived the battle described Lapu-lapu as *viejo*, the Spanish description of people 60 years or older. As an old person, Lapu-lapu would even be exempted from work and taxes imposed by Spain in its colonies, Gerona said.

'It is impossible that Lapu-lapu led the Battle of Mactán because, based on the description of the survivors, the chieftain was very old, about 70 years old [at the time],' he said.

Accounts also showed that Lapu-lapu recognized the authority of the Spanish Crown through Magellan and even agreed to pay tribute to the colonizers.

A portrait of Ferdinand Magellan

But the relationship soured after Magellan demanded that Lapu-lapu recognize his anointed supreme chieftain, Rajah Humabon, by kissing the latter's hand, a European way of recognizing authority, Gerona said. When Lapu-lapu refused, Magellan's troops attacked the chieftain's village twice, burning the houses. The colonizers launched a full battle to subdue Lapu-lapu and his allies.

Miscalculated

Gerona said Magellan miscalculated the capacity of the native warriors, who only had crude weapons. The Portuguese declined Humabon's offer to send hundreds of native warriors to reinforce the Spanish forces, who had better weapons and wore body armors.

The Battle of Mactán is recreated in this diorama at the Ayala Museum.

Fifty-seven members of the Spanish forces left their bigger ship on a small boat to launch the assault on Mactán. The Spaniards fought the more than 1,000 warriors Lapu-lapu sent to fight the foreigners.

Gerona said Magellan was first immobilized by a poisoned arrow that hit his leg. The leader of the Spanish expedition was then killed with a bamboo lance to the chest.

Gerona said 18 members of the Spanish forces were able to return to Spain. Nine survivors were given refuge by Humabon.

With Magellan dead, Lapu-lapu, the battle's victor, demanded that Humabon kill the survivors. Humabon refused and sold the survivors as slaves to Chinese merchants.

Gerona said that when Magellan arrived in the Philippines, Cebu was already a thriving port with vibrant communities headed by several chieftains and was actively involved in commerce.

Lapu-lapu was the supreme chief among four chieftains ruling Mactán at the time. From accounts by chroniclers, Lapu-lapu was involved in piracy. He would lure trading ships to his territory and demand tributes.

Gerona also discovered that Lapu-lapu was actually the brother of Humabon's principal wife but, for some reason, the two chieftains' relations were not cordial. They fought Spanish colonizers, but Gerona contended that Lapu-Lapu's

A replica of *Victoria*, the first ship to sail around the world, is shown at a port in Nagoya, Japan. It was one of five ships commanded by Portuguese navigator Ferdinand Magellan in an expedition bankrolled by the Spanish Crown, which led to the discovery of the Philippines by Europeans in 1521. After the death of Magellan in Mactán, his men fled Cebú and, under the command of Juan Sebastián Elcano, returned to Spain in 1522 to complete the first circumnavigation of the world.

heroism was based on the wrong belief that he killed Magellan, a Portuguese explorer who sailed under the Spanish flag.

An elephant in the room in this whole controversy is the only eyewitness account to this event by the Italian chronicler Pigafetta. His account of the skirmish in Mactán is crystal clear: no face-to-face combat ever occurred between Magellan and "Si Lapuklapuk."

The non-existent face-to-face combat between "Si Lapuklapuk" and Magellan is a perfect example of how history is blatantly falsified to satisfy a sectarian prejudice against Catholicism and the Spanish missionaries in this country.

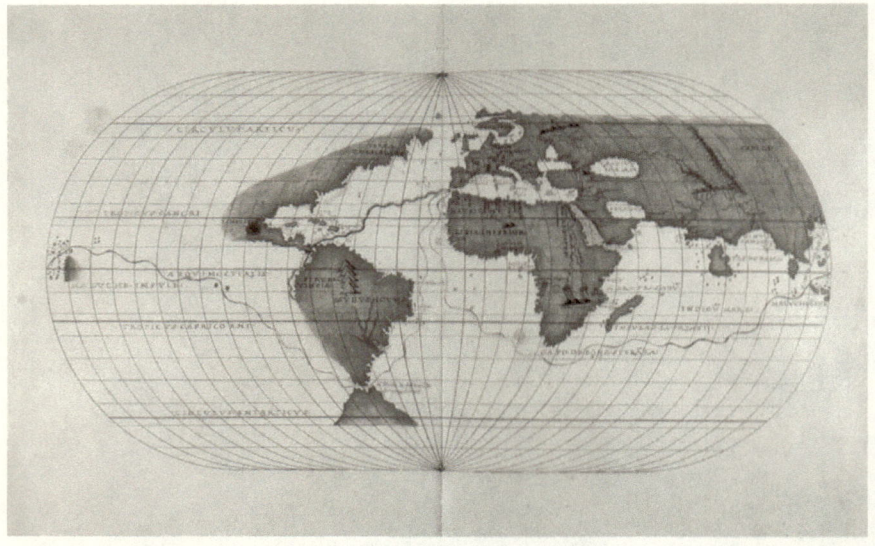

A map showing the route followed by Magellan from Spain to the Philippines and the one Elcano took to return to Spain, becoming the first circumnavigator of the world.

PART XIII

A BRIEF ANALYTICAL
HISTORY OF MINDANAO

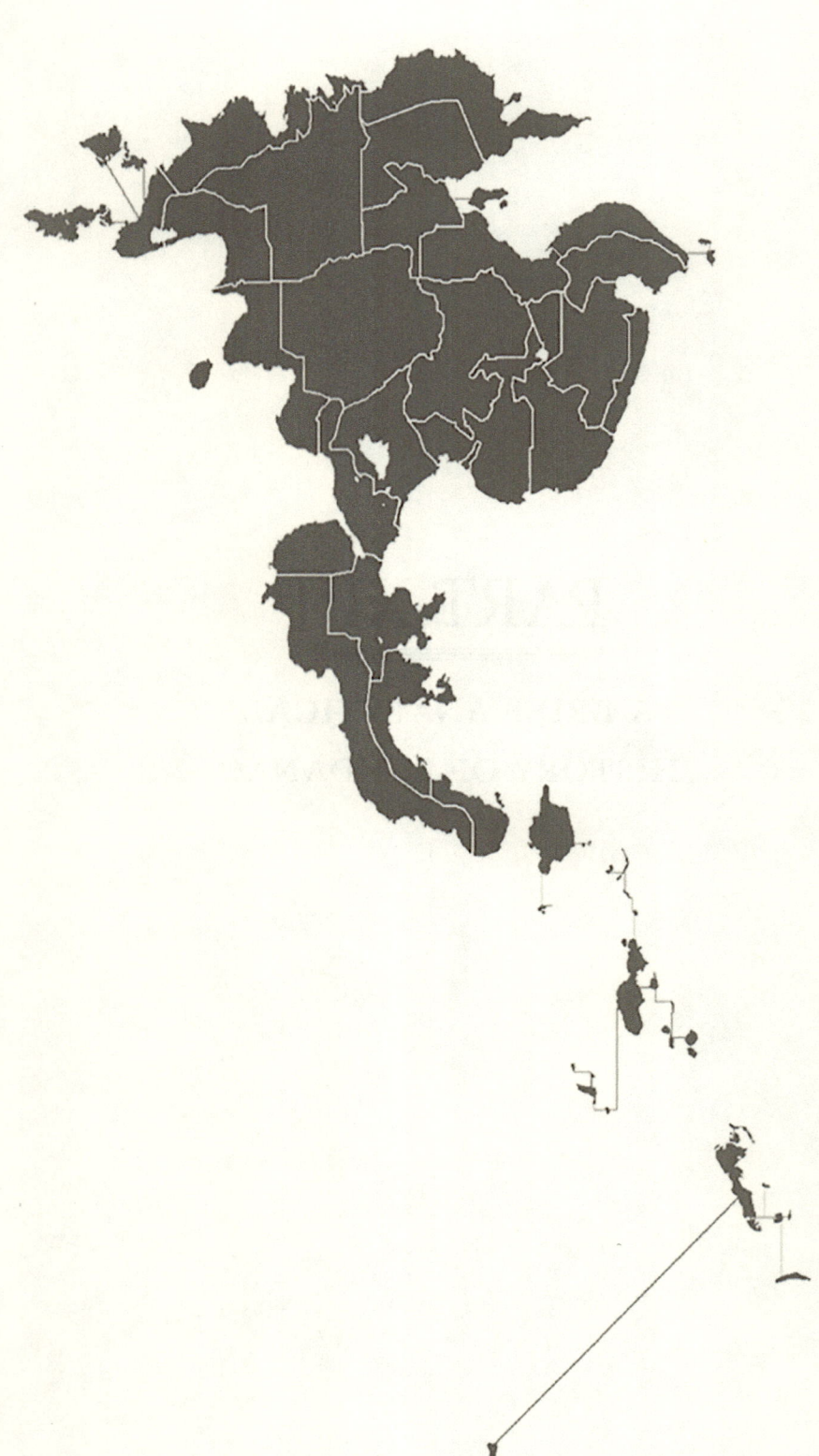

The troubled Philippine south has been wracked by violence for most of its modern history.

1. THE ORIGINAL MINDANAOANS, THE *LUMADS*

T he island of Mindanao and the Sulú archipelago, like the islands of Luzon and the Visayas, were originally populated by small ethnic states, in the form of tribes, collectively called *lumads*, the Cebuano word for aboriginals or indigenous people.

The equivalent of *lumad* in Tagalog is *katutubô*. In Spanish, the terms *lumad* and *katutubô* are equivalent to the word *indio*, which was synonymous to indigenous, *indigena* or *indigene* during Spanish times.

It was the Spanish missionaries who first drew an accurate map of Mindanao and Sulú where they listed the names of the different *lumad* groups (see table below) in the southern Philippines.

THE DIFFERENT GROUPS THAT COMPRISE THE *LUMAD* POPULATION	
1. AGUSANON	14. TAGABILI
2. MAMANUAS OF AGUSAN	15. TIRURAY
3. CARAGA	16. MAGUINDANAO
4. MANOBOS	17. THE TIBOLIS
5. MANDAYAS	18. MARANAO
6. THE DIBABAWON	19. SUBANON
7. ATAS OR ATI	20. YAKAN OF BASILAN
8. BUKIDNON	21. BURANON
9. TIGWASALOG	22. TAUSOG OF JOLO
10. BAGOBOS OF DAVAO	23. SAMAL
11. TAGAKAOLOS	24. ILANON
12. YULAMAN	25. BADJAU OF TAWI-TAWI
13. BILAAN	

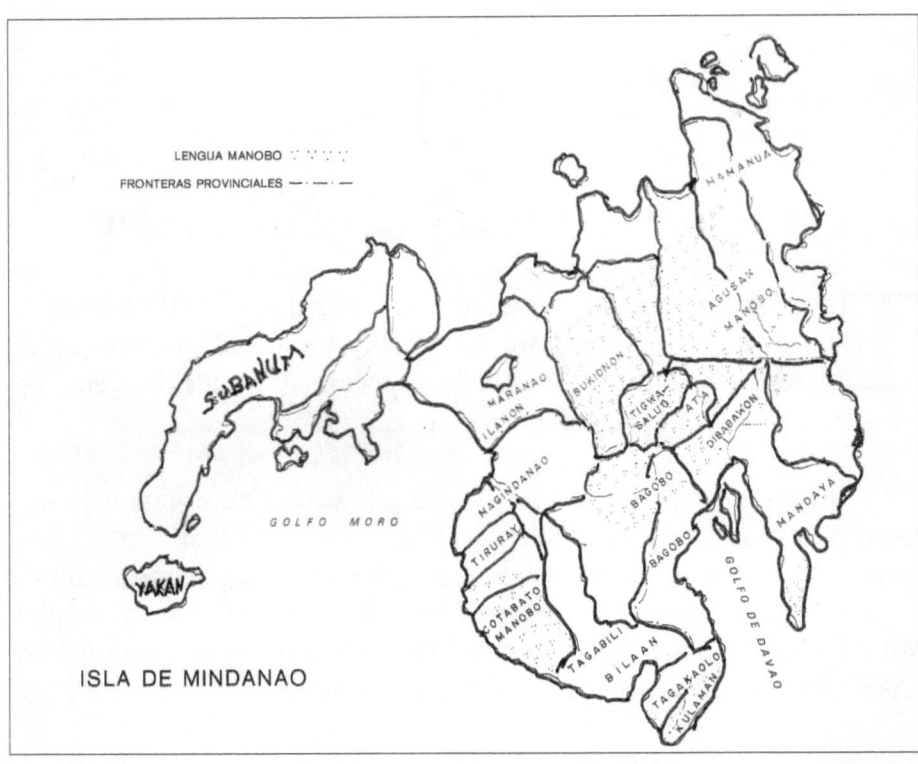

A representation of an old Spanish map created by Spanish friars during the Spanish colonial period shows the respective ancestral and territorial domains of the different *lumad* groups on the island of Mindanao and the Sulú archipelago.

2. THE MUSLIMS

THE MUSLIMS ARE NOT NATIVES OF MINDANAO. They came in the 14th century with their warrior-priests, or *punditas*, as slave traders with the aim of conquering by force of arms the Mindanao *lumads* whom they usually turned into slaves for themselves and the slave markets of Southeast Asia and Oceania. These warrior-priests combined their religious calling with piracy, violently raiding the *lumad* villages for food, women and slaves.

The Moros came to Mindanao only in the 14th-century as slave traders

According to Vicente Ilustre (1869-1928) from Taal, Batangas, who was appointed in 1905 as a member of the

Philippine Commission[1] to represent Mindanao, "the trade of the Moros did not involve money, but slaves used as currency which is reprehensible…" Don Vicente added that "they had the Balañgigui islands serving as their slave bank where they kept imprisoned all those Catholic Christian individuals they kidnapped, during their violent attacks and raids upon the Visayas and Luzon aside from the coastal and hinterland raids upon the *lumad* villages in Mindanao."[2]

The Vicente Ilustre *Notas* on the Moros of Mindanao candidly describes their often violent incursions into non-Muslim areas, especially their behavior toward women whom they abducted and forced into marriage:

The Moros' brutal treatment of areas they pillaged did not endear them to others

> By usually forced intermarriages of their so-called warrior-priests with *lumad* princesses, or 'principalia' women, the invading Muslim *punditas* were able to build modest mosques of bamboo and *kugon* leaves like in the case of the first Muslim mosque of Joló.

Of course, many present-day Filipinos perfectly know that it is the Arab petro dollars of later centuries that helped build the bigger mosques of modern times that we can see in some places of Mindanao and Sulú.

According to Don Vicente, the royal intermarriages did produce local palaces for the ruling Moro *maharlicás* whose followers were the slaves they owned. Like our animist ancestors in other areas of the country, the Moro rulers had two classes of slaves, namely the warrior slaves or *alipin saguiguilid* and the household slaves or *aliping pamamahay*. Eventually, these slave-owning ruling families and their followers evolved into tribal communities or clans that lived together like bees in a beehive.

---

[1] The Philippine Commission was created in 1900 by U.S. President William McKinley to help govern the Philippines. Invoking his executive authority, he vested the body with legislative and executive powers. Two years later, his action was codified by the U.S. Congress with the passage of the Philippine Organic Act. The law paved the way for the establishment of the Philippine bicameral legislature in 1907, with the commission serving as the upper house and an elected Philippine assembly representing the lower house.

[2] *Notas de Don Vicente Ilustre sobre Mindanao y los Moros*, compiled by Francisco Zaragoza y Carrillo (Manila:1950).

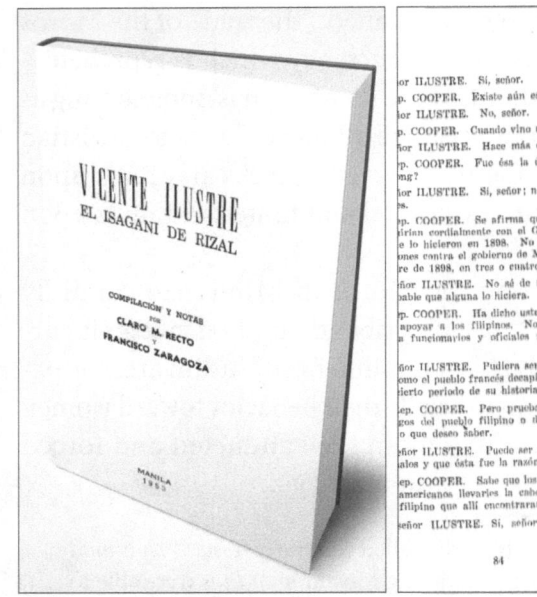

Don Vicente Ilustre, el Isagani de Rizal is a book authored by Claro M. Recto and Francisco Zaragoza.

Differences with other clans or tribes would often degenerate into bloody feuds and vendettas called *rido*. Some of these tribes kept a record of their genealogy and family histories in what is known as *társilas*. It was important to record family histories to keep track of the innumerable children of their patriarchs and the scions of these powerful men who would have as many as up to four wives.

The extent of the Moros' terroristic activities, according to Don Vicente's notes, was not confined to the *lumads* alone but also to other groups:

> To maintain themselves within their clannish or tribal system would often translate into a huge economic burden or problem usually passed on to the caste of slaves and would lead to the 'royal leaders or Sultans' to indulge in piracy and plunder of the non-Muslim neighboring communities, such as the animistic *lumads* and, or, the Christian Hispanized Visayans and the Hispanized and Christianized *lumads* of Luzon who were already productive farmers and industrialists that produced rice, corn, sugar, tobacco and abaca products and had an ongoing international galleon trade captained by the Spaniards and their *chino cristiano criollo* partners. So lucrative was the galleon trade that even the famous British pirates would park their pirate ships in the San Bernardino

sea lane with the objective of capturing one of these gold- and silver-loaded galleons returning from Acapúlco, Mexico.

It is a fact the Moros, unlike the Tagalogs, Bicolanos, Pampangos, Ilocanos and Visayans, do not have land titles, birth certificates, marriage contracts, business license, professional residence certificates or *cédula*, legal contracts, tax receipts, death certificates and countless other documents or reliable records in their own culture. This is one main reason they appear backward if not inferior, in the legal sense, to the general culture of Filipinos reared under the almost four hundred years of Spanish administration, education, influence and guidance. This circumstantial defect in their culture and society alienates them from daily business with Filipinos in general and the government administration in particular.

Most of the Moros are poor because they refuse to go into agriculture and the building of local industries. They fully depend on their *sacopes*, or slaves, for their daily food. Even their fishing and very scant farming is mostly left in the hands of their slaves because they are said to be of a more parasitic social class of people. They are feudal. That is why trade to them is violent piracy. They wait for the period of rice harvest among the Christian Visayans, Bicolanos, Tagalogs and even Ilocanos, and go out in droves to the sea with their swift and big *vintas* to confiscate the Christian rice and corn harvest of the said Visayans and Bicolanos.

And they are difficult to negotiate with because they are treacherous. The American military here say that there is no such thing as a good Moro. The only good Moro is a dead Moro. And this is confirmed by all the look-out towers built by the old Spanish administration by the sea along with almost all Catholic church bell towers near every seashore to warn the town's people of the arrival of the Moro pirate raiders who come for their rice and corn harvest, their jewelry, their young men and women for slavery and prostitution.

3. SPAIN CONQUERED MINDANAO AND MADE IT
AN INTEGRAL PART OF THE PHILIPPINES

DON VICENTE ILUSTRE CREDITED THE SPANIARDS for building fortifications in Mindanao that safeguarded peaceful communities there. Their long experience in dealing with Muslims in Africa and the Mediterranean helped them manage the constant Moro threat they faced.

Spain, having been a country with a long experience with the African and Mediterranean Muslims, did two important things for us Filipinos in order to safeguard and keep Mindanao for the future of our nation. Spain first established the city of Zamboanga with its Fort Pilar and surrounded the entire island of Mindanao with Christian Visayan *municipios* culminated by the founding of the present city of Davao spearheaded by *conquistador* Juan de Oyanguren. As Spain founded these Visayan Mindanao cities and municipalities, the importation of well-armed *barcos de vapor* (steamships) followed. And this modern acquisition greatly reduced if not totally defeated the pestilent and damaging Moro sea piracy that came in the form of violent and bloody raids upon the Christian Filipino settlements who had to defend themselves under the military command of their regular parish priest who would fight and even die for them.

It was both Teodoro Agoncillo and Cesar Adib Majul of the University of the Philippines Department of History who reportedly told a Muslim student activist that "Spain never conquered Mindanao." That U.P. student leader is the now aging Nur Misuari, chairman of the Moro National Liberation Front (MNLF) that fought a decades-long bloody rebellion against the government that claimed the lives of as many as 120,000 people.[3] He and the other Moro students of this American founded and controlled "state university" apparently believed this canard and decided to wage war against the government for the alleged historical injustice their people had suffered.

> *That Mindanao was never conquered is a debatable assertion by some historians*

The same half truth that Spain had never conquered Mindanao was reportedly repeated by MILF negotiator Mohagher Iqbal when he was exposed by the Manila media as a holder of a Malaysian passport because he would not say that he is a Filipino citizen unless the Bangsamoro bill was enacted into law.

He even taunted our legislature and the press that he would only reveal who and what he was if the said Bangsamoro bill was approved without any further delay by Congress.

Filipinos who know their history and who can read José Rizal's poetry, which is written in Spanish, will know that Mindanao and Sulú,

[3] "Philippines-Mindanao (1971–First Combat Deaths)." Project Ploughshares Web Site. January 17, 2018. http://ploughshares.ca/pl_armedconflict/philippines-mindanao-1971-first-combat-deaths/ (accessed November 2, 2018).

were conquered by Spain because they are integral parts of the Filipino State. Rizal celebrated the triumph of Spain in Mindanao when he sang to the Urbiztondo expedition against one Datu Mahumat of Joló. The conquest of Mindanao by Spain is attested to by Cebuano Visayan as the *lingua franca* of Mindanao and the reduction of Moro influence only to Sulú and the Lanao and Maguindanao areas since almost all the Mindanao cities and municipalities are predominantly Christian Catholic, therefore Hispanized Filipino communities.

Don Vicente Ilustre: His candid notes about the fanatical Moros and their terroristic activities resonate to this day.

4. MINDANAO UNDER THE AMERICANS

DON VICENTE ILUSTRE'S KNOWLEDGE of Mindanao history and the Moros cannot be disputed. Being a friend and contemporary of Rizal in Madrid, Spain, he was well respected among Filipino revolutionaries, even becoming the head of the Hong Kong revolutionary junta that edited a newspaper demanding immediate Philippine independence from the United States. It was also he who faced the anti-independence American military and neo-colonial politicians who ruled these islands. He came home in 1905 to Taal, Batangas, to campaign for freedom and to marry his long-time *novia*, Doña Rita Villavicencio

Vicente Ilustre was a contemporary of Rizal in Madrid and commanded people's respect

y Marella, daughter of the "Juana de Arco de Taal," Doña Gliceria Marella de Villavicencio. [4]

In 1907 Don Vicente faced an American commission that pompously proposed that America would grant Philippine independence but without Mindanao, "populated as it is by barbaric and wild Moros that needed to be civilized through proper education."[5]
This image of the Moros of that era was prevalent even among the Christian population of the Visayas. The American troops preferred the .45 caliber pistol as a close range weapon of the U.S. Cavalry to

U.S. soldiers pose for the camera with the casualties at the scene of the Bud Dajo massacre from which, out of an estimated 1,000 Moro men, women and children, only six survived.

defend themselves against the fanatical and ignorant Moro *juramentados* who would run amok over any trivial issue like not getting the favors they demanded.

---

[4] Claro M. Recto and Francisco Zaragoza, *Vicente Ilustre, el Isagani de Rizal* (Manila: General Printing Press, 1953).
[5] Ilustre, *Notas*, 84-85. The remarks were made by U.S. Rep. Henry Allen Cooper as recorded in the minutes of a session of the Philippine Commission. What provoked Cooper's remarks was an exchange between him and Ilustre who reported about the decapitation of Filipino functionaries sent to Mindanao. As chairman of the U.S. House Committee on Insular Affairs, Cooper pushed for the passage of a law calling for a popularly elected Filipino assembly to exercise power with the Philippine Commission.

The Americans, indeed, wanted to retain their control over Mindanao "to change the Moros or liquidate them completely as they well deserve." With this mindset, the Americans created the "Moro province" or "Moroland" and appointed Don Vicente Ilustre to deal with the Moro problem. In the meantime, Governor-General Francis Burton Harrison, who also spoke Spanish, came to know Don Vicente personally and greatly admired this highly educated and learned Batangueño lawyer for his personal capacities as a great leader.

There were also Moro leaders who, like Harrison, could speak Spanish very well. Among them was one Datu Piang, and he and the other Moro leaders used the language as a bridge to discuss local problems with Don Vicente. Don Vicente, a handsome Tagalog with a well-built and athletic physique of Malay stock, did impress many Moros with his appearance and ways. He told them that he was of their race and that they had to work

Don Francisco Zaragoza y Carillo, a great Filipino poet in Spanish.

together to negotiate triumphantly with the Americans to gain independence. He also urged them to continue upholding the Filipino State that they obtained from Spain, which most of them did recognize in the past. For, if they stayed under the control of Americans, a people of a different race, Don Vicente argued, the Muslim future could not be guaranteed, given the unforgiving approach of the then new colonial rulers toward the Moros.

As a member of the Philippine Commission, Don Vicente worked for and succeeded in giving the Moros the right to vote and to hold government administrative and elective posts since the early American administration. Datu Piang and his Muslim group, after many hesitations, agreed in the end with Don Vicente and made the Americans understand that Philippine independence without Mindanao is unacceptable. But during that turbulent era, as it is today, the Moros were divided among themselves. Their recalcitrance served to reinforce American iron resolve to wage a brutal "pacification" campaign in Mindanao, which included the massacres of countless civilians and combatants, the most searing and infamous of which was the Bud Dajo massacre in Joló in March 1906.

The deep wounds inflicted by the Bud Dajo massacre were reopened when in late 2016 then U.S. President Barack Obama, who was doing his valedictory trip to Asia as he was about to leave the White House, criticized President Rodrigo Duterte y Roa for the latter's war on drugs. An infuriated President Duterte reportedly called out the alleged hypocrisy of the U.S. leader by presenting him gruesome photos of the Bud Dajo massacre in front of other world leaders attending a closed-door regional summit in Laos.

5. THE BANGSAMORO FABRICATION

WHILE IT IS TRUE THAT THE MOROS HAD their own different and separate history, it nevertheless ran parallel to the history of the Luzon and the Visayan *lumads* or *katutubôs* under Spain. But as Don Vicente Ilustre pointed out in his *Notas*, as carefully compiled by Don Francisco Zaragoza y Carillo,[6] the Moros were never able to form a cohesive and orderly Muslim state as those *katutubôs* in other areas of the Philippines, notably in Luzon and the Visayas:

> [They] were never able to form a Muslim state of their own, by themselves, in the same way that the Luzon *lumads*, or *katutubôs*, meaning the Tagalogs, Kapampañgan. Bicolanos and Ilocanos, constituded, under Spanish guidance, the *Estado Filipino* with Manila as its capital and administration center. It is true that the Moros were already occupying parts of Mindanao at the expense of the persecuted non-Muslim *lumads*, but no Moro state was ever organized there and no significant Muslim or Moro capital city was either erected anywhere in Mindanao or Sulú outside of mere village-like

Progress in Mindanao has been hampered by fanatical Moros since Spanish times

---

[6] A native of Quiapo, Manila, Don Francisco Zaragoza y Carillo was a member of the *Academia Filipina de la Lengua Española* who devoted himself to erudition as a writer, poet and scholar. He annotated a collection of at least 37 rare books, magazines and documents on Philippines history.

Sultan Haji Hassanal Bolkiah Mosque in Cotabato City, named after the Sultan of Brunei who funded its construction.

sitios headed by some sultan or datu.

The pre-Hispanic Chinese Orang Dampuans were able to organize a trade center somewhere in northern Zamboanga which could have evolved into a big town or city, but it was the Muslims who, again, raided and plundered this trade center and massacred most of the peaceful Chinese traders. Even Joló owed to the Chinese traders what could pass for its first seaport for trading junks. But when the Spanish *conquistadores* started the international galleon trade in Manila, all the rich Chinese traders left the Moros of Joló to their own devices, and the Moro *sitio* quickly reverted to the state of impoverishment and decay it had wallowed in prior to the presence of the Chinese traders there. These Chinese traders left Joló and settled as *chinos cristianos criollos* in Binondo and San Nicolás, or what became the Spanish-sponsored *Parian de Manila*.

We may add that Marawi City, touted as "a Muslim city of Mindanao," is of recent foundation, courtesy of the present Republic of the Philippines. It used to be known as Dansalan, the name given to it by the Spaniards led by *conquistador* Francisco Atienza who founded the town in 1639.

It was only in 1956 when Dansalan was rechristened to Marawi by an act of Congress. Even under the American-organized "Moro province," it retained its Spanish name. But the modern Marawi was destroyed, thanks but no thanks to the evil Mautes whose banditry was bankrolled by drug lords and their own drug dealing activities. Sadly, not a few of its Moro residents themselves greatly facilitated, one way or the other, the infiltration of their city by the ISIS-inspired Maute group which caused its destruction. The irony is that Marawi is now being rebuilt by mostly Christian Catholic Filipino taxpayers whose system of government and way of life the Mautes and their followers had tried to supplant in their short reign of mayhem and destruction during the Marawi siege.

Misuari's corrupt record as elected official does not inspire faith in Moro self-rule

It was in the 1960s when Mindanao and Sulú began having separatist rebel movements against what they labeled as "imperial Manila." Many of these rebels are former U.P. students where they were taught to loathe this country's history, with Spain as the principal villain. Among the many lies they were told was that Mindanao was never conquered by Spain. They conveniently ignore the overwhelming evidence to the contrary as seen in the rise of municipalities and cities, with Spanish derived and influenced names and toponomy; the heavy presence of Christian Catholic Filipino natives that comprise 80 percent of the present total Mindanao population; and the use of a *lingua franca* which is not a Moro vernacular language but a Hispanized Visayan tongue, among other things. The Moro population remains a minority group mainly spread over the Sulú archipelago and the distant Lanao del Sur and Maguindanao areas, making up only 20

MNLF Chairman Nur Misuari

percent of the entire Mindanao population.

A typical example of an economically successful Moro rebel is Nur Misuari, a former student and even a former

Malaysia stands accused of financing Muslim rebel groups as part of destab plot

faculty member of U.P., who is the founder of the MNLF from where the more murderous Moro Islamic Liberation Front (MILF) broke away to intimidate an already weakened Filipino State with the threatening demand that they be granted a "Bangsamoro" sub-state or autonomy. Congress acquiesced to their demand with the passage of the Bangsamoro Organic Law. The law, which is still to be implemented, runs counter to many fundamental provisions of the present Constitution of the Philippines.

The name "Bangsamoro" is haphazardly coined from the Tagalog word for nation (*bansa*) and the Spanish word for Muslim (*moro*). The invading Muslims of Mindanao never had a national identity of their own like the Hispanized Filipinos clearly have. Given their acceptance and adoption of this Spanish word to define themselves as a distinct nation from the real Filipinos exposes them outright as fakes. There is, in fact, no "Bangsamoro people" but a band of Malaysian-sponsored invading terrorist Muslims trying to pull a fast one, which is another act of piracy against a weak and corrupted Filipino State that forgot its own history because of a subtle language change, on one hand, and a foreign dictated state policy and a grossly indebted economy, on the other hand. (The allegation that Malaysia is financing some of the Muslim rebel groups is plausible since it has a simmering land dispute with the Philippines over our historic claim to Sabah on the strength of the undisputed fact that the land is owned by the Sultanate of Sulú.)

To begin with, it is the pure and original *lumads* who are entitled to an ancestral domain and not the Muslims "funded and trained" by Malaysia. The MILF, in reality, does not have its own native constituency since the "Bangsamoro" they pretend to represent is inexistent in fact. This is the main reason they cannot really have any plebiscite as required by the unconstitutional Bangsamoro Organic Law. It is a fact that not all *lumads* are Muslims.

6. A MALAYSIAN-SPONSORED MUSLIM TERRORIST COLONIZATION OF FILIPINO MINDANAO *LUMADS*?

IF THE HISTORY OF THE MINDANAO *lumads'* long suffering in the hands of the invading and terroristic Muslims who come from Borneo and other islands and *sitios* that are now part of Malaysia and Indonesia remains unknown to most of our Manila policymakers, we have Hispanophobia to blame, according to the late Sen. Claro M. Recto.

He stated that "our Hispanophobic break with our Spanish past and our American legacy of ignorance about that same past along with its language, its record and its culture" has led us to this sorry state of being oblivious to our own history. But a recently opened Cotabato City museum called Museyo Kutawato has inadvertently explained that dichotomy by telling the story of two Maguindanao *lumad* brothers upon being confronted by the foreign Muslim invaders. These brothers, Tabunaway and Mamalu, were both leaders of their own *lumad* community. Upon being visited by the invading foreign *punditas* or the Arab-Malay warrior-priests, Tabunaway converted to Islam, but Mamalu decided to reject it, holding fast to the beliefs of their elders. As a consequence, the brothers parted ways, divided by their religious beliefs. Tabunaway and his followers stayed in the lowlands and Mamalu and his followers went to live in the mountains.

IT IS NOT THE SPANISH WHO ATTACKED THE MOROS. IT WAS THE MOROS WHO ATTACKED FOR SLAVES AND BOOTY THE SPANISH-DOMINATED VISAYAS AND LUZON. THE MOROS LIE WHEN THEY SAY THAT THEY "RESISTED" SPANISH COLONIALISM.

TO ISOLATE THE MOROS, THE SPANIARDS SURROUNDED MINDANAO WITH CHRISTIAN FILIPINO TOWNS AND CITIES LIKE ZAMBOANGA, OROQUIETA AND DAVAO.

This of course is plain revisionist oral history because in Don Vicente Ilustre's *Notas*, he observed that conversion to Islam in Mindanao was coercive, forcing people to join the faith under pain of death. People who refused to convert were beheaded when captured. And the *lumads* who resisted the proselytizers had to muster all their strength in an armed struggle to repel the invaders.

Our English-trained policymakers do not seem to care to defend the right of choice and freedom of our non-Muslim Mindanao *lumads* from the ongoing Malaysian-sponsored Muslim aggressors. By lumping the *lumads* together with the Muslim rebel separatists under the Bangsamoro Organic Law, the politicians responsible for this law are leading the non-Muslim *lumads* into a systematic kind of genocide in favor of the terrorists. These non-Muslim Mindanao *lumads* are the true Filipinos since birth and mostly law-abiding citizens. The way they have conducted their lives in peace is in sharp contrast to the aggressive Malaysian-sponsored Muslim terrorists, also known collectively as the MILF, who should still answer for the massacre of our SAF 44.

The Mindanao *lumad* resistance story against the Malaysian-sponsored Moro separatist rebels, who are also foreign aggressors, is not unique to the Maguindanao *lumads*. It is also true among the non-Muslim T'bolis who complain to this day about the massive grabbing of their land by Moros and even by government-sponsored settlers.

Datu Benito Blonto, a municipal tribal leader of the T'boli and Ubo tribes, recounted that "at the advent of Islam in the 14th century, the T'boli, Manobo and B'laan resisted the aggressive pros-elytizing of a succession of Muslim warrior-priests." Even writer and

> *Peace remains elusive in Mindanao, an island riven by conflict for decades*

language Professor Marina D. Suazo, in her famous novel *Davao*, recalled the many years of Bagobo armed resistance against the Muslim intruders who wanted to enslave them. The endless attacks of the Muslim pirates against the Bagobos of Davao was only stopped with the arrival and settlement of the Spanish forces in alliance with the Bagobos. Those Spanish forces were headed by Juan de Oyanguren who, with the Bagobos, established the Davao municipality that later became *la ciudad de Davao*. And since then, Davao has never ceded any part of the city to any Muslim control.

The Manila Spanish government later encouraged the Chavacano-speaking Binondo Chinese called *el caló chino de Binondo* to do business

in the main *población* of Davao City, which explains why Davao, like Zamboanga, also developed its own creole vernacular, which later assimilated Niponggo words when a group of Japanese abaca workers came to Davao.

7. A LAND OF PROMISE THAT LOST ITS WAY

MOST OF MINDANAO'S MODERN HISTORY has been marked with armed conflict. Whatever is to blame for this conflict, it appears that so-called Moro leaders would rather engage in terroristic activities and plain banditry than in providing long-term employment and a peaceful environment to their own people.

Under the leadership of Misuari, the MNLF succeeded in pushing for the establishment of an autonomous Muslim area in Mindanao under the Tripoli Agreement signed by the Marcos government and the MNLF and facilitated by Libya's Muammar Gaddafi. In the 1970s, Misuari effectively lobbied the leaders of oil-producing countries, like the then powerful Gaddafi. The threat of an oil boycott led by the Organization of Islamic Conference, many of whose members were part of the oil cartel in the 1970s, prodded the Marcos government to seek Gaddafi's help to resolve the Mindanao Muslim rebellion.

But the agreement collapsed when Marcos created two autonomous regions instead of one and fewer Muslim provinces than the MNLF had proposed. Under the Corazon Aquino government, Misuari's dream was resurrected with Aquino visiting him in his lair in Mindanao. A law creating an autonomous region in Muslim Mindanao would finally come to fruition a few years later.

So Misuari and his MNLF got to govern as they pleased the Muslim autonomous region especially created for him by law in Congress. Misuari and his cabal of corrupt administrators, however, got richer and richer but the ordinary Moro voter got poorer and poorer. He and his lieutenants ruled the autonomous region from 1996 to 2005 but had nothing to show for it except their incompetence and mismanagement that frittered away large financial and technical support from foreign donors.

After the MILF rebel group broke away from the MNLF, the former started recruiting and building its military camps without being bothered by successive Philippine presidents starting from Corazon Aquino to her inept son Benigno Aquino Jr., except for a brief period during the truncated Joseph Estrada presidency (1998-2001) when he ordered the Armed Forces to destroy those camps. With the ouster of Estrada, the MILF regrouped and exploited the weak-kneed Noynoy Aquino to demand for a much bigger territory.

Every Filipino should be given a voice in determining the wisdom of Moro autonomy

The peace situation in Mindanao slightly improved with the imposition of martial law by President Duterte in the face of the ISIS-inspired invasion of Marawi in 2017.

Most Filipinos, however, fear that after President Duterte steps down and once martial law is lifted, chaos will ensue. The terrorist group Abu Sayyaf, for instance, continues to engage in banditry, which includes kidnap-for-ransom activities, labeled as Sulú's "main industry." The terror group has horrified the whole world with its videotaped beheading of local and foreign tourists, mostly Americans, who could not pay any ransom.

The Abbu Sayyaf kidnappings, an activity done with regularity, appears to have the blessing of some local Muslim authorities since they are perceived to be doing almost nothing to stop it. It is even reported

that most of the townspeople cooperate with these terrorists, mostly relatives of theirs, in their dastardly deeds because, as kith and kin, they actually share in the ransom collected amounting to millions of pesos, if not U.S. dollars. These atrocities are rivaled in gruesomeness only by the Ampatuan massacre and the slaughter of the SAF 44 in Mamasapano, both committed with impunity in the Moro province of Maguindanao.

As we conclude this brief history of Mindanao, the local media reports about a plebiscite to ratify the Bangsamoro Organic Law. Many Filipinos believe that this plebiscite should be held nationally to give every Filipino a voice, not just limited to areas directly affected by the proposed law. And their clamor makes so much sense because, after all is said and done, the Bangsamoro Organic Law, once ratified and implemented, will be giving away a slice of the national territory to a rebel group whose "autonomy" will be financed by taxpayers' money to the tune of billions of pesos.

The Bangsamoro Organic Law is unconstitutional because it is just an ordinary legislation that cannot directly amend any provision of the existing Constitution which directly created the Muslim Mindanao Autonomous Region.

It remains to be seen if this kind of stiff investment will really bring peace to Mindanao. Perhaps while President Duterte is in power, there will always be peace in Mindanao, more so if martial law continues to be in effect. But what happens after he steps down?

Bad Moro actors masquerading as freedom fighters do not deserve autonomy

To aggravate further the situation, a Supreme Court ruling can still strike down the Bangsamoro Organic Law. As it is usually said in Filipino: *¡Abañgan!*

General Emilio Aguinaldo, president of the 1898 *Primera República Filipina*.

AN OLD INTERVIEW WITH PRESIDENTE AGUINALDO

My paternal grandfather, Felipe Gómez y Wyndham, a Mason, requested me not to immediately publish this interview in Manila's now defunct *El Debate*, a Spanish daily, while he was still alive. I wondered why. But now that he is gone, I believe it should be published as is, in Spanish, and let the readers who can understand the language find out for themselves why my grandfather did not want this interview to see the light of day in his lifetime.

ENTREVISTA CON EL PRESIDENTE EMILIO AGUINALDO Y SU SEÑORA, DOÑA MARÍA AGONCILLO, KAWIT, CAVITE
16 DE DICIEMBRE DE 1958

La Señora María Agoncillo de Aguinaldo me permitió la entrada en su casa cuando un ayudante le informó que un servidor, en representación de un grupo de baile filipino, quería saber su opinión sobre el traje nacional de Filipinas. Me recibió en lo que parecía ser la caida de su mansión.

GGR: Señora, en vista de la polémica en los diarios sobre el traje filipino tal como lo confeccionan ahora los "couturiers", "modistos" o "modistas", ¿qué dice usted?

SEÑORA DE AGUINALDO: Que el traje nacional sin su pañuelo, o alampay, sobre los hombros, deja de ser filipino.

GGR: Señora, ¿se opone usted a su modernización?

SEÑORA DE AGUINALDO: El traje nacional filipino debe respetarse. No se debe desfigurar. Se pueden hacer trajes con su influencia pero no se debe cambiar tal como aparece el traje nacional de la mujer filipina.

NOTA: *El Señor Aguinaldo (Don Emilio) estaba en la sala de su mansión y al oírnos hablar en español se acercó a donde estaba su Señora y se sentó en una silla próxima a ella. Nos dirigió la palabra.*

SEÑOR AGUINALDO: Es bueno que este joven todavia hable español. ¿Qué pasa con el traje nacional?

GGR: Señor Presidente, Su Excelencia, un servidor de usted, representa unos grupos folklóricos y su Señora acaba de decir que el traje filipino debe respetarse.

SEÑOR AGUINALDO: ¡Así debe ser! Ahora, aqui nada ya se respeta. No es costumbre mía criticar, pero ya que usted puede entenderme en castellano le digo que yo, el Señor Aguinaldo, está muy apenado por lo que ahora viene transcurriendo en este país por el que tantos sacrificios hemos hecho los veteranos de la República empezada en 1896.

GGR: Sí Su Excelencia. Un servidor le venera a usted como uno de nuestros héroes y padres de la Patria.

SEÑOR AGUINALDO: Aquí me vienen a entrevistar unos profesores de historia de la University of the Philippines de los yanquis. Y uno de ellos es un tal Agoncillo que dice ser pariente de mi Señora... Viene aqui y me habla en inglés y yo tengo que darle señales que me hable en tagalo porque sé que entiende muy poco de español. ¿Ha leido usted la historia de Filipinas que escribió? ¿Ha leido usted la biografía de Andrés Bonifacio que escribió?

GGR: No Su Excelencia. No he leido esos libros pero los voy a leer para enterarme de lo que dicen...

SEÑOR AGUINALDO: Yo no leo en inglés pero algunos conocidos me han dicho que no son libros a favor de Filipinas ni de los filipinos. Y creo que no lo son porque dicen mentiras hasta de la humilde persona de este seguro servidor.

GGR: ¿Qué cosa mala pueden decir de Su Excelencia?

SEÑOR AGUINALDO: Pues, lo que quiere la política Yanqui... Que servidor mandó asesinar a Don Andrés Bonifacio. Y eso no es verdad. Yo tuve mis diferencias con Andrés Bonifacio pero esta nueva corriente de cosas quiere dejarme mal parado a la vez que se va encubriendo injustamente los abusos y crueldades aquí del Yanqui para justificar su invasión y sangrienta anexión de Filipinas.

GGR: Me lamento escuchar estas palabras de Su Excelencia pero servidor está a la disposición de Su Excelencia para defenderle y dar a conocer la verdadera historia de nuestra Patria.

SEÑOR AGUINALDO: ¡Eso es! La verdadera historia de nuestra Patria particu-larmente la verdadera historia de nuestra revolución contra España y nuestra guerra de resistencia en contra de los invasores Yanquis que hasta a estas alturas me vigilan en mi propio país…

GGR: Tiene Su Excelencia un fiel seguidor, un soldado más, en este su servidor… ¿Puede resumirme Su Excelencia la historia de la revolución contra España?

SEÑOR AGUINALDO: En breve, bajo España, no estábamos económicamente controlados como ahora. Por eso, cuando aprendimos de los liberales españoles lo que es libertad, igualdad y fraternidad, hemos abrazado lo que es la Masonería y nos adherimos todos al Gran Oriente de España. Le hablo a usted de la Masonería porque conocí a los hermanos Gómez de Iloilo, Felipe y Guillermo, que son miembros de nuestra Masonería…

GGR: Sí, Su Excelencia. Servidor es nieto de Don Felipe y sobrino-nieto de Don Guillermo.

SEÑOR AGUINALDO: Los he conocido y les he leido en la revista *SEMANA* y en *La Voz de Manila* y otros periódicos de Manila. Por eso le hablo a usted con mucha franqueza porque estoy ya hasta la coronilla con lo que han hecho de este mi pobre país, nuestro país, nuestra Patria… Y lo que más me aburre es que me falsean la historia de la revolución y la historia de la guerra de la resistencia contra los Yanquis; contra los Estados Unidos… Esos historiadores que escriben nuestra historia en inglés americano vienen aquí para entrevistarme y hasta me hacen firmar cosas, pero nada de lo que digo publican cuando lo que declaro no va de acuerdo con la agenda de los invasores Yanquis… ¡Son unos desvergonzados!…

GGR: ¿Cuál es, entonces, la verdad, Su Excelencia?

SEÑOR AGUINALDO: El comienzo de la revolución filipina es trabajo de la Masonería; pero esa revolución terminó con el Pacto de Biacnabató. Los voluntarios filipinos ayudaron al Gobierno Español aquí a casi vencerme. Por eso, opté por firmar la paz mediante el Pacto de Biacnabató y opté por auto-exilarme a HongKón…

GGR: Y, ¿por qué aconteció la guerra con los Yanquis?

SEÑOR AGUINALDO: Sencillamente porque me engañaron los Yanquis. Se acercaron a mi como hermanos masones urgiéndome en nombre de la Masonería internacional que vuelva a Filipinas para reorganizar la revolución contra España dándome su palabra de hermanos masones que tras liquidado en nuestras islas el Gobierno Español que me otorgarían la independencia por la que luchamos.

GGR: ¿Es que no han cumplido los Yanquis con su palabra de hermanos masones de darle a usted y a nuestro pueblo su libertad?

SEÑOR AGUINALDO: ¡Nada de eso! Lea usted las Juntas Locales de Defensa que firmamos del Señor Apolinario Mabini… Le he pedido al Diputado Don Miguel Cuenco de Cebú que publique en los textos para la enseñanza del español ese decreto, esa proclama, que expedimos: las Juntas Locales de Defensa. Por eso que al llegar a Filipinas inmediatamente hice que se declare la independencia de Filipinas de España esperando que los Yanquis nos apoyen. Pero me traicionaron. ¡Nos traicionaron! En vez de apoyarnos como aliados nos provocaron la guerra muy adredemente porque su intención era robarnos la reserva en oro y plata que acumulamos en Malolos bajo la custodia del Gral. Antonio Luna y el Capitán Servillano Sevilla. Esa reserva vale más de CIEN mil millones de dólares y nos lo robaron al caer Malolos en manos de Arthur MacArthur. Y me persiguieron hasta Palanan, La Isabela, para capturarme. No se atrevieron a ejecutarme porque no les convenía hacer eso. Me quieren vivo para echarme la culpa del asesinato de Andrés Bonifacio y el de Antonio Luna.

GGR: ¿Cómo lograron intervenir los Yanquis en estos asesinatos, Su Excelencia?

SEÑOR AGUINALDO: Son muy astutos. Mediante la Masonería y el dinero pagaron a algunos hombres nuestros.. Si. Pagaron, intimidaron, amenazaron para que éstos, aunque supuestamente bajo mi mando y férula, asesinen a Andres y a Procopio Bonifacio tras un supuesto enjuiciamiento que duró sólo un día que los sentenciaron a muerte. Yo no quise confirmar esa sentencia pero me obligaron con amenazas hasta en contra de mi familia. Y aquí ahora estoy sufriendo porque se me apunta el dedo como el que mató a Bonifacio.

GGR: ¿Y lo del Gral. Antonio Luna?

SEÑOR AGUINALDO: Igual! Me lo manipularon y me lo montaron todo en Cabanatuan para luego echarme la culpa. Mataron al Gral. Antonio Luna como al Supremo Andrés Bonifacio a la manera masónica. ¡Con armas blancas! Es por eso que yo, en mi interior, ya he renunciado de la Masonería porque la Masonería de hoy es propiedad del imperio explotador de los Yanquis.

GGR: Mi General. Su Excelencia. Esta verdad debe publicarse.

SEÑOR AGUINALDO: Es precisamente por eso que te lo estoy contando ahora porque tu serás el que me lo va a publicar en el futuro para que nuestro pueblo conozca su verdadera historia.

GGR: ¿Está Su Excelencia arrenpentido de lo que ha hecho en su vida?

SEÑOR AGUINALDO: Sí. Estoy arrepentido en buena parte por haberme levantado contra España y, es por eso, que cuando se celebraron los funerales en Manila del Rey Alfonso de España, yo me presenté en la catedral para sorpresa de los españoles. Y me preguntaron por qué había venido a los funerales del Rey de España en contra del cual me alcé en rebelión… Y, les dije que sigue siendo mi Rey porque bajo España siempre fuimos sábditos, o ciudadanos, españoles pero que ahora, bajo los Estados Unidos, somos tan solo un Mercado de consumidores de sus exportaciones, cuando no parias, porque nunca nos han hecho ciudadanos de ningún estado de Estados Unidos… Y los españoles me abrieron paso y me trataron como su hermano en aquel día tan significativo…

GGR: Su Excelencia, ¿qué puede decirnos del futuro de nuestra Patria?

SEÑOR AGUINALDO: A estas alturas y a mi edad, barrunto que Filipinas ha de seguir siendo colonia de Estados Unidos porque la campaña de forzar el idioma inglés sobre nuestros niños es implacable y conduce a la desfilipinización de nuestras futuras generaciones. Y más aun cuando pierden el conocimiento necesario del idioma español, la oficial con la [lengua] tagala, de nuestra Primera República.

GGR; ¿Está usted en paz consigo mismo, Su Excelencia?

SEÑOR AGUINALDO: Sí. He vuelto a mi religión, la que heredamos como sábditos españoles. Y como el viejo soldado que soy, ya me iré poco a poco, a una vida mejor con la conciencia limpia y con nada más que con la satisfacción de haber servido honradamente a mi Patria dentro de mis posibilidades y a pesar de mis limitaciones.

GGR. Gracias Su Excelencia.

Photo Credits

Special thanks to the Office of the President, Republic of the Philippines for the official photo of President Rodrigo Roa Duterte which appears on the front cover of this book through the Web site of the Philippine embassy in Madrid. All other photos are courtesy of the Gómez Rivera photo archives, except for the following:

1. Photo of oil painting *Desembarco de Magallanes*, opposite page 1. Pierce Centina.
2. Miguel López de Legazpi, page 2; King Philip II of Spain, 4; Filipino overseas workers, 20; Leila de Lima, 35; Thomasite teacher and students, opposite page 53; USS *Thomas*, 55; U.S. soldiers with Filipino women and a child, 56; T.H. Pardo De Tavera, 74; dead Filipino soldiers, 87; replica of *Victoria*, 171; Bud Dajo massacre, 182; mosque, 185; Nur Misuari, 186. *Wikimedia Commons.*
4. Macario Sacay, page 9; President Ferdinand E. Marcos, 21; Sen. Claro M. Recto, 47; Laguna copperplate, 77. Presidential Museum and Library, Republic of the Philippines.
5. *Noynoying* poster, page 29. *anakbayan.org.*
6. President Rodrigo Roa Duterte, page 34. Presidential Communications Operations Office, Republic of the Philippines.
7. Real Numbers infographic, page 42. Philippine Drug Enforcement Agency.
8. Bayanihan through the years, opposite page 125; Bayanihan dancers, 128, 129, 130, 131; musician, 131; poster, 132. Bayanihan Philippine Folk Dance Company.
9. Calinog municipal hall and Catholic church, page 151. Evans R. Centina.
10. Diorama of the Battle of Mactán, page 170. Ayala Museum.
11. Portrait of Magellan, page 169; map of Magellan's route, 172. *xlsemanal.com.*
12. President Emilio Aguinaldo, opposite page 195. U.S. Library of Congress.
13. Nelly's Garden mansion, page 138. Nelly's Garden.
14. Destroyed buildings of Intramuros, opposite page 85. *Life* © C. Tewell through *theroguemag.com.*

Bibliography

Books

Aspillera, Paralúman S. *Basic Tagalog for Foreigners and Non-Tagalogs,* 1974 revised ed., 1. Manila: 1981.

Abecedariong Tagalog. Manila: Martinez Publication House, 1917.

Bowring, John. "Iloilo and Panay," in *Visit to the Philippine Islands, 359.* London: 3mith, Elder & Co., 1859.

De los Santos, Epifanio. *Filipinas para los filipinos.* 1908.

De Irrureta Goyena, Tirso. *Por el idioma y la cultura hispanos,* 122. Manila: UST Press, 1917. Also reproduced in the *Canadian Catholic Letter.* 1918.

Diksyunaryo ng Wikang Pilipino. Manila: Komisyong ng Wikang Pilipino, 1998.

Galende, OSA, Pedro. "Catechetic and Religious Instruction," in *The 450th Anniversary of the Santo Niño,* 79-81. Typescript.

García Martínez, Alfonso L. "The Imposition of English During the 1898-1901 Period," in *The Americanization of the Philippines,* 237-270. San Juan: Law College of Puerto Rico, 1982.

Goodno, James B. *The Philippines, Land of Broken Promises,* 33. Atlantic Highlands, NJ: Zed Books, 1991.

Joaquin, Nick. *Culture and History,* n.p. Manila: Anvil Publishing, 2004.

Lanza, Esteban. *Cronicas Visayas,* 296. Manila: UST Press, 1917.

Leddy Phelan, John. *The Hispanization of the Philippines,* edited by Renato Constantino, 25. Manila: Filipiniana Reprint Series, 1985.

Molina, Antonio M. *The Philippines Through the Centuries,* 41-46. Manila: UST Cooperative, 1960-61.

Stoll, David. *Fishers of Men or Founders of Empire?: The Wycliffe Bible Translators, (Summer Institute of Linguistics-SIL) in Latin America,* n.p. London: ZED Press, 1982.

—. *Is Latin America Turning Protestant?: The Politics of Evangelical Growth,* 17. Los Angeles: University of California Press, 1990.

Recto, Claro M. and Zaragoza, Francisco. *Vicente Ilustre, el Isagani de Rizal,* n.p. Manila: General Printing Press, 1953.

Varona, Francisco and De la Llana, Pedro. *The Life of Librada Avelino,* bilingual edition in Spanish and English, 241. Manila: Vera & Sons Publishing Co., 1935.

Zaragoza y Carrillo, Francisco. *Notas de Don Vicente Ilustre sobre Mindanao y los Moros.* Manila:1950.

Government Publications

United States. "The Use of English," in *The Ford Report,* 368. Manila: Bureau of Printing, 1916.

United States. *The School Report,* 96. Manila: Bureau of Printing, 1908.

Philippines. Vide General Provisions. 1973 Philippine Constitution.

United States. *A Survey of the Educational System of the Philippines,* 24-26. Manila: Bureau of Printing, 1924.

Dissertation

Sevilla de Alvero, Rosa. "Crítica del sistema educacional de Filipinas." Diss., University of Santo Tomás, 1936.

Periodicals

Bresnahan, Mary I. "English in the Philippines," *Journal of Communication*, vol. 29, issue 2, 1 (June 1979). 64–71. https://doi.org/10.1111/j.1460-2466.1979.tb02948.x

Cabán, Pedro. "Subjects and Immigrants During the Progressive Era," *Latin American, Caribbean, and U.S. Latino Studies Faculty Scholarship*, vol. 16. (2001). http://scholarsarchive.library.albany.edu/lacs_fac_scholar/16

Campbell, James A. "Letters to the Editor." *Los Angeles Times,* November 3, 1991.

Contreras, Volt. "The AGILE Factor, Unseen Hand Behind 50 Laws, Executive Orders." *Philippine Daily Inquirer*, March 19-23, 2003.

Hernández, OSA, Policarpo. "A Church Built for the Ages." *Search, The Augustinian Journal of Cultural Excellence* 15, no. 2 (2004). 111-113.

Pacqueo-Arreza, Elisa. "School Reforms: Mission Impossible?" *Philippine Daily Inquirer*, March 21, 1999.

Reyes, Modesto L. *ISAGANI,* June 1925 and September 1925.

Robertson, James Alexander. "The Evolution of Representation in the Philippine Islands." *The Journal of Race Development*, 6, no. 2 (1915).155-66. doi:10.2307/29738120.

Online Sources

Andrade, Pio. Jr. "'Padre Damaso' and the Friars: Myth Versus Reality." *inquirer. net*. Accessed October 10, 2018. https://lifestyle.inquirer.net/220264/padre-damaso-and-the-friars-myth-versus-reality/

Burmila, Edwin. "The Invention of Christopher Columbus, American Hero: How the Founding Fathers Turned Christopher Columbus, a Mediocre Italian Sailor and Mass Murderer, Into a Historical Icon." *thenation.com*. Accessed November 2, 2018. https://www.thenation.com/article/the-invention-of-christopher-columbus-american-hero/

Donahue, Bill. "Media Passionate About Anti-Catholic Bias." *catholicleague. org*. Accessed October 20, 2018. https://www.catholicleague.org/media-passionate-anti-catholic-bias-3/

Escandor, Juan Jr. "Lapu-lapu As National Hero? Not So Fast." *inquirer.net*. Accessed November 3, 2018. https://newsinfo.inquirer.net/790091/lapu-lapu-as-national-hero-not-so-fast

Lulunka, Barbara. "Ethnocide." *sciencespo.fr*. November 3, 2007. Accessed October 27, 2018. https://www.sciencespo.fr/mass-violence-war-massacre-resistance/en/document/ethnocide

Morallo, Audrey. "Defense Chief: Bulk Of Marawi Siege Funding Came from Drugs." *philstar.com*. Accessed May 21, 2017. https://www.philstar.com/headlines/2017/09/25/1742536/defense-chief-bulk-marawi-siege-funding-came-drugs

Tatad, Francisco S. "Clueless on Sabah, Messed Up on Jabidah, Toothless on China." *manilastandard.net*. Accessed May 10, 2018. http://manilastandardtoday.com/opinion/89468/clueless-on-sabah-messed-up-on-jabidah-toothless-on-china.html

Tiglao, Rigoberto. "Malaysians Fund Abu Sayyaf." *rigobertotiglao.com*. Accessed October 10, 2018. http://www.rigobertotiglao.com/2016/06/21/malaysians-fund-abu-sayyaf/

"Joanna Demafelis: Employers of Filipina Maid Found Dead in Freezer Arrested." *bbc.com*. Accessed October 10, 2018. https://www.bbc.com/news/world-middle-east-43177349

"Miriam Wants Probe on Alleged Bribery of Senators." *philippinestar.com*. Accessed October 9, 2018. https://www.philstar.com/headlines/2014/07/02/1341452/miriam-wants-probe-alleged-bribery-senators#wRdFcVyTAT89UjtB.99

"Arroyo Spokesman Claims PNoy Personally Asked Corona to Block the Distribution of Hacienda Luisita to Farmers." *politics.com.ph*. Accessed October 1, 2018. http://politics.com.ph/arroyo-spokesman-claims-pnoy-personally-asked-corona-to-block-the-distribution-of-hacienda-luisita-to-farmers/

"Noynoying." *wikipedia.org*. Accessed June 1, 2018. https://en.wikipedia.org/wiki/Noynoying

"Duterte Supporters Allege Cheating in Presidential Polls." *rappler.com*. Accessed October 12, 2018. https://www.rappler.com/nation/172141-duterte-youth-cheating-presidential-elections-comelec

"The Philippines Genocide Three Million Filipinos Killed." *britsinthephilippines top*. Accessed October 20, 2018. https://britsinthephilippines.top/philippines-genocide-3-million-filipinos-killed/

"How the U.S. Hispanic Population Is Changing." *pewresearch.org*. Accessed November 1, 2018. http://www.pewresearch.org/fact-tank/2017/09/18/how-the-u-s-hispanic-population-is-changing/

"Buying Power of Hispanic Consumers in the United States from 1990 to 2017." *statista.com*. Accessed November 1, 2018. https://www.statista.com/statistics/251438/hispanics-buying-power-in-the-us/

newamericamedia.org

"Pope Alexander VI Divides New World Between Spain and Portugal." *litencyc.com*. Accessed November 2, 2018. https://www.litencyc.com/php/stopics.php?rec=true&UID=13912

"Philippines-Mindanao (1971–First Combat Deaths)." Project Ploughshares Web site. January 17, 2018. Accessed November 2, 2018. http://ploughshares.ca/pl_armedconflict/philippines-mindanao-1971-first-combat-deaths/

When José Morán entered the monastery, it was to pursue the highest form of chivalry. But his fate as a religious priest takes a precipitous turn when social paroxysm grips the fictional island-nation of Islas e Islotes after the downfall of the government. To cover up his own misdeeds, his abominably corrupt religious superior leading a double life seizes the ensuing chaos and collaborates with human rights violators in the military to accuse the completely innocent friar of a fabricated heinous crime. The plot unravels as those who claim to follow Christ wade into politics, taking for granted his injunction to "render therefore unto Caesar the things which are Caesar's and unto God the things that are God's." In this novel, cassocked hypocrites are unmasked and only the weak are spared.
ALSO AVAILABLE IN KINDLE EDITION.

Triptych and Collected Poems represents over forty years of Gilbert Luis R. Centina III's poetic works, which critics have described as "modern poetry at its best," "lyrical" and "eloquent." It cements his reputation as a religious poet who "honors the [Catholic] church's fortitude, individual spirit and conviction, belief and the voyage thereof." Written in four different continents (Asia, Europe and the two Americas), it echoes his own personal quest for that Beauty ever ancient, ever new, as described by Saint Augustine, the spiritual founder of his religious order. That pursuit is by no means without its struggles, considering that it is a part of the human experience, with all its foibles, disappointments and triumphs. But it is a search rooted in the belief that when all is said and done, our heart is restless until it finally rests in God's presence.

Getxo and Other Poems is the fifth poetry collection of prize-winning poet Gilbert Luis R. Centina III. Critics have described his poetry as lyrical, modern poetry at its best and deeply rooted in religious history, mythology and mysticism. He continues that trajectory with the flash pieces contained in this collection, which he has masterfully crafted "with the strength and magnitude of prayer" that is palpable through the pages not only of this volume but of all his works. The title of this collection is derived from a Basque town in northern Spain, where the author is currently assigned as a religious priest of the Order of St. Augustine.

Somewhen is a hymn of praise to the living God, a theme that resonates throughout the book. This collection marks the return of Gilbert Luis R. Centina III to poetry writing after a long hiatus during which he devoted himself to his work as a Roman Catholic religious priest, only writing newspaper columns and editing a cultural journal on the side. It honestly lays bare the pharisaical clericalism found inside the cloistered walls, even as it finds deeper spiritual meaning in the arid cityscape of a secularized world. In the dross of human despair, it reassures readers that "when God seems asleep, he is very much awake."

Glass of Liquid Truths is a prize-winning poetry book. In the words of one critic, it's "a tankard rich with memories and feelings, thoughts and imaginations bred of the cloister and of the hearth, talented by the light streaking in from the varicolored windows of a cathedral that cannot but glitter with the painful awareness of man's frailties" where one can find "Augustine confronting Genet in the same cubicle of grief and suffering" and "a friar hovering between earth and heaven, uncertain whether to fall or to rise, to clasp the earth for what it is worth or to go searching for a God who plays 'hide-and-seek.'"

Our Hidden Galaxette is the first poetry book by prize-winning author Gilbert Luis R. Centina III. Cloistered within this seminal volume are hymns of praise of "nobler geometries," jeremiads against the "gilt nihility" of contemporary society, epistles to friends turning and turning "in a spin of madness," tragic observations on "lichens feasting on purple robes." In this lyric cloister, Teilhard de Chardin walks with Saint Genet. With the latter, he does not see synoptic, being Genet's *advocatus diaboli* while expressing a wish to be Chardin's disciple. This is a type of Christian literature "sans the megalophones of Blay, the mystic ecstasies of St. John of the Cross or the pastoral paeans of Gerard Manley Hopkins but endowed with a tremulous lyricism which is entirely its own."

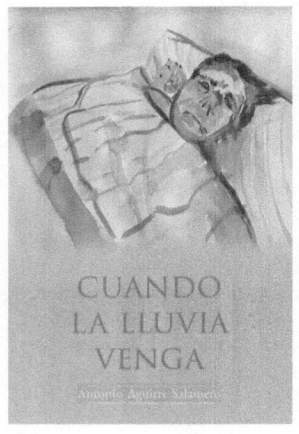

Antonio Aguirre Salamero es un poeta con gravitas. Su poesía recoge su amor por la naturaleza, belleza creada por una Belleza increada, visible en ella. Simbolista y naturalista, cree que los árboles que hayamos plantado nos sobrevivirán en el tiempo, una vez hayamos partido. Su poesía es poderosa y conmovedora, y convierte cada línea en una afirmación filosófica, una estrofa en un aforismo. Su amor por la familia y por la amistad es palpable a lo largo de este libro, y se renueva, libre, como un torrente que se desborda con fuerza cuando llega la lluvia. Nace en Bilbao -España- en 1964, estudia en el colegio Gaztelueta de Leioa, y obtiene la Licenciatura en Derecho por la Universidad de Deusto – Vizcaya.

Escrito por **José María Alonso Alonso de Linaje**, *La soledad como oportunidad* es una guía para encontrar sentido en la vida en las diferentes etapas de la vida, incluso en medio de la soledad causada por la enfermedad a la vejez. Es útil tanto para el paciente como para el cuidador. José María es un hombre del Renacimiento: autor, educador, músico y hacendado. Se graduó en la Universidad de Valladolid con un título en educación, un campo en el que ha dedicado la mayor parte de su vida profesional. Hasta la fecha, ha publicado un total de 52 libros y artículos para diversas revistas en España.

Gilbert Luis R. Centina III, OSA, poeta conocido y multipremiado tanto en EE.UU. como en Filipinas, habla hiligaynón, tagalo, inglés y español, es autor de seis libros de poesía, dos novelas y un libro de crítica, y buen conocedor de las labores de los hispanistas de Filipinas, dedicados a difundir, defender y enaltecer el idioma español. Es de esta noble pelea de los hispanistas en Filipinas de donde obtiene su inspiración para escribir *Dyptich/Díptico*. Durante más de tres siglos–conviene recordarlo–las Islas Filipinas formaron una muy querida parte del Imperio Español.

www.ingramcontent.com/pod-product-compliance
Lightning Source LLC
Chambersburg PA
CBHW031926060726
47496CB00007BA/2261